B1 C000085076

A Strange World

A Biographical Novel

Gretta Curran Browne

SPI
Seanelle Publications Inc.

First published in November 2015 by GCB Publications

ISBN: 978-1-912598-17-5

Typeset in Georgia 10/18

Cover image by permission of Mr Alain Delon.

www.grettacurranbrowne.com

For my husband Paul

With all my love

The Boy ... The Man ... The Legend

PART ONE

New Beginnings

"He had a power of fascination, rarely, if ever, possessed by any man of his young age."

John Cam Hobhouse

Chapter One

~ ~ ~

Before finally retiring for the night, Joe Murray decided to venture up to the private apartment of his young master to see if there were any last instructions to be carried out prior to his lordship's journey down to London the following day.

Although now seventy-two years old, Joe climbed the spiral stairs up to the North-West wing quickly and nimbly, a strong man with a soft heart who was now feeling very sad that his lordship was leaving Newstead again.

He knocked at the dressing-room door and, receiving no answer, entered it quietly, wondering if Lord Byron was already asleep or sitting at the desk in his bedroom writing as usual; although why a young man should prefer to spend his time doing so much writing was still beyond Joe's comprehension. Yet when he had once said so, his lordship had merely smiled and said, *"Joe, if I did not write to empty my mind, I'd go mad."*

And what a mind! Although still only twenty-three-years young, Lord Byron had the cleverest mind in the whole of Nottingham in old Joe's opinion. And it was not only poetry he wrote, but letters – always writing *letters* was his lordship.

"I like writing letters, Joe, because it's a way of keeping in touch and chatting socially to people while remaining alone and undisturbed by them."

Joe walked quietly through the dressing room and listened at the bedroom door. He had to be careful and do this because that hussy of a maid Susan Vaughan, pretty and sneaky as she was, would sometimes creep into his lordship's bed at night whether he wanted her to or not. Although once in, his lordship rarely threw her out again, and for this reason Joe detested her. She was so mad with love for him she had no shame.

Joe pressed his ear against the bedroom door and listened, but there was not a sound, not even the scratch of a pen flying across paper ... He knocked softly, receiving no answer from this room either ... was he asleep?

Opening the door slowly inch by inch, Joe finally got his head around the door ... and saw that the room was empty, the bedclothes on the four-poster untouched ... which was strange, because his lordship was not in any of the rooms downstairs either, and it was almost midnight.

Joe rushed down the stairs again with all the worried panic of a father looking for his wayward son. After all, his lordship had been very low in spirits these past few weeks, what with the death of his mother as well as three of his friends, all four dying about the same time. His heart had been near broken at the sadness of it all. And then to top it all, he had accidentally met Mary Chaworth again.

By the light of his lantern, Joe finally found Lord Byron standing at the edge of the great lake at the front of Newstead Abbey, leaning against a tree and gazing up at the stars.

"You've been gazing up at those stars since you were ten years old," Joe said impatiently. "They never change, you know, the same old stars in the same old sky."

"Ah, that's where you are wrong." Byron smiled at the old man. "There's been warfare up there tonight, Joe, meteors crashing here and there and shooting stars all over the sky. Money couldn't buy such a wonderful sight."

Joe looked up at the night sky, which did indeed look very bright tonight.

"I saw it all from my window and came out here to get a better look," Byron said. "Do you see that bright stream of vapour up there, Joe? That's where a meteor shot across the sky like a rocket, probably a fragment of some comet ... oh yes, the celestial fires are burning tonight."

Joe Murray looked up at the sky but could not see any bright vapour.

"I don't see it."

"It's gone now," Byron said, his eyes still searching the expanse of the sky.

"Or was it just your imagination?" Joe put down his lantern. "Ever since you were a boy, my lord, you have always had a vivid imagination."

"No, I have always had vivid *sight*," Byron replied. "Just because *you* cannot see it with your old eyes doesn't mean it's not there ... or was not there. If you miss seeing a flash of lightning in a thunderstorm, it doesn't mean it has not happened."

"I know all about storms and stars," Joe insisted, "being a boy in the Navy as I once was, and I was young then with *good* eyesight. Our ships were navigated by the stars, that's how we got from one place to another."

"And the help of a compass," Byron grinned.

"Aye, that too," Joe shrugged. 'Course I was just a cabin boy so I saw no compass. My job was to keep the captain's uniforms and shoes clean and ship-shape and bring him his coffee in the morning. I was fourteen when I ran away into the Navy, and nineteen when I ran out of it. Did I ever tell you about the time ..."

Byron had heard it all before, but he let Joe talk on while his eyes continued to watch the beauty of the night.

After a silence, when he suddenly realised that Joe had stopped talking, Byron looked at him.

"What were you thinking?" Joe asked.

"Oh ... about the Navy ... and about what you just said," Byron lied, because not even the threat of death would ever permit him to hurt Joe's feelings about his old-time reminiscences. After so many years together, the old butler was more like a beloved grandfather to him than a servant.

In the light of the lantern he saw the smile of pleasure emerging on Joe's face. "Great things I tell you, eh, my lord?"

"Great things indeed. But still ..." Byron sighed, his blue eyes on the sky again, "if I was star, I would hate to be a fixed star."

"A *fixed* star – what d'you mean?"

"Those fixed stars that ships navigate by. Always in the same position in the sky. Always watched by sailors and citizens alike. I would rather be a bright glorious meteor that flames across the sky in one bright magnificent flash than be any fixed star in one place for all eternity."

Joe chuckled. "Didn't I just say you had a vivid imagination."

"Just as I would rather have *one* glorious passionate night making love to the girl I love, than have *years* married to a woman I was only fond of."

Joe knew he was thinking of Mary Chaworth again, and that was an obsession no person could cure him of, except himself.

"In London," said Joe encouragingly, "you'll no doubt meet lots of those high-class society young ladies and find that one of *them* will suit you and your aristocratic rank much better than a country girl like Mary Chaworth."

When Byron gave no answer, Joe felt sad again, certain in his own mind that Lord Byron still believed that Mary had rejected him for Jack Musters because of his lordship's afflicted right foot and his slight limp when he walked, but God in Heaven! — that was crazy, that was ridiculous, because limp or not, Lord Byron still had to be the best-looking young man in all England, and there was not a man or woman in the whole of Nottingham who would deny that.

Both men turned abruptly at the sound of running feet. Joe jumped alert. "Who can that be at this hour?"

There were two different estate gates and the sweep of two different carriage drives that led up to the lake and the mansion of Newstead Abbey and both were almost a mile long, so no place for an unauthorised stranger to be running in the dark.

"It could be a poacher," Joe said, holding up the lantern. "I'll go and get my gun."

"I have mine," Byron said, for he never walked around the estate late at night without wearing a fully-loaded pistol under his jacket.

"So *how*," said Joe indignantly, "did whoever it is get past the gate-keepers and the gamekeepers?"

Seconds later Fletcher came running into the light of the lantern, panting hard from his running.

"Fletcher — you damned adder!" Joe exclaimed. "You've been out when you should have been in! So what would his lordship have done when he needed your help to get his shoe off before bed! And *you* being his *valet* employed and paid for that purpose!"

"I went, my lord," said Fletcher, still panting from his run, "to say farewell to my kin before moving to London, but there was a discharge —"

"And there will be another discharge," said Joe Murray angrily. "*You* being discharged from his lordship's service if you carry on like this in London, Fletcher."

"A discharge from a gun!"

"A gun?" Byron could see Fletcher was very distressed. "Are you hurt? Who fired the gun?"

"Jack Musters, the son of the Sheriff," said Fletcher. "Oh, there's been bad trouble in Nottingham tonight with the Luddites getting into the factory and breaking more of the machines, but someone betrayed them to Jack Musters and he came with his militia ready to shoot them all. I thought he was going to shoot *me* even though all *I* was doing was walking by. I knew nothing about the secret machine-breaking of the Luddites."

"And if you *had* known?" Byron asked. "What would you have done?"

"I would have joined them and smashed a few more," Fletcher said defiantly. "Once a Nottingham man always a Nottingham man."

"Did Jack Musters speak to you?" Byron asked coldly. "Did he put his hands on you?"

"He was ready to haul me in until I said I was Lord Byron's personal valet, so he quickly let me go."

"Did he indeed?" Byron's tone was sardonic. Jack Musters was not only the son of the Sheriff of Nottingham, but Mary Chaworth's husband. They had met a few times and Byron despised him.

The three men went into the house where Joe Murray, feeling more conciliatory towards Fletcher now, poured him a glass of ale.

"Although you shouldn't have been out," Joe said sternly. "And as for saying farewell to your kin, it's not like his lordship is taking you abroad over the Continent for two years again. Egad! it's only down to London you'll be going, and back every few weeks no doubt."

Byron was looking curiously at Fletcher. "What's going on in Nottingham? And who are these Luddites?"

Fletcher stared at him. "You don't know?"

"How can he know?" Joe responded. "When he's been abroad for two years and has had four deaths to cope with, and I'm not one for wasting his lordship's time with tittle-tattle about the commoners."

Byron and Fletcher exchanged a knowing glance. It had often amused them both how Joe, after his forty years in service at Newstead Abbey as personal valet to two Lords during that period, now also considered himself not only above all the other household staff at Newstead, but also above the common people of Nottingham.

"Although I *will* say," Joe added, "it's brutal what's going on out there, depriving poor men and women of their livelihoods, and now the government is threatening to *hang* them for protesting!"

Only now did Byron realise what a secluded life he had been living here at Newstead, surrounded by acres and acres of the estate's parklands and countryside, and unaware of what was happening in the lives of the townspeople only fifteen miles or so away.

"Fletcher..." Byron put his palm up to Joe Murray in a gesture for him not to say another word —"Fletcher, tell me what is happening in Nottingham?"

"Well, they say it's happening in Lancashire and Yorkshire too, but it's the people of Nottinghamshire who have been the first to rebel."

"Rebel against what?"

"Poverty," Fletcher said. "Bad poverty. Apart from the farm workers, Nottingham has always been a textile county, you know that, my lord. A place where our workers are known all over the kingdom for being *artists* – the framework knitters in the factories, and then the women 'stockingers' – many of whom make the hosiery at home on their own frames. It's been the industry of Nottingham for a century. But now ..."

Fletcher shook his head in disgust — "*now* the factory owners are bringing in these big *wide* frames that will do the work of seven men instead of one, putting men and women out of work and leaving them and their families to starve. And also – to add insult to injury – these new machines are ruining the reputation of the whole county, producing garments that are cheaper but inferior in quality to those made by the workers, degrading the dignity of their trade – *as well as* putting men out of work."

"And to be fair to the Luddites," said Joe Murray, giving away the fact that he knew a lot more than he pretended to know, "they do *warn* the factory masters to remove their new machines from the premises, and if the masters refuse, the Luddites go in a smash the machines in night raids using big sledgehammers. Brave men, I say, because they know it's the hangman or transportation to a convict colony if they get caught."

"But what else can they do in the face of poverty and destitution," Fletcher added, and then he looked at Joe Murray with a frown of suspicion. "How do *you* know what size sledgehammers they use?"

Joe put on his most superior face. "I knows what I know, which is usually everything. So mark that, young

Fletcher, and mark it well."

"Why are they called Luddites?" asked Byron.

"It's the name of their leader, General Ludd," said Joe Murray. "*He's* the one that's organised all the secret societies and the swearing of oaths amongst the people to support the machine-breakers and never betray them to the militia, and that's why they're called *Ludd*-ites.*"

Fletcher groaned with impatience – he'd had enough of Joe Murray thinking he knew everything. "There's no such person as General Ludd! He's made up – doesn't exist! It's just a name the frame-breakers use to frighten the militia and remind them of our own *Robin Hood!* See – Ludd – Hood – sounds the same."

Fletcher suddenly caught himself and realised he had made a grave mistake. He looked at Lord Byron with eyes of fear. "That's a secret, my lord, you mustn't tell anyone, or *I'll* be hung."

"Aye, by me!" Joe Murray was furious at this revelation. "No General Ludd? You mean he's just a made-up country myth, like Robin Hood?"

"Robin Hood is not a myth." Now it was Byron who was indignant with Joe. "He's documented in all the records of Sherwood Forest since the time that all of its lands were owned by the Byrons. Robin Hood and his men hid out here in Sherwood Forest after he had supported the Earl of Lancaster in the rebellion against King Edward the Second – although I doubt that Robin and his men were as *merry* as the legend says, especially in the freezing snows of a Sherwood winter."

Fletcher and Joe Murray were stunned into a long silence, their two faces agog, until Joe said – "King Edward the Second – the same king who slept *here* in Newstead Abbey?"

Byron nodded. "The same one."

"Maybe that's why King Edward was sleeping here?" Fletcher said excitedly. "Maybe it was during one of his searches for Robin Hood?"

Byron shrugged. "I've no idea; but regarding the Luddites ... I think they should continue to use the memory of Robin Hood to enforce the Sheriff of Nottingham's fear of this mythical General Ludd."

"Don't do it, my lord!" Joe Murray warned in a fearful voice, inwardly damning Fletcher for bringing all this business to his lordship's attention. "Don't place yourself on the side of the common people! If you do so, you will be damned by your own class and lose the honour of your coronet!"

The mention of his coronet suddenly inspired Byron with an idea.

"There is one way that I can personally try and help the people of my own Nottingham, and that would be down in London, in Parliament."

"How so?" Joe asked.

"I'm due to make my maiden speech in the House of Lords in a couple of months. And now, at last, I believe I have found something worth speaking about."

~ ~ ~

Early the next morning Joe Murray and Fletcher stood at the front door of Newstead Abbey, watching Lord Byron riding off in the company of his young page Robert Rushton.

"Now see what you've done!" Joe Murray said accusingly to Fletcher. "He was all set to go down to London today, but now you've got him riding up a different road altogether. I just hope it's not one that leads him into trouble."

"So..." said Fletcher, feeling equally as peeved at this

unexpected event, "did he tell you *when* we will be going down to London now?"

"No, he said very little, other than he was not going to London, but he *was* going to see for himself what was going on in his own county."

And as he rode towards Nottingham Byron saw ... families in their cottages who had always appeared quite happy and self-sufficient before he had gone abroad two years ago, were now standing by the roadside trying to sell bundles of sticks cut down in the forest, or the women trying to sell a few spare carrots from their under-stocked vegetable gardens.

When he reached the road leading to one of the factories in the centre of Nottingham, the town was filled with militia, and an uproar going on beyond the cordon of soldiers.

Slowing his horse, two soldiers approached him with their hands up for him to halt, but seeing from his clothes that he was clearly a gentleman, waved him through.

Nearing one of the factories and seeing the crowd, Byron turned to Robert Rushton and gestured for him to dismount. "Find out what's going on and why the militia have the town surrounded."

Minutes later Robert came back and spoke quietly. "Four more stocking-frames were broken last night and the militia have come to collect the evidence, and they are warning the people there will be a few transportations to convict colonies before the week is out."

Byron would probably have stuck to his intentions and remained an observer if, at that moment, he had not seen Jack Musters riding onto the scene with all the pomp of the arrogant upstart that he was.

The sardonic smile was back on Byron's face ... Jack Musters, the man who had married Mary and who had been told by some gossip that Mary and Byron had been seeing speaking together after Byron's return from Greece – all innocent of course, a chance meeting when the two of them had merely talked for a few minutes – but enough to make Jack Musters declare to one and all that he would – "give Lord Byron "a sound thrashing" if he ever saw him again."

Well, now Musters was going to see him again.

Byron dismounted from his horse and walked towards the front of the crowd and began to mingle with the people, shaking hands and smiling in a very friendly way as he introduced himself. Most of the men, surprised that he should do such a thing as shake a commoner's hand, shook his hand back vigorously, while many of the women curtsied as the word spread through the crowd of who he was.

Jack Musters pulled his horse up, shocked at the effrontery. As a magistrate, and captain of the Militia, as well as being heir-presumptive to the title of Sheriff of Nottingham, Musters had ordered all members of the gentry to keep away from the town today.

"You, sir! What are you doing mixing with these people? Who are you?"

Byron stood at the front of the crowd with his back to the militia, but now he turned and looked up at Jack Musters, proud and defiant and – according to the gossip of the crowd afterwards – *"looking as fine and as handsome as any young prince!"*

"Good morning to you, Captain Musters."

Muster's was taken aback. "Lord Byron!"

"Of Newstead and Rochdale, as you know. And amongst these people, I believe, are some of my own tenants. So why should they be of interest to you and your militia?"

"Anarchy was carried out here last night," Musters replied. "Villainous anarchy. And the militia are here to collect the evidence."

"The evidence? ... Oh, the *evidence* ..." Byron bent down and picked up a small fragment of a broken stocking-frame lying on the ground and held it up in mock amazement.

"Is *this* the evidence of such anarchy? A broken *stocking* frame?" He looked around at all the mounted soldiers. "Why, at the sight of all these soldiers, Captain Musters, I thought the *French Revolution* must be happening all over again here in Nottingham, but no ... the militia are out in force and all due to a broken stocking frame!"

"More than one frame, Byron, and it was not broken, it was deliberately smashed!"

"Even so ..." Byron responded in the same mocking tone, "does it really require all this marching and counter-marching of your militia? Prancing along with all the pride and pomp of soldiers going to *war!* And when your detachments arrive at their destination, what is it they do? Why – they collect fragments of broken stocking frames! Next you'll be calling in the *army* to assist you in defeating such mischief."

The crowd were all laughing now, delighted at Lord Byron's sarcasm, and Jack Musters seemed at a loss as to how to respond further – aggression he could fight brutally, but such *mockery* from one of the aristocracy was something he had never encountered before.

And of all the aristocrats – Lord Byron! A man whom his wife Mary would not hear a word against, nor tolerate any criticism of Byron whatsoever. And if this got back to her ... Jack dreaded to think of the silent condemnation on her face that could often last for days!

Minutes later the militia reluctantly complied with their captain's order to turn about their horses and leave, and set off back to their quarters amidst the laughing derision of the women and the loud hootings of the children.

In the days that followed, Lord Byron continued his tour of every part of Nottinghamshire; and in the nights that followed the Luddite men were heard in the taverns loudly singing a new song –

"Chant no more your rhymes about Robin Hood.
His feats I but little admire,
I will sing of the achievements of General Ludd
Now the hero of Nottinghamshire!"

It was a song which some claimed Lord Byron had personally written and sent to the Luddites by way of a secret messenger, but few knew if that was true or not.

Overnight Lord Byron had become a hero of the Nottingham people, but none saw him after that week, because he had removed himself down to London, where – rumour had it — on behalf of the people of his own Nottingham, he intended to speak to all the Lords of the Realm within the Palace of Westminster.

Chapter Two

~ ~ ~

London, at its heart, was a town of true majesty in the year of 1811.

The triumph of Georgian architecture in buildings of light stone, stood with a solid yet airy grace, mingling amidst streets of town-houses with walls of yellow or cream plaster, the front doors all painted in glossy black and adorned with gleaming brass handles and knockers, above which the fanlight windows allowed sunlight to flood into the huge halls.

The town houses of the *haut monde* were even more eye-catching in their fantastic elegance; Palladian homes with Grecian porticoes and marble pillars, spaced between Green Park, Hyde Park and Regent's Park, all enjoying the combination of town and country in a London that had a total population of seven hundred thousand, out of which *London Society* consisted of no more than a select collection of five hundred persons, headed by the Prince Regent.

In Fleet Street, in John Murray's bookselling establishment, Robert Dallas and the bookseller were facing a conundrum about Lord Byron and his epic poem " Childe Harold's Pilgrimage".

"He denies it," Dallas said, "but of course it *is* based on his own pilgrimage through Portugal, Spain, Greece and Turkey during the past two years. How else would he be able to describe events in such detail? Especially those parts in Turkey – a barbaric land where few Christian men would ever *dare* to venture, yet we all know that Lord Byron did so."

"And his descriptions are glorious ..." John Murray was determined to become a publisher, and divined himself as *a publisher of the future*. And he also believed that Lord Byron would be the *poet* of the future. He looked fretfully at the manuscript in his hands. "I'm holding gold in my hands, Mr Dallas."

Dallas nodded. "I thought the same when I read it. A true treasure."

"You have *got* to persuade Lord Byron to allow me to publish it. It has always been my dream to become a publisher and not a mere bookseller ... and with this wonderful manuscript I know it will make my name as such – as a *publisher*, and a great one – and for that I am prepared to invest any amount of money."

"Yes, but I don't think any amount of money will persuade him," Dallas replied. "The manuscript he gave to me for publication was entitled '*Hints from Horace*', and that has now gone to Cawthorn's as usual."

John Murray, a shrewd and clever businessman aged thirty-three, wore a face of sheer determination. "I lost Jane Austen to Egerton's, but I am *not* going to lose Lord Byron or this manuscript."

Dallas was feeling as frustrated as John Murray. Authors could be such difficult people to deal with when it came to their work, especially Miss Austen who insisted on disregarding all literary agents and publishers, preferring instead to self-publish her book *Sense and Sensibility* and keep most of the sales profits for herself. She was using Egerton's merely as her book *seller*, paying for all of her own printing and holding on tight to her copyright, paying Egerton's no more than the usual percentage commission from any sales they made.

Yet now, with a manuscript by Lord Byron, John

Murray was offering to pay for the printing and advertising and all other expenses out of his own pocket, *and* possibly a small fortune to purchase the copyright – so keen was he to become the publisher of Childe Harold's Pilgrimage.

And Dallas, being so desperately in need of money, was eager to get his own agent's commission out of it all, if *only* Lord Byron could be persuaded.

Dallas shook his head regretfully. "It's ridiculous, I know, but Lord Byron is convinced that Childe Harold is nothing more than his own *'personal scribblings'* – as he put it, and unworthy of publication. All of my persuasion is used up. I have no persuasion left."

John Murray was frowning. "Why does he have such a low opinion of it? Do you know why?"

"Yes. In the first year of his travels Lord Byron was accompanied by his Cambridge friend, John Cam Hobhouse. They went as far as Greece together before Byron continued travelling on into the Morea alone. But while they were down in Athens, Byron showed Hobhouse the first two cantos of Childe Harold for his opinion. Well, it seems that Hobhouse was not at all impressed; his opinion being that that it had "*very little to recommend it, and much to condemn.*"

"*What!*" John Murray was astounded. "Is this Hobhouse an illiterate nincompoop?"

"No, indeed no. John Hobhouse is very clever. He won the Hulsean Prize at Cambridge and Byron has great respect for him, but I think Hobhouse's opinion may have been tainted by a touch of jealous rivalry."

"Oh, how so?"

"Lord Byron told me that during the first year of their travels, Hobhouse spent much of his time writing travel notes for a future book – so it must have come as a great blow to Hobhouse when he discovered that Byron had been writing his own account of their journey, and not in regular prose – but in beautiful and dramatic *verse."*

John Murray randomly opened a page of the manuscript in his hands, and read the first verse that his gaze fell upon – Byron's first view of a Moslem mountainous country:

Land of Albania, let me bend mine eyes

On thee, thou rugged nurse of savage men!

The cross descends, thy minarets arise

And the pale crescent sparkles in the glen ...

"Oh how his friend must have *hated* Byron while he was reading this." John Murray smiled. "It's so absolutely splendid, it would wipe any travel-book about the same journey clean off the table. No wonder his jealous friend condemned it."

~ ~ ~

John Cam Hobhouse had often felt jealous of Byron, jealous of his poetic talent, jealous of his stunning good looks, jealous of his natural wit and ready laughter – but he had never *hated* him, not once, not for a minute – and not even when he had *pretended* to hate him during their early days at Trinity College, Cambridge.

In truth, John Cam Hobhouse had always loved Byron, almost to the point of worship, although he could not show it for fear of people thinking he was homosexual, which he was not, and Byron knew he was not – although Byron would not have cared a jot if he was. All Byron knew for sure was that John Cam Hobhouse was his greatest and truest friend.

Now Byron was in London, in the company of Scrope Davies who had now almost recovered from the tragedy of losing Matthews, and was now determined to enliven poor Byron, who had also lost his mother.

Byron was already enlivened, because he always enjoyed the company of Scrope Davies. And the thing he liked most about Scrope, was that he never sought to change him, whereas John Hobhouse never got tired of attempting to *improve* him.

And Scrope Davies had a good heart, a *kind* heart; and now, knowing how much Byron loved the theatre, Davies had reserved for them a box at the Haymarket Theatre.

"The last time I was here," Byron said, looking down at the crowded seats below, "the old-price riots were going on, so I couldn't hear a word from the stage."

Scrope laughed. "Ah, the old-price riots. They finally ended when the management were forced to reduce the price of the seats in the pit back down to their old price, but they made up for it by *doubling* the price of the boxes."

The red velvet curtains on the stage began to move, some of the torches were dimmed, and a hush descended on the theatre.

Scrope was grinning. "You will enjoy this, By," he whispered. "In fact, I know you will *love* it."

Byron was not so sure. "No disrespect to you, Scrope, but the last play you took me to see was deplorable – Robert Coates, a man of over forty – playing *Romeo.*"

Scrope Davies laughed. "Ah, Coates, *Coates,* will we ever forget him? A wealthy and hapless eccentric who hired a theatre because he fancied himself to be a great actor. But be honest, it was very funny to watch."

"It was *hilarious*," Byron agreed, "especially when

Romeo sat up and refused to die at the end because the orchestra had forgotten to herald his tragic death with a drum-roll."

The orchestra suddenly struck up a drum-roll now and the audience hushed, but the curtain did not rise. Instead, one of the actors walked onto the stage in costume with an announcement —

"Ladies and Gemmen ... a most *melancholy* accident has happened to the actor who undertook to play the part of Altamont ..." the actor paused for the audience to take in the tragic effect of this sad accident, his head lowered ...

And from then on Byron and Scrope Davies and the rest of the audience knew they were in for a rum night of it.

Byron was still laughing when he got back to his rooms in St James Street after midnight. He immediately sat down to write a letter to John Hobhouse in Ireland, and tell him all about it.

8, St James Street

My dear Hobhouse — Our friend Scrope is a pleasant person, a facetious companion, and well respected by all who know him; he laughs with the living, though he don't weep with the dead, yet I believe he would do that also, could it do them good service, but good or bad we must endeavour to follow his example, and return to the routine of business or pleasure.

I, this night, saw ROBERT COATES again, but this time performing "Lothario" and the house crammed. Damn me if I ever saw such a scene in my life; the play had to be closed in the 3rd act; after Coates was boo-ed off the stage. He had been interrupted several times before, because he made speeches that were nothing to do with the play, and every soul was in hysterics. And all the other actors were of his own ridiculous model.

A farce followed in dumb-show after Coates had been hooted from the stage AGAIN – for a bawdy address he attempted to deliver. "Love a la mode" was damned, Coates was damned, everything was damned, and *damnable.*

His acting I need not describe, you have seen him at Bath. But never did you see the OTHERS. Those fellows defied burlesque. Oh, Hobby! eye hath not seen, ear hath not heard, nor can the heart of man conceive tonight's performance.

Baron Geramb was in the stage box, and Coates in his address NAILED the baron, to the infinite amusement of the audience and the discomfiture of Geramb, who grew very wroth indeed and shouted back at Coates..

I meant to write to you on other topics, but I must postpone. I can think, and talk, and dream only of those buffoons — Heighho! Goodnight.

*Your ev*er, *BYRON*

Chapter Three

~ ~ ~

Robert Dallas was bewildered and confused. There was something very *chameleonic* about young Lord Byron that was hard to grasp. Words alone could not describe him; one had to actually meet him to understand the rare *fascination* of the young man.

"Are you serious, my lord?"

Dallas stood staring at Lord Byron, as dazed in his mind as if he had been hit on the head with a hammer.

"If *you* think Childe Harold is so good then you have it, keep it, I give it to you as a gift."

"But, Lord Byron ... I cannot accept it."

"Of course you can. I'm sure your mother once taught you that it is rude to refuse a gift."

Byron was looking at the white and weird expression on Dallas's face. "It's reward enough for me that you like it so much, Mr Dallas. So do what you like with it, earn what you can with it, although I shall retain ownership of the copyright."

"And John Murray can publish it?"

"John Murray? Never heard of him. But if it *is* going to be published, then it must be done properly. I'll have nothing to do with any publisher who prints a number of copies, shoves them into his catalogue and merely *hopes* they will sell without any further effort on his part. I want no hole-and-corner publishing that leads to the quick death and disappearance of *Childe Harold*. If that were to happen, I can assure you of a duel and the quick death and disappearance of the publisher also."

"A duel?"

Byron nodded. "In my youth I learned to be a good shot with a pistol, and then during my time abroad I became an absolute *wafer-splitter* with the same pistol."

"Indeed? Well, I can assure you, my lord, that a duel will not be necessary, because Mr John Murray is the man for the job, a man of true sincerity, and a man of good *business*. He will not take your work and waste it. And I will personally be consulting with him at every stage, especially as you have done me such a great favour by placing the manuscript in my hands."

Byron picked up some papers on his desk. "Now will you do me a favour in return, Mr Dallas?"

"Oh, anything, my lord. To help you in any way would be my pleasure."

The smile was back on Byron's face. "You may not think it such a pleasure at the end, but it's your *honest* opinion I need, Mr Dallas, no false praise, just the honest truth."

Dallas inclined his head respectfully. "I gave you my honest opinion about Childe Harold's Pilgrimage did I not? And I shall do the same now. What is it? A new manuscript?"

"No, it is the first draft for my maiden speech in the House of Lords. It's a very important speech, not only to myself, but the people of Nottinghamshire. So, in presenting it, tell me if I *declaim* too much, and at the first hint of a yawn, stop me and tell me why."

Dallas nodded and sat down on a chair. "Very well."

"My lords ..."

Dallas listened as Byron read his speech aloud, constantly stopping to correct himself by hastily grabbing his pen and scratching out a word here and there — "That word's no good, too *mild*. I don't want to send them to sleep, I want to pelt them *awake* long enough to hear my argument."

When are you due to deliver your speech?" Dallas asked.

"Oh, not until the new year. The first slot they can give me is sometime in February – no wonder it takes so long for the Lords to pass or reject *any* Bill put before them. Still, I am damned nervous, and want to be well prepared."

Dallas thought the speech was very good, but he was not given any opportunity to say so, interrupted as they were by his lordship's valet who knocked and poked his head around the door.

"Lord Byron, I'm sorry to disturb you ... but Mr Hobhouse is at the door."

Byron dropped the pen and papers in his hand. "Hobby? *Here?* In person?"

"Aye," the valet smiled, "and he said to tell you he has brought a friend back from Ireland with him."

"Then show them in, show them in —" Byron turned to Dallas. "You don't mind if we stop here? Mr Hobhouse is one of my dearest friends and —"

The expression on his lordship's face turned to absolute delight – but Dallas saw that it was not the sight of his dearest friend that had ignited such happiness in his lordship's eyes, but the small golden-brown dog that his friend led into the room.

"Sorry, Byron, I could not get you an Irish wolfhound," Hobhouse said, "and I'm afraid this young pup is a poor replacement. The Irishman who sold him forgot to tell me that the dog is obviously a bit of a dunce, nervous and shivering all the time."

The pup was indeed very quiet as he stood looking around the room with nervous eyes, but as soon as Lord

Byron bent down and began to fondle him, lifting him up into his arms in a very loving way, the dog came alive with a few small barks and began sniffing Byron's neck excitedly, while Byron gleefully sniffed him back until man and dog were happily nuzzling each other. "Oh, you have given him no *love*, Hobby!"

"I don't give love to animals," Hobhouse retorted. "And the beast made it clear from the start that he did not like me, shivering and shrinking away from me all the time."

"*No* animal likes you, Hobby, because you are such a very crabby and unpleasant fellow at the best of times."

Dallas could see that with the arrival of his new canine friend, Lord Byron had forgotten all about the manuscript of Childe Harold and his speech to the Lords and everything else. He decided it was time to leave and head straight back to John Murray with the good news.

"Lord Byron ..."

"Hobby, this is Mr Robert Dallas, my book agent."

"Mr Hobhouse ..." Dallas shook hands with Lord Byron's friend who was pleasant enough, apart from a puzzled expression on his face. "Book agent? What book are you talking about?"

"Childe Harold's Pilgrimage," Dallas said proudly, knowing that Hobhouse had given Lord Byron his own very negative opinion of the work. "I think it is very original, full of beauty and talent, and I must confess I was somewhat surprised that you, Mr Hobhouse, thought the manuscript had little to recommend it, and much in it to condemn."

Hobhouse appeared startled. "I did not say that!" He looked at Byron. "I said it was not the *best* work you are capable of, and it's not."

"Of course it's not," Byron shrugged, more interested in his new dog. "Everyone gets better as they go along. Now this pup is of the *mastiff* breed. Did the seller tell you anything else about him?"

"No, other than that he was from the litter of a Dutch mastiff."

"Dutch? Then I can expect him to grow into a big dog in time – a man's dog! What shall I name him?"

"Dunce," Hobhouse suggested.

Byron laughed. "No. I think ... as I am the *first* man in the world to have swam across the Hellespont in imitation of Leander in Greek mythology, then I will name this beauty 'Leander' in honour of that event."

Hobhouse was smiling, not at the name of the dog, but at Byron. "It's good to see you again, Byron. My English friends in Ireland were all very dull."

"Then we will have dinner at the Cocoa Tree to catch up. I'll send a note to Scrope Davies to let him know you are back and to come and join us."

Robert Dallas decided it really was now time for him to slip out and leave.

At the open door of the drawing-room he looked back at the two men, thinking them a strange pair to be such close friends — Byron, taller than average, slender yet manly, beautiful and charismatic – and Hobhouse, shortish and stocky with a pugnacious face and cynical eyes.

Now Dallas understood why John Hobhouse was often referred to as "Byron's Bulldog" due to his long habit of always protecting Byron and his interests like a protective bodyguard.

And now Dallas realised how fortunate he was to have acquired the manuscript of Childe Harold's Pilgrimage in less than an hour before Hobhouse had arrived on the scene.

He was certain now, having met the man, that if John Hobhouse knew that Byron had so generously *given* the manuscript to him, as well as all profits from any sales, he would have grabbed the manuscript back and prevented such generosity.

In his Fleet Street office, John Murray was also very surprised. "Are you sure?"

"Oh yes, he was quite clear about it, although he is retaining ownership of the copyright."

John Murray was a shrewd businessman, but also a fair and ethical one. His delight at the news that he could publish the manuscript was tainted by this.

"Nevertheless, Mr Dallas, I shall require a contract between Lord Byron and myself, giving me the right to publish his work, and the contract to be *signed* by Lord Byron himself. After that, if his lordship wishes for you to have *his* share of any profits from sales, then I must have a separate document from Lord Byron confirming that fact. A letter in his own hand and signature will do."

After a pause, John Murray changed his mind. "On second thoughts, I think it would be preferable if I visited Lord Byron myself, not only to discuss the publication of the manuscript, and have the contract signed by him in my presence, but also to acquire a document or letter from him direct to *myself,* instructing me that all his royalties from *Childe Harold* be paid to you for your own use. Yes, I think that would be enough legal clarification of the matter."

Dallas was frowning. "Surely you are not doubting my honesty about Lord Byron's gift to me, Mr Murray?"

"Not at all, I assure you." John Murray smiled his

slow smile. "It's simply the way of sound business, Mr Dallas, sound legal business."

~ ~ ~

John Murray did not rush to request an appointment with Lord Byron; that was not his way. He waited a week and then sent a formal business request for a meeting to discuss the publication contract for Childe Harold's Pilgrimage.

When the two men finally met, in Lord Byron's drawing-room, they instinctively liked each other. After an hour or so of easy and friendly conversation, they decided to continue their discussions over an early dinner in one of the Albany dining rooms, where John Murray found himself being introduced to one of Byron's friends, the famous *Beau Brummell*.

"Byron, you handsome devil! Is it true what I hear? You have spent the past two years ravishing every female between Spain and Greece?"

Byron laughed. "It was not always *me* that did the ravishing ..." and then enigmatically, "if any ravishing was done at all."

Beau Brummell, six foot tall, a handsome and elegant young man, exquisitely dressed, was just as friendly in his manner to John Murray, who also liked him on sight.

"And what about you?" Byron asked Brummell. "Scrope Davies tells me that you and the Prince of Wales have had an altercation. Is that true?"

Brummell sighed as he sat down and helped himself to a glass of champagne. "Prinny and I have been close friends since my boyhood, you know that, so only God knows why he has suddenly turned so bitterly against me."

"Scrope says the rumour around London is that you had the nerve to tell the prince he was getting very fat."

"I am certain I did not." Brummell sipped his champagne. "But now that you mention it ... the man *is* beginning to look more like an elephant than a prince."

Byron laughed; he liked Beau Brummell immensely and had always found him charming and amusing. "So what actually happened in the altercation?"

"It was not an altercation, Byron, it was a *farce*. And one which makes me wonder if Prinny is not on his way to becoming as mad as his father."

Brummell took another sip of his champagne. "It happened at Carlton House when we were all gathered in the prince's Circular Room as usual, having dinner around his huge circular table with me sitting on his right, as usual, and all *seemed* to be going well, until suddenly – without even a hint of a warning – the prince turned to me and threw a glass of wine in my face."

"Good grief!" said John Murray, shocked at such bad behaviour from a royal.

"So what did you do?"

Brummell shrugged. "The only thing I could do. I picked up my own glass and threw wine into the face of the person sitting next to me on my right with a loud instruction — *'The Prince's Toast tonight! Pass it around.'* "

Brummell laughed. "And they *did,* like puppets, all dutifully throwing wine into their neighbour's faces until everyone was dripping and drenched – and Prinny sitting there staring around the table before declaring to me that *they* were all mad. Of course I *had* to agree with him."

When Byron and John Murray had stopped laughing,

Byron asked, "So are you and the prince friends again?"

"*He* may think we are," Brummell said, "but it will be a long time before he gets the pleasure of my company in Carlton House again."

Brummell lowered his voice, a wicked grin on his face. "And being as fat as he is, and suffering so badly with wind as he does, I've given the Prince of Wales a secret new nickname – *Big Ben*, after the thundering clock – *pass it around.*"

When Brummell had left them, John Murray looked at Byron. "Are you going to pass it around?"

Byron shrugged. "No, the insult was not to me, so the revenge should not be mine."

~ ~ ~

The following morning Robert Dallas arrived in John Murray's office in a state of great anxiety. His *need* of a better income for himself and his family was getting quite desperate.

"Well?"

"Not really," said John Murray, putting a hand to his head. "A hint of a hangover, I believe, from all the champagne I drank last night with Lord Byron; although it was a very enjoyable night. Yes, very enjoyable indeed."

"And the contract for Childe Harold?"

"Oh, that was all signed and settled before we left his apartment."

"And as to the matter of my ... commission on sales?"

"That was agreed and signed also. *All* royalties due to Lord Byron are to go in full to you. He seems incredibly obliged to you for all the hard work you have done in finding a publisher for the manuscript."

"But *you* are the first and only publisher I have

shown it to."

"Yes, lucky me." John Murray smiled cynically. "And of all the men alive this day in London – *you*, Mr Dallas, must be the luckiest man of all."

A hint of red embarrassment touched Dallas's face. "His lordship is *too* kind."

Chapter Four

~ ~ ~

During the following weeks John Murray and Robert Dallas discovered that Lord Byron could be as abrupt and as difficult to deal with, as he could be easy and friendly.

Of the *money* that might be gained from his publication, Byron appeared to care nothing; but of the poetry itself, he appeared to care deeply and would accept no changes induced by any other mind or hand.

To Mr. John Murray

Sir, — The time seems to be past when (as Dr Johnson said) a man was certain to "hear the truth from his bookseller." You have paid me so many compliments; it is only fair that I now give equal credit to some of your <u>objections</u>.

With regard to the political parts, I am afraid I can alter nothing; I am too sincere in them for recantation. On Spanish affairs I have said what I saw, and every day confirms me in the notions I formed on the spot.

My work must make its way as well as it can; I know I have everything against me, but if the poem is a true POEM, it will surmount these obstacles, and if not, it deserves its fate.

You have given me no answer to my question—

tell me fairly, did you show the manuscript to any of your corps? – I sent an introductory stanza to Mr Dallas to be forwarded to you; the poem otherwise will open too abruptly.

I am, sir, your most obedient, &c., - BYRON

Within a few days of Fletcher posting the letter to John Murray, a note from Robert Dallas arrived, which incensed Byron — his handwritten manuscript had been shown privately to Mr William Gifford, a man very highly-esteemed in the literary world.

"Of your Satire he spoke highly," Dallas wrote, *"but this poem (Childe Harold) he pronounced not only the best you have written, but equal to any of the present age."*

Byron immediately fired off a letter to John Murray:

Sir, — Since your former letter, Mr Dallas informs me that the manuscript has been submitted for the perusal of Mr Gifford, contrary to my wishes.

I hardly conceived you would so hastily thrust my production into the hands of a stranger, who could be as little pleased by receiving it, as the author is at the Manuscript being offered in such a manner, and to such a man.

You have placed me in a very ridiculous situation, but it is past, and nothing more is to be said on the subject. You hinted to me that you wished some alterations to be made; if they have nothing to do with politics or religion, I will make them.

> I am, Sir, &c &c. — BYRON

And then a reply to Robert Dallas:

Sir — As Gifford has ever been my "Magnus Apollo" any praise, such as you mention, would be more welcome to me than all of Bokara's vaunted gold.

I am not at all pleased with Murray for showing him the manuscript; and I am certain that Gifford must see it in the same light that I do. His praise is nothing to the purpose — what else could he say? He could not spit in the face of one who has praised him publicly in every possible way (me).

I must own that I wish Gifford to know that I did not have any part in such a paltry transaction. It is bad enough to be a scribbler without having to resort to BRIBED praise. It is anticipating, it is kneeling, it is begging, — the devil! the devil! the devil! And all without my wish and contrary to my expressed desire.

I wish Murray had been tied to PAYNE'S neck when he jumped into the Paddington canal, and

*so tell him – that is the proper receptacle for all
publishers – the canal! And you will ask him to
excuse me for saying so, as I am not one for cant
or hypocrisy.*

I am also etc., etc., – BYRON

In John Murray's office, Byron's literary agent was
feeling extremely worried. "I do believe that he is very
angry with *both* of us," said Dallas.

John Murray was thoughtful. "Yet I like the fact that
he is not in any way *hypocritical*, as he says. Rather
refreshing, wouldn't you say? Especially coming from
one of the aristocracy."

Dallas was taken aback by Murray's unperturbed
manner.

"And his wish for you to have jumped with Payne into
the Paddington canal?"

Murray laughed. "Oh, that is no more than the
friendly banter he and Beau Brummell were exchanging
between themselves during our first dinner together."

"Nevertheless," Dallas was still fretting, "I wish you
had not shown it to Gifford when he asked you not to.
And Cawthorns are being quite *savage* with me for
offering Childe Harold to you first, and not to them."

John Murray remained unperturbed. "Then I shall
have to make sure that neither Lord Byron nor yourself
regret that offer to me. I know I shall not regret it."

The man's suave confidence did not console Dallas,
who rushed home and wrote a grovelling letter to Lord
Byron, pleading with him not to be angry with Mr
Murray.

Lord Byron *boomeranged* a reply back via a
messenger, which did little to console Dallas in any way.

I WILL be angry with Murray. It was a back-shop, Paternoster-row, paltry proceeding, and if the procedure turns out as it deserves, I will raise all Fleet Street, and borrow the giant's staff from St Dunstan's church to IMMOLATE that betrayer of trust. I have written to him, as he has never before written to by an author, and I hope you will amplify my wrath, until it has an effect upon him — B

And so began one of the closest and most famous friendships ever forged between a publisher and his author, and one which was to last a lifetime.

Chapter Five

~ ~ ~

A chance remark made by Samuel Rogers, another poet, suddenly put Thomas Moore into a state of great alarm.

"So Lord Byron is back in England, and about to publish again."

Rogers lowered his newspaper. "And according to this, he is rumoured to have included a few stanzas in clear condemnation of Lord Elgin for his vandalism and theft of the Greek sculptures from the marble walls of the Parthenon. And quite right too. Elgin had no moral or legal *right* to do it."

When Thomas Moore gave no answer, Samuel Rogers looked at him more directly, and saw that Moore had put down his glass and was looking quite unwell."

"Something wrong with you, Moore?"

"No..." Thomas Moore's face had gone very pale, "but now you have mentioned Lord Byron ... I suddenly find myself in a bit of a perilous scrape."

"With Lord Byron? How so?"

"He might shoot me dead in a duel."

Samuel Rogers, a man of fifty, was almost twenty years older than the Irish poet Thomas Moore, and Rogers knew for certain that Moore did *not* know Lord Byron, and had *never* met him.

"So how can you be in a scrape with him? You know Lord Byron no better than I do, which is not at all."

Moore stood up, confused as to what to do next. "It's all due to that damn book of his ... *English Bards and Scotch Reviewers* ... after his criticism of me in that book, I wrote and challenged Lord Byron to a duel."

"*You* challenged Lord Byron?"

Rogers looked disbelievingly at the dapper little Irishman.

"Even though you had heard the rumour that Byron always carries a pistol on his person and spends all his time on that estate of his shooting at everything except the animals? They say all the outside doors at the back of his mansion are pock-marked with bullet holes from his years of practicing his aim."

"I know, I know, but I lost my head, because his criticism of me in that book was so unfair. But everything has changed now. I'm married *now,* with a baby on the way, so I cannot risk being shot dead *now.* Bessy would be widowed and heartbroken if I was."

"Calm down, calm down; you haven't been shot dead yet."

Moore found it hard to calm down. The responsibilities of marriage and impending fatherhood were too important to him now to take any risks. "I must get back to Bessy. I have stayed too long as it is."

He found his hat and looked appealingly at Rogers. "If there is a duel, will you be my second?"

"Certainly not."

"Then thank you and good day!"

Moore left the house and rushed straight home to Bessy, wishing he had not been such an utter *fool* when sending that letter to Lord Byron; but then he had been in his cups, had drunk too much wine, intoxicated and full of himself due to the success of his *Irish Melodies*, indignant with the aristocrat for scathing him – *and* he had also been safely far away in his own country of Ireland.

"So why *did* you send the letter challenging him?"

Bessy asked. "How did you expect Lord Byron to respond?"

"To be perfectly honest, I expected him to send me a letter of apology, but all I got was a letter from one of his friends informing me that Lord Byron had gone abroad to Greece and the Levant, but he would pass the letter on to him as soon as he got back ... and now he's back!"

"Oh, Tommy." Bessy could see how distraught her dear husband was and pitied him. They had been married for less than two years and still doted on each other.

"It's not that I'm a coward, you must understand that, Bessy. When I first sent the challenge two years ago I was ready – for the sake of my honour and good name – to risk death if necessary. But that was before I married *you,* and now *we* have a coming child to think of."

"We do indeed," said Bessy; a beautiful girl who was not yet nineteen, twelve years younger than her husband, but her mind and manner had always been very sensible.

"Why don't you write a nice letter to Lord Byron," she suggested, "explaining the change in your circumstances since you sent the challenge, telling him that all you want is an apology, and that will settle the matter. Is that not a good idea, Tommy?"

Thomas Moore stared at his wife, his blue eyes as always filled with adoration. "Bessy, it's a *perfect* idea!"

Tommy then searched through his papers and finally found the copy of his first letter to Lord Byron:

22, Molesworth Street
Dublin. January 1, 1810

To The Right Hon. George Lord Byron
Newstead Abbey, Notts.

My Lord,

Having just seen the name 'Lord Byron' prefixed to the <u>second edition </u>of a work entitled "English Bards and Scotch Reviewers" in which, it appears to me, the <u>lie</u> is given to a public statement of mine, respecting a duelling affair with Mr Jeffrey some years since.

I shall not, I fear, be able to return to London for a week or two: but in the mean time, I trust your Lordship will not deny me the satisfaction of knowing whether you avow the <u>insult</u> contained in the passages alluded to.

It is needless to suggest to your Lordship the propriety of keeping our correspondence secret.

> *I have the honour to be*
> *Your Lordship's very humble servant*
> *THOMAS MOORE.*

Reading it again now, Tommy considered it a very good letter; but he was also very uncertain as to the consequences of the letter if Lord Byron *had* been in England at that time.

What did anyone know about the man? Few of Tommy's English friends had ever met him or even seen him. All had only heard of him due to his book, *English Bards*.

But then, Tommy realised, Lord Byron's circle of friends would be very different to his own social circle.

The members of *Haut Monde* were not in the habit of socialising with commoners. And according to Samuel Rogers, Lord Byron was reputed to be a close friend of Mr George 'Beau' Brummell, and they did not come any more *haut* than Brummell.

No, if an Irish poet hoped to reach the pinnacle of literary *success* in London, as Tommy did now, he could not afford to make an enemy of one of the upper class. Why else had he dedicated his last book of poetry so sincerely to 'The Prince of Wales.'

He dipped his pen into the inkpot and began his letter to Lord Byron, telling him that since writing to him in the first instance, he had taken upon himself obligations, both as husband and father, "*which make most men – especially those who have nothing to bequeath to their family – less willing to expose themselves unnecessarily to danger.*"

Tommy then rambled on about his doubts now of that first letter ever having reached his lordship, due to the noble traveller having journeyed to Greece some months before the arrival of the letter, so —

"The time which has elapsed since then, though it has done away neither the injury nor the feeling of it, has, in many respects, altered my situation; and the only object I have now in writing to your Lordship is to preserve some consistency with that former letter, and to prove to you that the injured feeling still exists.

It would give me sincere pleasure if, by any satisfactory explanation, you would enable me to seek the honour of being henceforward ranked among your acquaintances.

> *I have the honour to be*
> *Your Lordship's very humble servant*
> *THOMAS MOORE*

~ ~ ~

Byron was in Cambridge with John Hobhouse when Moore's letter finally reached him, and utterly perplexed him.

He showed the letter to Hobby. "Do you have any idea what *insult* he is talking about?"

Hobby was staring thoughtfully at the letter. "Thomas Moore ... isn't he the one —"

"Yes, one of my favourite poets. When I was sixteen I read his poetry all the time. It was all so romantically voluptuous it would have stirred the innocence of any adolescent mind. Moore was accused of being *immoral,* and then when Francis Jeffrey savaged him in the 'Edinburgh Review', so Thomas Moore challenged Jeffrey to a duel."

"And now Thomas Moore is challenging *you* to a duel. Perhaps duelling is one of his regular leisure pursuits."

Byron laughed. "It would seem so. But in 'English Bards' it was Jeffrey I was satirising over that duel, not Moore. Although both men were ridiculous from the outset."

"How so?"

"Well, Moore for challenging a critic to a duel in the first place. Did *I* go around threatening to shoot people when the Edinburgh Review savaged me?"

"No, but you were on the verge of shooting *yourself.*"

"True, but I more sanely fired back by writing 'English Bards' wherein I savaged Jeffrey in return. And as for Thomas Moore, it was the *duel* I lampooned, not him."

"What was so funny about it?"

"To be fair, all I know is what Grubb Street wrote about it."

"Grubb Street?"

"Fleet Street – those dogs that described me as *'a lord with a limp'*, hobbling around Cambridge writing my poetry as if I was some *Richard the Third* character. They probably still think I hobble around hunched up and muttering rhymes to myself with one eye cocked – *'What do I fear? – Myself? – There's none else by – Richard loves Richard – that is, I and I!'*"

Hobby had to laugh at Byron's comic mimicry, and also the ridiculousness of such a comparison. "You would make a good actor, Byron."

"Oh, that reminds me – last week I saw John Kemble playing Coriolanus at the Haymarket Theatre. His performance was glorious!"

"Forget all that. The duel between Jeffrey and Moore?"

"Oh yes, the famous duel. It took place at dawn in a park at Chalk Farm, but the police had been notified and arrived on the scene and stopped it, hauling both men off to a cell in Bow Street police station where – according to Grubb Street – when the pistols were examined by the police they found – not bullets – but *pellets* inside both guns."

After a second of disbelief, Hobhouse roared with laughter. "A schoolboy duel!"

"But worse was to come," said Byron. "Grubb Street exaggerated the story for days, as those hacks always do, until the pellets were then reported to be made of nothing more lethal than *paper*, running with the headline *'The Paper Pellet Duel!'*

When Hobhouse had stopped laughing he asked, "So what are you going to do now – tear up a piece of Shakespeare and load it into your pistol to meet Moore in a duel?"

Byron was reading the letter again...

"It's nonsensical," Hobby went on, "challenging a man to a duel for simply lampooning a ridiculous affair."

"No ... now that I read his letter more carefully, Hobby, his original challenge was due to me – in *English Bards* – implying that he was a liar in some way. Now that *is* a very grievous offence to any gentleman."

"But you never received that first challenge, did you?"

"No."

"Then I should just ignore this one."

Byron was inclined to agree. "I'm not even sure if it's a duel he wants..." He read aloud the last sentence of the letter again ...

"In conclusion, it would give me sincere pleasure if, by any satisfactory explanation, you would enable me to seek the honour of being henceforward ranked among your acquaintances."

Hobhouse shrugged. "Well, there, it's obvious isn't it? The man is a *social* climber, using this as an excuse to make your acquaintance and be ranked amongst your friends."

Byron looked at Hobby, thinking he could be incredible dense in all matters *not* relating to politics.

"Moore is a well known poet in both Ireland and England, and as yet I am *unknown* as a poet to all but a few thousand."

"You are a lord. Any commoner would love to have a

lord amongst their acquaintances."

Byron grinned. "You are a commoner, Hobby, albeit the son of a very wealthy man. So is it my *title* you like, or me?"

Hobhouse shrugged. "It's your title of course. I detest you."

"And Moore has enough aristocratic friends from what I know," Byron continued. "Princess Charlotte is one of his most ardent admirers."

"Of his *poetry*, not of him personally, probably never set eyes on the man. And probably no other members of the aristocracy have either. So, are you going to take up his challenge or not?"

"Of course I'm going to take up his challenge, although I'm not quite sure what his challenge is. He seems to be reaching out to me with *both* hands — one holding a pistol, and the other to shake."

"Ignore him," Hobby advised again. "His first letter is a mystery that no one has ever received, and his second is stupid, so just ignore him."

~ ~ ~

If Thomas Moore had a grievance against Lord Byron before, he had an even bigger one now. Three weeks had passed, and still no reply from his lordship.

"Such *discourtesy!*" Moore complained to Samuel Rogers. "Such arrogance!"

"I think you may have been too quick on the draw, Tommy," said Rogers, busily searching through his bookshelves. "Lord Byron may have been offended by *your* lack of balance between gratitude and anger."

"What are you talking about?"

"This!" said Rogers, pulling out a book and flicking through it. "Lord Byron may have offended you in

'English Bards', but he gave you great praise in his *Hours of Idleness* before that."

"What?"

"Here, read it ... Byron obviously included this poem in defence of *your* earlier castigation by Jeffrey in the Edinburgh Review. The sympathy of one poet for another, I suppose."

Confused, Moore took the book into hands. "Lord Byron wrote about *me*? When was this?"

"It was when you wrote under the pseudonym of *'Thomas Little'* for your more amorous poetry, although every reviewer knew it was Thomas Moore who had written those poems, and obviously so did every other poet."

"And Lord Byron —"

"Sprang to your defence. Read it."

Moore began to read the poem, his face reddening with every line:

POOR LITTLE! sweet, melodious bard!

Of late esteemed it monstrous hard

That he who sang before all;

He who the lore of love expanded,

By dire Reviewers should be branded

As void of wit as of morals.

And yet, while Beauty's praise is thine,

Harmonious favourite of the nine!

Repine not at thy lot;

Thy soothing words may still be read,

When Persecution's arm is dead,

And Critics are forgot.

Moore was almost in tears. "Why did you not tell me about this when it was published?"

"I didn't know you then, and you lived over in Ireland, so how could I tell you?"

"So *why* have you not told me since?"

"Because I read it myself only yesterday. I had read only the first half of the book before I put it away and forgot it. The first half is not very brilliant in my opinion. It was your conversation to me about Lord Byron that prompted me to search it out again."

Moore was so furious with Samuel Rogers he made a quick excuse and left, rushing home to Bessy, still clutching Byron's *Hours of Idleness* in his hand.

"I feel so embarrassed now. Not a word of gratitude when he supported me *in print* – and then a bitter letter of complaint when he annoyed me. No wonder he has simply ignored my letter to him now."

"Oh no, he has not ignored you, Tommy." Bessy moved over to the sideboard and lifted a letter. "This came this morning. It has Lord Byron's seal on it."

Shocked, Moore took the letter from Bessy. "Oh, pray God it is not his angry acceptance of my challenge! I am distraught enough without having to contemplate the possibility of a duel with a man who has supported me in the past."

"Shall I read his letter first?" Bessy asked gently. "To give you fair warning of what to expect before you read it yourself?"

Tommy knew the reason she had made such a suggestion was because she was impatient to know what was in the letter. He quickly broke the seal, opened out the letter, and saw that the address at the top was in the town of Cambridge –

Sir, — Your letter followed me from Notts to this place, which will account for the delay in my reply. Your former letter I never had the honour to receive. The public statement you mention, I know nothing of

At the time of your duel with Mr Jeffrey, I had recently entered College, and remember to have read a few squibs about the occasion; and from the recollection of these, I derived all my knowledge on the subject, without the slightest idea of "giving the lie" to a statement by you, which I never saw.

When I put my name to the production which has occasioned this correspondence, I became responsible to all whom it might concern. My situation leaves me no choice: it rests with the injured and the angry to obtain reparation in their own way.

Tommy looked up. "He's ready to meet me in a duel! Oh, dear God, what am I to do?"

"There's more," Bessie pointed, and Tommy read on:

With regard to the passage in question, YOU were certainly not the person to whom I felt personally hostile. On the contrary, my thoughts were engrossed by one, whom I had reason to believe was my worst literary enemy, Francis Jeffery, nor could I foresee that his former antagonist was about to become his champion. You do not specify what you wish to have done; I can neither retract nor apologise for a charge of falsehood, which I never advanced.

In the beginning of the week, I shall be at No. 8 St James's Street. Any gentleman delegated by you, shall find me ready to adopt any conciliatory proposition which shall not compromise my own honour —or, failing in that, to make the atonement you deem it necessary to require.

I have the honour to be, Sir,
Your humble servant
BYRON

Bessy read the letter herself, but made no comment about the content, other than remarking on the address: "St James's Street", why, that's just a few streets away. Oh, Tommy, it is never a good thing to quarrel with one's *neighbours*."

When Tommy gave no reply, Bessy waited ... until Tommy finally shrugged. "Well, that's a satisfactory explanation enough. He did not see my public statement in the Press, so he could not have called me a liar over it. I shall write to him now, accepting his explanation."

My Lord,

Your Lordship's letter is, upon the whole, as satisfactory as I could expect. It contains all that I could require of you.

As your Lordship does not show any great wish to proceed beyond the rigid formula of explanation, it is not for me to make any further advances.

Allow me to add that I still have the <u>copy</u> of that first letter sent to you, if your Lordship should feel inclined to see it – because I confess I do not feel <u>quite</u> easy under the manner in which you have dwelt upon the miscarriage of my first letter to you ...

"Oh, Tommy, now you are insinuating that *he* could be a liar! Of course he did not receive your first letter if he says he did not, so why are you now casting some doubt on that?"

Looking over his shoulder at the letter he was writing, Bessy was losing patience. "It will end in a duel if you are not careful!"

Tommy frowned, wondering about that ... but he decided to take the risk. He rather enjoyed the idea of hearing from *Lord* Byron again.

Chapter Six

~ ~ ~

It was winter, dark and dreary weather, the snow upon the ground, and a strangling gloom was depressing Byron, as it always did whenever he came back to Newstead Abbey, so near to Annesley Hall and Mary Chaworth.

He had mounted his horse with the intention of seeing the current situation of the textile workers in the town of Nottingham, but his old horse seemed to know better than he did where he *really* wanted to go.

He had ridden carefully through the parklands and the broad acres of Newstead, and on through the fields that led to Diadem Hill, overlooking Annesley Hall.

Reining his horse to a halt on the hill, he sat and gazed down at the black trees standing rigid in the white snow, their branches no longer opulent and green, but barren now, thick black twigs jutting up to the grey sky.

Yet in his mind he could see again the trees as they looked in springtime, alive with delicate green buds, and Mary on her horse riding beside him, as she had so often done in their teenage years. He could still hear her voice, talking, laughing ...

The air around him was damp, like a cold mist, but his mind had moved on to summer, that last wonderful summer with her, when the white blossoms of spring had all fallen, and the wild roses were in full bloom under the sunshine, and they had sat by a tree together, here on Diadem Hill.

She had taken his hand in both of her hands, clasping it tight as she looked at him with love and said — "Your friendship has made my life so sweet, Byron. I will always cherish our friendship, and I hope you will too."

"It's *you* I want to cherish," he had said emotionally, but she put her fingers to his lips and smiled, "Tell me one more poem by Thomas Moore, do you know any more?"

"I know them all – *'The Minstrel Boy* to the war has gone, in the ranks of death you will find him— "

"Oh no!" she interrupted. " Too sad."

"The Last Rose of Summer?"

"Even sadder."

He had stared at her. "How can a dead rose be even sadder than a dead boy?"

Her face had become tinted with a flush of pink. "I was not being callous, just thoughtless in my words and request for something more cheerful."

Her face was beautiful, perfect in its oval shape, her large dark eyes silently beguiling him to forgive her, her firm bottom lip slightly pouting at his rebuke.

He had wanted to cover those lips of hers with his own and devour her with passion.

"You are an angel," he said. "An angelic being."

She laughed away his adoration. "Speaking of angels, here's a question for you, Byron ... How many thousand angels could dance on the point of a very fine needle, without jostling one another?"

Laughing, they had debated the number, until he remembered one of Moore's poems about a girl who always acted like the purest of angels.

"Although," he said, "this one was written under his pseudonym, 'Thomas Little'. "

"Say it then," she said smiling; so he did —

"Oh! why should Platonic control, love,

Enchain an emotion so free?

Your soul, though a very sweet soul, love,

Will never be sufficient for me.

If you think, by this coolness and scorning,

To seem more angelic and bright,

Be an angel, my love, in the morning,

But, oh, be a WOMAN tonight!"

Mary's face had flushed into a pink tint again. "You are incorrigible, Byron, your thoughts are always on romance."

"With *you*," he agreed.

"Then you are foolish." A sadness had come into her dark eyes. "I must go home now," she said, standing up. "The sun is low, I have stayed out with you too long."

And yet ... and yet ... he remembered, when walking silently back down the hill together to her home, their hands had touched, and clasped, and her fingers had tightly clung on to his as if he was the dearest friend she had ever known.

And then they had paused by a tree and she had hesitantly told him that she was promised in marriage to Jack Musters.

His rage, his *rage* ... but all that rage had gone now, because when they had met again, a few years later at a dinner at Annesley Hall, he was sure those dark eyes of hers were looking at him with love again ... the hopeless love of a girl now married to someone else ... a good girl, a *respectable* girl who would prefer to suffer silently than damage her reputation. He knew her so well.

He reached under his cloak and took out his watch ... not quite noon ... He knew she always left the house to take a walk or a ride every day, so if he stayed here long enough, he would *see* her again. Should he do so? Was it worth it? Even from a distance?

Yes, yes, *yes*.

~ ~ ~

The cold hours went by slowly. He began to freeze. He pulled his cloak tighter around him to warm him and stop his slight shivering.

Was he mad? Sitting here on a horse on a hill just to get a glimpse of his goddess. The only warmth in the air was the two funnels of smoke shooting up from his horse's nostrils.

He looked down at Leander, his mastiff, sitting on his front paws so quietly, as good as gold as he patiently waited with his master.

Some time later the north wind at his back began to blow up stronger, and even Leander gave one or two barks of protest at the long wait.

Finally he sighed, deciding that, yes, he must be mad to remain sitting here waiting like the love-struck teenager he had once been.

He urged his horse forward: why had he not realised that she was unlikely to come out in this cold?

He rode back to Newstead Abbey where everyone was busily preparing for Christmas and the arrival of John Hobhouse, Francis Hodgson and William Harness the following day.

Old Joe Murray was up the stairs shouting orders at some of the servants. Fletcher was missing – as he usually was when he was needed – so it was Nanny Smith, the housekeeper, who came rushing to help him remove his snow-slushed boots.

She urged him over to the large fire in the ground-floor parlour, but his bounding dog got there first, shaking himself and flopping down in front of the flames as if all he wanted was the feel of some *heat* on his coat.

Also needing warmth, Byron sat down in the nearest armchair, and Nanny Smith sat down on a low stool in front of him, ready to pull off his boots and have a gossip with him while she did so, as usual. It was something she had been doing since he was ten years old, so they were both practised and knew what to expect.

"Is it true that the ladies in London have stopped wearing stays under their frocks?" she asked eagerly.

Byron's blue eyes popped wide at her. "Now how would *I* know that?"

"Oh God!" Nanny's hands went to her face in shame. "Oh, forgive me, my lord, but for a minute there I forgot myself. Although they do say you have plenty of lady friends down there."

"Who's *they*?"

"Fletcher."

Fletcher walked into the parlour in perfect time to meet Byron's glare. "Fletcher, the *first rule* of being a valet is never to disclose any of your employer's private business or affairs."

"And I never have," Fletcher insisted.

"So why is Nanny asking me about my lady friends?"

Now it was Fletcher's turn to glare at Nanny Smith. "All I said in answer to *her* questions was that his lordship had many friends in London, and some were ladies."

"That's all?"

"That's all."

Byron looked at Nanny, who nodded meekly. "That's

all."

"So why did you ask me such a question, Nanny? Do you think I go around like a naughty child lifting up the dresses of ladies to peek at what they are wearing underneath?"

Fletcher's laughter broke the strain, but Nanny was still confounded with shame and red-faced.

"I'll do that!" Fletcher said, waving Nanny aside. "You're too old to be pulling off boots."

"No I am not *too old* – how dare you!" Nanny Smith had never looked so insulted. "I was pulling off his lordship's boots when you were still learning how to wipe your nose, William Fletcher, so don't you dare take that uppity tone with me."

"No, no, let her continue," Byron said, waving Fletcher away. "It will give Nanny and I a chance to talk about events in Nottingham."

"Well *I* could tell you that – all you need to know," declared Fletcher. "I've just been told it by my Uncle Phebus. The anger of the machine-breakers is even worse now."

"You can tell me later," Byron said. "But now, if you would be so kind as to scram, Fletcher, I would like some time alone with Nanny."

As soon as they were alone, and Fletcher had gone, Nanny knew he was going to ask *her* about the frame-breakers, because she lived here, day in and day out, and so obviously she knew more than Fletcher or his deaf old Uncle Phebus.

"Nanny ... Mary Chaworth ... is she well, do you know?"

"I didn't want to talk about *her*," Nanny Smith said later to Joe Murray, "not *her* who had hurt him so much and broken his heart in the past. And God knows why he don't just forget her like any sensible young man would do. But well, he asked me a civil question, so I was forced to give him a civil answer."

"I'm sure I couldn't say, my lord."

"You've heard nothing about her of late? Does she live a quiet life then?"

"On the *contrary*," declared Nanny, unable to stop herself. "If she spends more than a few hours a day in her home I'd be very surprised to hear it."

Byron smiled; knowing he would learn all there was to learn from Nanny.

"She's a lady of course ..." Nanny motioned for him to stretch out his leg and put his right boot into her lap, and when he did so, she tugged gently and carefully on the boot, knowing his right foot was the damaged foot.

"And like so many ladies of her class," Nanny said, "Mary spends a lot of her time doing her *charity* work."

"Charity work? What — with the families of the unemployed frame-breakers?"

Nanny stopped what she was doing and stared at him. "The frame-breakers? Why would she help them or anyone belonging to them? Not when her husband is the biggest enemy the frame-breakers have – him and his militia! There's not a working man in Nottingham that has a good word to say about Jack Musters ."

Byron had no interest in talking about Mary's husband. "So what charity work does she do?"

"At the hospital, with the orphaned children of those mothers who have died in childbirth. She has two children of her own now, so I suppose that's where she gets her sympathy."

Byron was startled. "*Two* children? When did she have the second?"

"Some time last year, while you were away in Greece."

Byron's mood was darkening, yet he listened to every word Nanny said as she rambled on.

"I suppose the reason you and she got on so well in the past is because you were both so similar. She without a father and so made a ward of the Chancery Court because she was the heiress of Annesley ... and you also with a dead father and also made a Ward of the Chancery Court because you were the heir to Newstead Abbey."

Byron sighed. "Mary could have united two loving hearts and two great houses, yet she threw it all away for the son of the Sheriff of Nottingham. And why?— because she thought I was too young for her, although I was only *two* years younger than herself, but he was ten years older. She could have waited – there was no need for her to rush into a marriage with anyone."

"Oh there was," Nanny said knowingly, "and the rush was all on *his* side, frightened he would lose her."

Byron yanked his boot back, and sat up. "What do you mean?"

"Oh, you wouldn't know, because you were up at Cambridge at the time," said Nanny. "The delay was all due to the man her mother married, her new step-father, Reverend Clarke. He learned something about Jack Musters that made him and Mary's mother turn against the marriage. They would not allow Mary to marry Jack Musters under any circumstances. They were determined that Jack Musters would *not* inherit the Annesley estate."

Byron was now alarmed. "What did the stepfather know about Musters?"

Nanny shook her head. "No one knows that, not even Mary I suspect. And all I know is what your dear mother told me about it."

"My mother? My *mother* knew about this?"

"Yes, but she said you weren't to be told."

"What?" Byron's frustration was rising. "What wasn't I to be told?"

"That not only Jack Musters, but the entire Musters family mounted a legal challenge against Mary's mother and stepfather for not allowing the marriage to take place. And Jack Musters' mother, in particular, Sophia Musters, was very pushy and behind it all. The whole Musters family went down to the Court of Chancery in London to get the rule of Mary's guardians set aside. Jack Musters brought witnesses to testify that he was a man of good character and behaviour, and the Court agreed there was no sound reason why Mary Chaworth's earlier pledge of marriage should not be fulfilled, but only *if*, Mary herself wished it."

"And did she?"

"She must have done, because they were married shortly afterwards, while you were away at Cambridge. And the rush was nothing to do with Mary being pregnant or anything like that, because almost a year passed before a child was born."

"So then ... she must have been no more than sixteen or so when she had agreed to marry Jack Musters."

"Aye. You would have been away at Harrow at the time when Jack Musters first set his eye on her. As lovely a girl as Mary was then, she was also a very sweet and innocent type of girl, wasn't she?"

When Byron did not answer, his eyes dwelling thoughtfully on his sleeping dog, Nanny Smith continued:

"The marriage ceremony took place in the drawing-room of the Muster's house at Colwick, and not at the bride's home of Annesley Hall, as you would expect. So

Mary was married without a single relative of her own present, not even her own mother, nor her stepfather, because both refused to attend."

Byron pulled his right boot back on, beside himself with frustration. "So all this was going on and not one word about it was said to *me* – not even by you or Joe Murray!"

"Oh, neither of us would have dared to say anything, my lord, not when your mother was alive. And neither of us told a word of it to any of our own servants either, in case it got back to your mother."

"And *why* did my mother not want me to know?"

Unable to think of a kind answer, Nanny shrugged and decided to be honest.

"Because she wanted to keep you as far away as possible from Mary Chaworth. She did not like the girl one bit, nor the way Mary always teased and flirted with you here at Newstead. *I* said it was because Mary was a happy-natured girl and so fond of fun, but your mother insisted it was because Mary wanted to get her hands on the estate of Newstead Abbey and become mistress of it, and displace your mother."

"Mary didn't give two hoots about Newstead Abbey. The only estate she cared about was Annesley!"

Byron wished he could rage at his mother now, pacing up and down the parlour with his hand to his head as his mother's words came roaring back to him — "*Even if you were of a proper age, and even if she was disengaged, that young lady would most definitely not be my choice for you!*"

"Well, it's all gone and past now, just like your dear mother," said Nanny with a deep sigh. "Even Mary's mother and stepfather have gone."

"Gone? You mean ... dead?"

"Oh no! Nothing like that!" Nanny shook her head. "At the time of the wedding, in accordance with the usual marriage settlement, as soon as Jack Musters changed his name to Jack Chaworth and became the inheritor of Mary's estate of Annesley, Mary's mother and stepfather packed their bags and moved out to Gonalston Rectory. They refused to live under the same roof as Jack Musters or have anything to do with his family, because they were certain the main reason he had been anxious to marry Mary was to get his hands on her inheritance."

"Mary's mother moved out? But of all people in this world, Mary adored her mother."

"Aye, I know." Nanny nodded. "And Mary must have known how appalled her own dead father would have been to know his wife had been more or less forced out of the grand home he had provided for her."

Byron was looking quizzically at Nanny Smith. "How do you *know* all this?"

"Like I said, I heard it all from your dear mother. She and I were very close – well, we could *not* be anything but close, could we? Seeing as I attended on her day and night. And let me tell you, your mother knew *everything* that was going on at Annesley Hall, always most interested in it. Until, of course, Mary was safely married to Jack Musters, and then all her interest vanished."

Nanny folded her hands in her lap. "But, you know, your mother wasn't *all* wrong. As she said to me later — 'You see now, Nanny, the way Mary Chaworth allowed her own mother to be forced out of her own home, and that's what she would have done to me if she had got a chance to marry my George – forced *me* out of Newstead Abbey and into some lonely cottage somewhere."

"Mary is not that kind of person, mean and selfish," Byron insisted. "Mary undoubtedly suffered more over the removal of her mother than anyone could know."

"Aye, happen you're right," Nanny said. "I'm only telling you what your mother said to me.."

Byron had not loved his mother. His life from childhood with her had been extremely difficult. At times he had even hated her – hated her cruel jibes and her insane possessiveness towards him, and her jealousy of any person he had liked. And now .... now he did not want to start hating her again.

He said to Nanny: "Speak to no one of this ever again. Do you understand me, Nanny? It's over and finished and my mother's sins must be allowed to die with her. And as for Annesley and Mary Chaworth, I don't want those names to be ever mentioned again in this house. No whispering. No more gossip about Mary. Understand?"

As he walked to the door Nanny called out –"Where are you going now?"

"Back out to the snow – to cool down!"

~ ~ ~

Walking through the snow, Byron thought over all that Nanny Smith had told him, his mind going back to the unexpected dinner he had been invited to at Annesley Hall some months before he had left for Greece. It was a strange invitation, coming when it did, because he and Mary had not seen each other once throughout his years at Cambridge.

He had expected her to be lively and full of fun as was her nature, and very happy in her married state; so much so that he almost did not go, believing he would be unable to bear seeing her so happy with another man.

Yet, it was not so. There were fourteen people in all sat down to dinner that night, but neither he nor Mary spoke barely a word to anyone else, nor to each other. Both seemed frozen at the sight of each other again, their eyes constantly meeting across the table over the tureens and candles and lingering silently.

Although we never silence broke,

Our eyes a sweeter language spoke.

~ ~ ~

Later that night, in the Blue Room, Byron was sitting at a table covered in books when Joe Murray entered the room. He neither heard nor looked up, and Joe knew why. Even as a boy his lordship's reading was extensive, but his special delight was the study of voyagers and their travels. He would sit up all night reading them, devouring every detail in the pages, his whole mind absorbed in their adventures. No wonder he had gone off to Spain and Greece and Turkey and did so much travelling himself.

"My lord."

Byron looked up, and saw Joe Murray carrying a letter on a platter.

"Did you not see this, my lord? I *did* tell you about it, and it's been sitting on the post table all day."

Byron took the letter.

"Will I wait up?" asked Joe, glancing at the clock which showed almost midnight.

"No, you go to bed now."

"Is there anything else you need?"

"Yes, I need you to go to bed and leave me alone."

Joe smiled. "Then I'll say goodnight, my lord."

The letter was from his half-sister, Augusta, opening her heart and fretful mind to him.

He read the letter slowly and carefully, due to Augusta's muddled way of thinking and writing when she was upset, yet as he read on he could understand her alarm and distress, and all due to the thorny Prince of Wales.

Augusta's husband, George Leigh, had long been a trusted and valued equerry to the Prince, but now they had quarrelled due to the Prince *"accusing George of cheating him in selling a horse for him, claiming George had kept for himself part of the sale money..."*

Byron laid down the letter, moved his book to one side lifted his pen and ink and a pad of Vellum, and wrote back to her:

My dearest Augusta, — I wrote to you yesterday with all my news, and now I shall fill up this one sheet before I go to bed.

I can't help regretting, on your account, that so long an intimacy with the Prince should be dissolved now when your husband might have derived some advantage from HRH's friendship.

However, at all events, and in all situations, you have a brother in me, and a home here — I am led into this train of thinking by a part of your letter which hints at financial losses.

Pray can't you contrive to pay me a visit? I really

do not perceive anything so formidable in a journey here, but all this comes of Matrimony. You have a Nurse and the children and the weight of a family to carry with you. If you did come, you could do what you please without us interfering with each other. This place is so extensive that two people might live together without ever seeing, hearing, or meeting — but I cannot feel the comfort of this myself unless I also marry.

In short it would be the most amiable matrimonial mansion — my future wife and I shall be so happy, one in each Wing, and never seeing the other — If this description won't make you come, I can't tell what will.

But I am wandering — in short I only want to assure you, that I love you, & you must not think me indifferent because I don't show my affection in the usual way. Goodnight, I have to walk half a mile to my bedchamber.

Yrs ever
BYRON

Before sealing the letter, he wrote a cheque for three hundred pounds, payable to George Leigh, the equivalent of one year's salary as an equerry to the Prince of Wales.

Chapter Seven

~ ~ ~

When John Hobhouse arrived at Newstead in a cheerful mood for Christmas, Byron looked at him accusingly. "The night that you and I went to dinner at Annesley Hall, before we went to Greece? Do you remember?

Hobby paused to think back. "Yes, I remember. What about it?"

"In the carriage coming back, *you* insisted that Mary Chaworth appeared *very happy*, content in her marriage and idolising her husband."

"So?"

"You lied."

"Oh for goodness sake, Byron!" Hobby irritably threw off his cloak. "Not this Mary Chaworth nonsense again! If I lied to you – which I don't believe I did – it was based on the best and kindest motive."

"Which was?"

"That she was *married*. Face up to it, Byron, she *could* have had you, but she chose a superior man instead."

Byron's eyes narrowed. "Superior?"

"In age, superior in *age*, that's all I meant. At the time of your romance you were a young calf of seventeen but he was a buck of twenty-nine, and a *soldier* to boot!"

"Whereas *I* was not only too young – I also walked with a limp*!*"

"I did not mean it in that respect," said Hobby fretfully, "and you know I didn't."

After a long pause, Byron's face relaxed. "I know you

didn't, Hobby, and it's pointless for me to be challenging you about it now, because it's all over and done with ... finished."

Hobhouse was not so sure about that, but he was glad to change the subject, and even more pleased when a welcome interruption arrived.

"A glass of brandy, Mr Hobhouse?" said Nanny Smith, appearing with her usual warm smile. "Your favourite?"

"Yes, thank you, Nanny, a glass of brandy would be most welcome now."

She looked at Byron, who waved his hand in refusal. "I'll wait until the others have arrived."

Nanny frowned. "Now, I know Mr Hodgson, but Mr Harness ... who is *he*, my lord?"

"A friend of mine from as far back as my schooldays at Harrow."

"Harrow? As far back as that? So you must know him well?"

"Quite well."

"So does he have any particular likes or dislikes in food that we should know about? Any particular requirements we should prepare for?"

Byron thought about it. "No, I don't believe so ... although he may not wish to eat meat on any day that is a Friday."

"No meat on a Friday? Why is that?"

"He is preparing to go into Holy Orders. High Anglican. And like the Catholics they don't eat meat on a Friday, do they?"

"Oh good grief!" exclaimed Hobby in horror. "First Hodgson and now Harness – so what kind of bally awful Christmas is this going to be for *me* then?"

He glared at Byron. "How am I, an avowed *atheist*,

supposed to jolly along through Christmas in the company of *two* future priests of the Church?"

Byron grinned wickedly. "It will be fun to watch you do it, Hobby, and thumping the table throughout dinner will not be allowed."

"And what if Hodgson gets all 'Holier than thou' with me?"

Byron laughed. "Hodgson would never act holier than thou, Hobby. It's not his way."

"And Harness?"

"Ah, well, like me, he's five or six years younger than Hodgson, and he's as chaste as myself. So watch what you say in front of him, that's all."

"You – *chaste?*"

"In my soul, yes."

Even Nanny Smith had to sigh at that, although she turned her face away from Byron as she did so ... His lordship might have his own private rooms in the North-West wing, at the opposite end of the building to where all the other rooms of residence were, but it was common knowledge that he had been sleeping on a regular basis with Susan Vaughan, his favourite of all the maids, and the poor girl was besotted with love for him, often weeping for him when he was away in London, and driving Joe Murray near to the end of his patience.

Nanny again sighed her disapproval of it all, and walked towards the door. "I'll get your brandy, Mr Hobhouse."

~ ~ ~

Christmas, a time of happiness; and it was the best Christmas everyone at Newstead had ever enjoyed. Byron had ensured that all the particular things that each of his friends enjoyed was available to them. They dined every evening in his own private dining room in the North-wing, the food and drink rich and plentiful, as was the food on the table in the Servants' Hall.

William Harness had initially been taken aback when he saw the outside of the Abbey, so huge and gothic in the winter darkness of a December evening, but once inside he smiled with pleasure at finding the rooms that Byron had furnished for his own residence so comfortably appointed, glowing with crimson hangings, and cheerful with capacious fires, and all the furniture consisting of a rich gleaming mahogany and green and red upholstery.

Byron's dining room in the north-west wing was beautiful, every piece of furniture in it beautiful, and especially the wall above the fireplace which was a mosaic of marble tiles in a combination of numerous beautiful colours.

The only disappointment for William Harness throughout the Christmas week, was that Byron always refused to join the men on their regular morning shoots in the forest, even though his friend John Pigot, from Southwell, often came over to join them in the fun.

"You don't shoot at all?" Harness asked.

"Not animals, no," Byron replied.

"Not even a few birds?"

A strange expression came on Byron's face, as if the question brought back an unwanted memory.

"I shot a young eagle once," he said. "In Greece, on the southern shore near Vostizza. I still don't know why I did it. I saw it flying up there, so cocky in its swoops, and before I knew it I had raised my gun and shot it down with one bullet. When I ran to it lying on the ground, I saw it was only wounded, and I did my best to save it ... his eye was so bright, so golden, and he looked at me as if to say 'Why did you shoot me? I was only *flying around* in my own sky.' So I nursed it, but it pined and died in a few days. I swore then that I would never willingly kill another bird."

John Pigot and William Harness both saw the sadness in Byron's eyes as he remembered his young eagle, mortally wounded by his own gun; and as the two young men set off with their own guns on their shoulders, John Pigot said to Harness, "Byron has always been like that, too soft-hearted, and not a spark of malice in him."

~ ~ ~

Later that evening there was much malice in Hobhouse's amusement when it was Byron, and not himself, who came under fire from the two future priests on the subject of religion.

William Harness spoke of his beliefs quietly and seriously, but Francis Hodgson showed a hint of emotional tears in his eyes as he implored Byron to give the Christian faith more serious thought. Even the old Calvinistic beliefs of his childhood would serve him better than no belief in God at all.

"The worst of it is, I do believe in some great power above and around us," Byron replied, "I just don't know *what* I believe."

Hobhouse sat forward, shocked. "So Scrope Davies was right then? At Cambridge you were only *pretending* to be an atheist?"

"No, I pretended nothing at Cambridge."

"Then Matthews was right," Francis Hodgson accused. "Matthews always insisted that you were a Platonist."

"I'm no Platonist, I'm nothing at all," Byron replied irritably. "But I would sooner be a Paulician, Manichean, Spinozist, Zoroastrian – *anything* other than one of the seventy-two religious sects who are tearing each other to pieces for the love of God and hatred of each other."

"And spoken like a *true* atheist," Hobby supported.

Byron ignored him, his attention focused on Hodgson who had raised the subject – "Just look to Ireland and the Protestant and Catholics, or the rest of the world's hatred of the Jews. And as to *your* religion – if Christ came to save all *good* men, then a good Jew must go to Heaven and a bad Nazarene straight to hell. Is that not so?"

Hodgson hesitated, not sure of the answer.

"And what about the rest of mankind?" Byron asked. "People in Africa and those unknown parts of the world that Christians have not yet reached or preached? Who will believe that God will damn those people for not knowing what they were never taught?"

"That's why we are sending missionaries to as many parts of the world as we can," Hodgson replied. "To spread the word so that every man alive will hear the message."

"Do you honestly believe that the *only* passport into Heaven is Galileeism?"

"Yes."

"And is God a Galilean, and *only* a Galilean? Tell me God is not that small?"

"Why are you getting so heated?" Hodgson demanded. "Surely we can be more rational."

"I am being rational," Byron insisted. "All I am saying is that I would prefer ten Jews and five Moslems to even *one* of your fox-hunting curates!"

"Aha!" Hodgson exclaimed. "So this is more about *your* love of animals than *my* love of God."

Byron lowered his eyes, his fingers fiddling with the stem of his wine glass. He was very fond of Francis Hodgson, and always had been, but he knew they would never agree on the subject of religion.

"Hodgson," he said quietly, "I will always rejoice to see you ... but let us say no more on this endless theme of religion. Let me live, well if possible, and die without pain. That's all I ask of life. The rest is with God."

"Amen," said John Hobhouse, sitting back smiling, knowing that Francis Hodgson would never rudely bring up the subject of religion at a dinner table again. At least, not at Byron's dinner table.

Chapter Eight

~ ~ ~

After spending Christmas in his hometown of Dublin, Thomas Moore arrived back in London without his darling wife.

Bessy had stayed behind in Ireland for another month or two because she had been so happily spoiled throughout Christmas by her mother and two sisters who were all delighting in her pregnancy, and even Tommy agreed that Bessy should be allowed to continue enjoying her pampering, rather than returning to lonely London where, with the services of only one maid, she would have to fend for herself.

Tommy's main concern now was business. There was his contract with Longmans to be received and signed and returned, and then there was much *writing* to be done to fulfil that contract.

The buff quarto packet containing the contract from Longmans was already there and waiting for him when he entered his lodgings in Bury Street, but there was another letter beside it which immediately caught his eye, because the red wax bore the seal of Lord Byron.

"Good gracious!" Moore was completely taken by surprise at the sight of the letter. Having heard nothing further since his last letter, he had been sure that Lord Byron had simply ignored it.

8, St. James's Street

Sir,

My friend Mr. Hodgson apprised me that a letter for me was in his possession (which may probably be *your own) and is still <u>unopened</u> in his keeping. If examination of the address, and the similarity of the handwriting, should lead to such a conclusion, it shall be opened in your presence, to the satisfaction of all parties*

With regard to the latter part of both your letters, I felt myself at a loss in what manner to reply. Was I to anticipate friendship from one who believed me to have charged him with falsehood?

I should have felt proud of your acquaintance, Mr Moore, had it commenced under other circumstances, but it must rest with you to determine how far it may proceed after such an inauspicious beginning.

I have the honour to be &c, your etc.,

> *BYRON*

Thomas Moore was rather astounded by the letter, comprising as it did of such good sense, self-possession, and frankness on the part of Lord Byron.

Tommy sat down at his desk and immediately wrote back:

My Lord, – I answer your letter with great pleasure. I was afraid your Lordship had totally mistaken me. I find however that my reliance on your generosity was not misplaced.

I shall now mention the subject to my friend Samuel Rogers, and as I know that he has long

*wished for the pleasure of your Lordship's
acquaintance, we cannot have a better person or a
better mode of bringing us together, and I believe the
sooner we shake hands in amity the better.*

> *I have the honour to be, my Lord
> Your Lordship's very humble Servant
> THOMAS MOORE*

P.S: You may now destroy my original letter to you.

~~~

Lord Byron though, to Tommy's disappointment, was
not ready to destroy the original letter or to shake hands
just yet.

*Sir — You must excuse my troubling you once
more upon this very unpleasant subject. It would be
a satisfaction to me if the unopened letter in Mr
Hodgson's possession (supposing it to prove your
own) should be returned "in statu quo" to the writer;
particularly as you expressed yourself "not quite
easy under the manner in which I had dwelt on its
miscarriage".*

*I felt, and still feel, very much flattered by those
parts of your correspondence which held out the
prospect of our becoming acquainted. If I did not
meet them in the first instance, let the situation I was
placed in be my defence.*

If, therefore, you still retain the wish, I shall be

happy to meet you, when, where, and how you please.

I have the honour to remain &c.,

BYRON

Once again, Thomas Moore was rather astounded by the frankness of Lord Byron's letter. It gave him pause for thought ... According to the reviews for his *English Bards and Scotch Reviewers,* Byron was reputed to be a young man aged twenty-one, so now he would be aged no more than twenty-four, yet his letters displayed him to be mature, open, and very manly-minded in every respect.

Moore showed the letter to Samuel Rogers saying, "I can understand his initial caution. I had placed him in a position in which he was ignorant as to the character of the person who addressed him. Hence, his judicious reserve to my advances towards any acquaintance."

"And yet," said Samuel Rogers, "have you never once wondered or asked yourself *why* he would be happy to meet you? And why he felt 'very much flattered' at your suggestion that the two of you should become acquainted?"

"Because of my ludicrous allegation against him," Tommy said artlessly. "I was offended, and so he now wishes to make amends."

Samuel Rogers sighed with impatience. "In *English Bards*, Byron deliberately offended almost every poet alive, with the exception of myself of course, because he *praised* me and defended me against the hacks."

"So ..." Tommy was confused, "what are you saying?"

"That he likes you, Moore! And although he doesn't know you personally, he knows your *poetry*. He's probably been an admirer of yours for years. Why else would Byron be *flattered* at your suggestion of becoming acquainted?"

Tommy's blue eyes began to sparkle. "You know, I never thought of that ... young lords of the *English* aristocracy reading my work and becoming *admirers* of mine."

Rogers' face relaxed into a grin. "So when are we to have the honour of Lord Byron's company?"

~ ~ ~

The meeting, and return of the letter, followed by dinner at six, was arranged to take place in Samuel Rogers home in St James's. Yet as the hour of six drew near, Thomas Moore was overcome with trepidations and embarrassment.

"I feel such a fool now," he said to Rogers. "I feel, in my mistake, I have been left standing on the wrong-foot, which is always an embarrassment. When Lord Byron arrives, will you speak to him on your own first, and explain how it was such a *genuine* mistake on my part? And also – also say that I reacted in the way *any* honourable gentleman would have done in the same circumstances."

Rogers smiled. "Don't worry, Tommy, I know exactly what to say to Lord Byron."

When the door-knocker announced a caller, Tommy pushed Rogers into the hall in a state of nervous agitation. "Go on, go on – say what you have to say to him first so as to *smooth* his way in before he meets me. I don't want him to start the evening thinking badly of me."

The maid had already opened the door and the caller was *not* Lord Byron, but Thomas Campbell, another poet, and a friend of Rogers who was just "popping in."

"You can't pop in – not now!" Rogers said irritably. "I'm expecting a guest."

"What guest?"

"Lord Byron."

"Byron? You mean ... the young author of *English Bards?*"

"Exactly. So watch your step as you go now, and I'll see you when you pop in tomorrow."

"Hold on, Rogers, this is no way to treat a friend. I would very much like the opportunity to meet Lord Byron, as I believe I am the only living poet he spared in his diatribe against us all."

"So that makes two of us because *I'm* not dead yet. Oh come in then, come in, but Moore may not like you being here."

Tommy was indeed vexed to see Campbell enter the back parlour where he was stood in nervous hiding, but before he could utter a complaint, the front door knocker announced another caller, and Tommy pushed Rogers back out to the hall. "Now you know what to say, Rogers?"

"I do."

"And when you have said it," Tommy instructed, "then you can come and lead me in to the drawing-room and introduce me to his lordship."

As he made his way back to the hall, it suddenly occurred to Samuel Rogers that not one of three men had ever *seen* Lord Byron, so what to expect?

The maid was in the process of taking Lord Byron's cloak when Rogers arrived in the hall, and paused ... and then moved forward to reach out and shake Lord Byron's hand with a smile and an apology for the reason that necessitated their meeting in this way.

"I apologise for the lamentable way that Moore has

handled this situation, my lord. It has all been, well ...
rather *Irish*."

In the back parlour, Moore and Campbell stood alert
when Rogers returned and said quietly: "I have taken
him into the drawing-room, so if you come in now,
Moore, and then you, Campbell, can join us in a few
minutes."

"What does Lord Byron look like?" Campbell asked.

Rogers made a face, unable to resist – "As the
newspapers described him, short and ugly and walks
with a limp like *Richard the Third*."

"Oh dear," said Thomas Campbell in disappointment,
and looked at Moore. "But then they *do* say, Tommy,
that most of the aristocracy are as ugly as sin. Just look
at the Prince of Wales! Do they come any uglier than
him?"

"I don't care what he looks like," Tommy said
truthfully. "He's a lord and he writes a good letter and
he has come here for *my* benefit and not his own. So
take me in, Rogers, take me in."

When Thomas Moore quietly entered the drawing-
room he stood and stared at the tall young man
standing by the window, gazing out to the street. He
turned his head and looked at Moore in rather a *haut*
manner; an aristocrat at a glance.

Rogers said: "Lord Byron, it is my pleasure to
introduce you to Ireland's most famous poet, Thomas
Moore."

Byron and Moore stood looking at each other in
silence, and then both smiled. It was instant and mutual
liking at first sight.

Byron had a letter in his hand, and held it up — "Your
letter, I believe, Mr Moore, still sealed and unopened."

From then on, Rogers had to agree, a wonderful night

was had by all. Lord Byron was an extremely charming and agreeable young man, and Moore was at his very best; his Irish stories and anecdotes kept them all in constant laughter, and Rogers could see that Byron was delighted. They spoke about the savaging Moore had received from the Edinburgh Review for the eroticism of his amorous poems written under the name of Thomas Little.

"Oh, that was *nothing* compared to the savaging I got from some of the women on the streets of Dublin," Moore told Byron. "They accused me of trying to corrupt the innocence of Ireland's youth and wanted me hanged, drawn and quartered. Although *one* woman was slightly more lenient when she forced me to a stop in my walk along Ainger Street. She asked me — 'How many Gods are there?' So thinking of the Trinity I said 'Three' — to which she bawled — 'Then I pray you will never get the chance to see even *one* of them!'"

Later that night, back in his lodgings, Thomas Moore was feeling so happy he decided he could not wait until the following morning to write and tell his darling Bessy all about the success of the evening, and his impressions of Lord Byron.

The first things I chiefly noticed about him was the nobleness of his air, his beauty, the gentleness of his voice and manners, and – what was naturally the biggest relief and attraction – his marked kindness to myself.

Being still in mourning for his mother, the colour black, of his dress, as well as of his glossy black hair, gave more effect to the pure, spiritual paleness of his

features, in the expression of which, when he spoke,
there was a perpetual play of lively thought.

And then Tommy went on to tell Bessie about the most *remarkable* event of the evening, which happened near the end, when all except Byron were sipping their last glass of brandy.

Samuel Rogers could not resist taking down his copy of *'English Bards and Scotch Reviewers'* and asking Lord Byron to sign it with his own signature. "As a memento," Rogers said.

Byron agreed, but when the pen and ink were brought to him, he sat looking at the front cover, hesitated for a long moment, before finally lifting the pen and starting to write.

"Surely we have time for one more brandy," Campbell had suggested to Rogers, and Tommy had agreed with Campbell, and Rogers was happy to oblige.

So while the three chatted as their glasses were topped up, Byron had opened the book and began to glance down each page, shaking his head sadly here and there, and then writing something in the margins.

When he stood to leave, the farewells were very friendly all round; but Moore and Campbell held back from leaving the house with him, because now all three poets were very curious to see what Byron had written in the margins of his own book.

And when they looked, and *saw* what Byron had written inside Rogers' copy of *English Bards,* all three were shocked.

On the front page he had written —

The binding of this volume is considerably more
valuable than its contents. Nothing but the

> *consideration of it being the property of another*
> *prevents me from consigning this miserable record*
> *of misplaced anger and indiscriminate acrimony to*
> *the flames —BYRON*

Wide-eyed, Rogers turned the pages and found that along the whole of Byron's severe verses against William Wordsworth, he had written – '*Wrong, and Unjust'*.

And the same verdict was affixed to those verses against Coleridge: '*Wrong also. Too ferocious – this is mere insanity.'*

Yet he was not always repentant; against another writer he had written – '*Do not regret – he is an ass.'*

Against the poetess, Rose Matilda, he was equally unrepentant: '*They tell me she has married the Morning Post newspaper – a good match.'*

On Hewson Clarke, a vicious critic for a magazine, he had remarked: '*Right enough — this was well deserved.'*

On the last page, he had written his own opinion of *English Bards*:

> '*The greatest part of this satire, I most sincerely wish had never been written. Not only on account of the injustice of much of the critical and some of the personal part of it, but the tone and temper of it I cannot now approve.'*

Samuel Rogers' face was beaming with elation. "You know what this means?"

"That he has *defaced* your copy of his book?" said Thomas Campbell.

"No, you fool, it means that one day, who knows, this copy of mine containing the author's own regretful

notes in his own hand, could be worth not *one* pound –
the price I paid for it – but *hundreds* of pounds!"

Tommy and Campbell looked at each other and
laughed at such a possibility. Byron was practically
unknown as a poet, and even worse, what he had
written so far was considered – even by Byron himself –
to be unworthy of the paper it was printed on.

Chapter Nine

~ ~ ~

Thursday, 27th February 1812 was a very important day for the people of Nottinghamshire.

So many of the textile workers had now been thrown out of their jobs in the factories and had been replaced by the wide frames, leaving them unemployed and unable to provide for their families.

Adding insult to injury, the ruling government in Westminster had now resolved to crush the protesters and protect the machines. Any man known to be a *Luddite* would be either jailed or transported to a convict colony. Any man known to have participated in the destruction of a frame, would be hanged. The Bill sanctioning the death penalty for machine-breakers had been approved and passed by the House of Commons.

Now, on the 27th February 1812, five weeks after Byron's twenty-fourth birthday, the Bill was due to be approved or rejected by the Upper House, after consideration and debate by all members of the House of Lords.

Lord Byron entered the Palace of Westminster that morning knowing that the people of his own county were relying upon him, and *him* alone, to speak up for them. Their political representative in the lower house had gone along with the Tory government and voted for the Bill to be passed into legislation.

As he entered the lobby adjoining the chamber he was greeted and introduced to Lord Holland, the leader of the Whig Party. It was their first meeting.

"Are you with us?" asked Lord Holland. "With the

Opposition?"

"Yes."

"Do you have your speech with you?"

"Yes."

"May I take a glance at it before you go in?"

Byron smiled apologetically. "I'm afraid that's impossible, my lord. My speech is in my head."

"What?" Lord Holland stared at him. "No notes? No papers at all? Lord Byron this really is not *good* enough. In an important debate such as this, a member must come to the chamber fully *prepared.*"

"I am fully prepared, my lord. I know what I want to say and I find consulting with notes and papers very restrictive to my thinking process."

"But at the very least notes are a *prompt.* If one's mind goes astray or gets distracted, notes are the essential *prompt* to get you back on track."

"My apologies, my lord."

Lord Holland sighed dismally. "Lord Byron, I know this is your first speech to the House, and therefore some allowances must be made for you, but if you are going to sit with us Whigs on the Opposition benches, then I would ask you in future to *please* come with your speech better prepared. Oh, and it is also usual for *me* to see any speech you intend to make, at least a week or two *before* you deliver it."

Byron frowned. "Why? So you can censor what I say?"

"So I can *advise* you on what to say and what *not* to say."

It still sounded like censorship to Byron, but he decided to be respectful enough not to argue the point with his elder.

And now that he was here, surrounded by all these red robes, including the wearing of his own red robe, he was beginning to feel quite nervous.

The chamber was packed, filled to capacity; the lords supporting the ruling Tory government sitting on one side, the Whigs on the other. Byron took his seat as far away as possible from Lord Holland, in case the party leader felt the need to occasionally *prompt* him down a mental track he did not wish to go.

He needed to sit in his own quietness and think, and strangely enough, it was not only the Nottinghamshire workers he was thinking of, but also the factory *owners*.

In the past few weeks he had spoken to a few of the proprietors, and they too had voiced their bitter grievances against this despotic government. Nor did they welcome the sight of the Army and Militia patrolling their streets and disrupting the daily freedoms of the people – dragoons patrolling through every field and searching houses at random.

"It's a disgrace," one factory owner had complained. "These are our people, have always been our people, and we have to live amongst them now in their hunger. And in truth *we* are seeing no financial benefit to us from these machines, but we have been *ordered* to use them."

But it was the *Bill* under debate that Byron knew he must speak against, the *Death Penalty Bill* against the frame-breakers, the biggest disgrace of all.

The Lord Chancellor had stopped speaking and resumed his seat. Byron heard his name called.

"Lord Byron!"

Byron stood and appeared perfectly at ease, although a quick glance at Lord Holland showed him that the Whig leader was watching him very carefully.

"My Lords ... to enter into any detail of the riots would be superfluous, as the House is already aware of them. The town and county of Nottinghamshire are burdened with large detachments of the military. The police are in motion. And the *police*, however useless, are by no means idle. Several notorious men have been detained on the clearest evidence of the capital crime of *poverty*. Men who had been guilty of lawfully begetting several children, whom – thanks to *this government* – they are now unable to maintain."

A buzz of annoyance was rising from the Government benches. Few of the noble lords knew this young Lord Byron, but the very *least* they had expected from him was loyalty and solidarity with the fellow peers of his own *class* – yet here he was, like a *French revolutionaire* – raising his voice in contempt on behalf of the mutinous unemployed frame-breakers of Nottingham.

"And considerable injury," Lord Byron continued, "has also been done to the proprietors of the new frames. These machines were presented to them as an advantage, inasmuch as they superseded the necessity of employing a number of workmen, who were then left, in consequence, to starve.

"Yet it is observed, that the work executed by these machines was inferior in quality, not marketable at home, and merely hurried over with a view to exportation to foreign countries. Meanwhile, the rejected workmen, in the blindness of their ignorance, in the foolishness of their hearts, believed the maintenance and well-doing of the industrious poor were objects of greater consequence than the *enrichment* of a few individuals."

"Impudence!" exclaimed an old lord on the Government benches. "Who is this *impudent* young man?"

"And it must be confessed," Lord Byron continued, "that although the adoption of the enlarged machinery might have been beneficial to the master without being detrimental to the servant, – yet it benefits *neither!*

"Every garment manufactured by the new machines lies rotting in the warehouses without a prospect of exportation because of its inferior quality. And with the demand of work and workmen equally diminished, frames of this construction tend materially to aggravate the distresses of all – the masters *and* the workers.

"But the real causes of these distresses and consequent disturbances lies deeper. When we are *told* by the Government, that these men are in league together for the destruction of their *own* comfort – can we forget that it is the bitter policy and destructive *warfare* of the last eighteen years that has destroyed their comfort, your comfort, all men's comfort?

"That policy of *war,* which, originated with *'great statesmen now no more'* has survived the dead to become a curse on the living."

The Government benches were in uproar at the "*impudence*" of the young lord, but sitting on the opposite side of the House, Lord Holland's face was a picture of enchantment and delight.

"The punishment should fit the crime," Byron continued, "but I did hope that any measure proposed by His Majesty's Government would have had *conciliation* for its basis – and *not* that we should all have been called at once, to pass sentences by wholesale and sign death-warrants blindfolded."

The noise was deafening. The Lord Chancellor motioned for silence; politeness in the House in response to a speech must prevail, and once silence eventually resumed, Lord Byron continued –

"Why were the military called out to be made a mockery of – if they were to be called out at all?? As the sword is the *worst* argument to be used, so it should be the last – but in this instance it has been the *first.*"

He looked around at the lines of sitting men. "All this has been happening within one hundred and thirty miles of London, and yet you *'good easy men'* have sat down to enjoy your foreign triumphs in the midst of domestic calamity. But all the cities you have taken, all the armies which have retreated before your leaders, are but paltry subjects of self-congratulation if your own land divides against itself, and your dragoons and executioners must be let loose against your fellow citizens "

Someone shouted out — *"The young man should now place himself at the head of the mob."*

"The mob?" Byron replied angrily. "Are any of you aware of your obligations to the *mob?* It is the *mob* that labours in your fields, and serves in your houses, and mans your Navy, and recruits into your Army It is the *mob* that have enabled you to defy all the world! But be warned — they could also defy *you* when your neglect has finally driven them to despair."

Standing in the gallery were John Cam Hobhouse, Thomas Moore, Samuel Rogers, Thomas Campbell and Robert Dallas; and standing a few feet away and unknown to them, was a young man named Percy Bysshe Shelley, his eyes glowing like lamps – all were absolutely stunned at Byron's performance in front of his peers.

After another burst of outrage and uproar, Lord Byron was allowed to continue his speech, and he continued where he had left off, with no change in mood or tone or *impudence.*

"And now, on behalf of the people, I *must* remark on what quickness you are accustomed to fly to the succour of your distressed allies, while leaving the distressed of your *own* country to the care of Providence. When the Portuguese suffered under the retreat of the French, every arm was outstretched to them, every hand was opened, from the rich man's largess to the widow's mite, all was bestowed to enable them to rebuild their villages and replenish their granaries.

"Yet, at this moment, when thousands of our own unfortunate countrymen are struggling with the extremes of hardship and hunger – as your charity began abroad – so it should now end *at home.* A mere *tenth* of the bounty bestowed on Portugal would have gone a long way to help your own people – even if these men could not have been restored to their employments, it would have rendered as unnecessary to send them to the tender mercies of the bayonet and the gibbet."

The government benches were rustling with fury again, red robes flapping irritably.

"So how will you carry this Bill into effect? Can you commit the men of a whole county to their own prisons? Will you erect a gibbet in every field and hang up men like scarecrows? Or will you proceed, by decimation, to place the county under martial law, de-populate and lay waste all around you, and restore Sherwood Forest to its former condition as an asylum for outlaws? Are these your remedies for a starving and desperate populace?"

Standing in the gallery, Thomas Moore had tears in his eyes, because there was something about Lord Byron now, in his brave defiance of the ruling establishment, in his speech that bowed to no one, which reminded Moore so much and so sadly of his younger days in Ireland and his friend Robert Emmet ... Byron and Emmet — both young men, both of the upper class, and both speaking up with such passion on behalf of the common people.

"When a proposal is made to their Lordships to emancipate or relieve, you hesitate, you deliberate for years, you temporise and tamper with the minds of men, but a *Death-Bill* must be passed offhand!

"And yet, suppose the Bill *is* passed – suppose one of these men, as I have seen them weak with hunger and sullen with despair, suppose this man surrounded by those children for whom he is unable to secure food – and there are *ten thousand* such men from whom you may select your victims – suppose this man is dragged into court for this new offence, by this new law – you will still need two things to convict or condemn him, and these are, in my opinion, *twelve butchers for a jury* and a bloody Jefferies for a judge!"

Thomas Moore was startled. "Is he referring to Francis Jeffreys the critic?"

"No," Hobhouse replied, "Judge George Jefferies, notorious for his brutality in the seventeenth century."

Lord Byron had resumed his seat, his speech now

over, and it was clear from the murmuring all around the chamber that many of their lordships did not know what to make of him.

Yet Lord Holland now knew *exactly* what to make of him. Byron had entered the chamber full of youth and energy and blasted all the decades of stale air up to the rafters and out through the sunlights with his passion and eloquence. He had made every man sit up and listen, whether in anger or agreement, didn't matter.

"Now *that* is the kind of man we need at the front of the Whig Party," Holland said to his neighbour. "Young and handsome and *fresh* with indignation. We have become too fusty in our image, too dusty in our thinking, almost as bad as the Tories, yet Lord Byron appears to have double-vision and the capacity to see things from both sides of the situation, rich and poor. Bring him to me during the tea-break."

Lord Byron was not to be found in the tearoom or anywhere along the corridors during the break. He was outside in the Great Hall with his friends, displaying mock fury to Robert Dallas who had offered him his left hand to shake in congratulations.

"Your *left* hand, Dallas, you offer me your *left* hand on such an occasion!"

Dallas, who had never been to Turkey or Greece and so did not understand the *offence* of such an act, looked at the rolled-up umbrella in his right hand and said meekly to Byron, "It's raining outside, that's why I brought it."

"Then switch it."

Dallas quickly switched the umbrella to his left hand and held out his right, which Byron shook vigorously with a delighted smile. "The supporters of this foul Government are *cursing* me back there! Is that not worth a right-hand shake?"

Rogers and Campbell also gave him their right hands, followed more slowly by Thomas Moore, who was now looking at Byron with different eyes: a lord he may be, but now he knew there was a lot more to Byron than a title.

"What say you, Hobby?"

"Are you satisfied that you went too far?" Hobby asked.

"Very satisfied."

"Even though you spoke, with a sort of *modest* impertinence, followed by some very violent sentences, and abused every thing and every body and put the Lord Chancellor very much out of humour?"

"Even though," Byron confirmed.

Hobhouse grinned, and held out his right hand. "Then well done, my friend, well done!"

When the others had left to keep their various appointments elsewhere, Byron returned to the House and Hobby returned to the gallery.

Lord Grenville of the Whigs was the first to stand and compliment the speech of the young lord, but Lord Eldon and Lord Harrowby both followed, one after the other, to ferociously oppose him.

While sitting and listening to the drone and huff and gruff of the Lord Chancellor, Byron's eyes were ranging over all the lords on the Tory side ... and counted twenty-six *bishops* ... placemen who had been given their Bishoprics in order to secure their votes whenever the government needed them ... political corruption at its highest level.

The session ended with the announcement that the vote would be taken the following night.

"Not even *one week* allowed for the members to have time for due thought," Byron said to Hobby with disgust, "just one day to decide life or death for the textile men of Nottinghamshire."

Hobby had to agree. "It's damnable, but then if the truth be known, all the votes in support of the Bill were bargained and bought and secured weeks ago."

The following night, Lord Byron returned to the House and registered his vote against the Bill alongside many of the Whigs – although he was shocked to notice that a fair number of the opposition had *abstained* from registering their vote.

The Bill was passed, the Death penalty was now law for all frame-breakers, and Byron left the Palace of Westminster in a state of despair.

"Whigs, Hobby, *Whigs* – members of the Opposition *abstaining* – unable to make up their minds, and allowing the other side to win. So what kind of *minds* do they have?"

"Slow ... very slow ..." Hobby said slowly. "Some are so old it will probably take their slow minds a week to think over all you said and grasp your argument. And then clarity will dawn in a *eureka* moment and they will then torment their families with repeated pesterings of — "You know, I *should* have voted with that fine young man who seemed to know what it was all about ... now *what* was his name?"

Byron laughed at Hobby's mimicry of an old lord in his dotage, but his laughter was interrupted by Sir Francis Burdett who insisted on shaking his hand, saying, "Lord Byron, I have to say, that was the *best* speech made by a lord since ... well, since the Lord knows when!"

"Thank you, sir."

"And *one* vote, the Bill was passed by only one vote instead of the expected one *hundred* votes – so many of the government supporters must have secretly defected. If only some of our own side had done their duty and not abstained."

"If only," Byron agreed.

"I will be sending you an invitation to come to dinner next Sunday," said Sir Francis. "Please do come, and bring along some of your friends – including young Mr Hobhouse here, I know him well, always up there in the gallery in the House of Commons."

Sir Francis rushed off, and a moment later a Tory peer caught Lord Byron's arm and offered congratulations on his maiden speech to the House. "Astonishing, quite astonishing!"

Byron's surprise was visible – a *Tory* congratulating a

new member of the Whig Opposition!

"But as an old hand at these things, Lord Byron, may I offer you some advice? The next time you wish to make a speech like that, you might have more success if you unleash your eloquence in a *theatre,* and not the House of Lords. Or better still – in the House of *Commons,* where the politicians down there would feel more at home with your dramatic attacks on their lack of virtues and judgement."

He stormed off, and Byron looked at Hobby, who was grinning. "I believe I have just been insulted."

Hobby's head was shaking. "Oh no, that was the best compliment that Tory could have given you – his *rage!"*

Byron was watching the Tory peer getting into a carriage.

"His rage? What about mine? And even *worse* is what faces the weavers and textile workers now if they dare to break a damned stocking frame – death! Is that the British freedom our politicians boast about? Is that liberty?"

"No, but you did your best, and so did the Whigs, yet still the government won. The Bill has been ratified, and now nothing more can be done. So let's leave it at that."

And Byron might have left it at that, had he not been sickened by all the gloating over the Government's victory in the newspapers the following day.

A day later, on March 2nd, the *Morning Chronicle* published a piece entitled *'An Ode To The Framers of the Frame Bill'* written by *Anonymous,* which silenced all the gloating and left quite a few nobles faces looking very red with embarrassment; while the textile workers throughout the country roared their cheers as the Ode was read out to them:

Oh, well done Lord Eldon and Lord Ryder!
Britannia must prosper with councils like yours;
Hawkesbury, Harrowby, help you to guide her
Whose only remedy must kill ere it cures.
Those Villains the Weavers are all grown refractory,

Asking some succour for Charity's sake --
So hang them in clusters round each manufactory
That will at once put an end to YOUR mistake.

The rascals, perhaps, may take to robbing,
The dogs to be sure have got nothing to eat --
So if we can hang them for breaking a bobbin,
Twill save all the Government's money and meat:
Men are more easily made than machinery--
Stockings fetch better prices than lives --
Gibbets on Sherwood will heighten the scenery,
Showing how Commerce, how LIBERTY thrives!

Some folks for certain have thought it was shocking,
When Famine appeals, and when Poverty groans,
That life should be valued at less than a stocking,
And the breaking of frames leads to the breaking of
bones.
If it should prove so, I trust, by this token
(And who will refuse to partake in the hope?)
That the frames of YOU fools be the first to be broken,
Who, when asked for a remedy – sent down a ROPE!

At his breakfast table, John Hobhouse lowered the newspaper. No one else would know, or even be able to guess, but *he* knew that voice, that sarcasm.

A moment later he started to smile. 'Trust Byron to pour vinegar all over their puff-pie of gloating.'

Chapter Ten

~ ~ ~

Later that afternoon John Murray sent a note to Lord Byron by messenger, informing him that he was bringing forward publication of *Childe Harold's Pilgrimage,* on March 10th, in order to take advantage of the publicity of his maiden speech in the House of Lords.

Byron's surprise at the note made him stare at Fletcher. "March 10th ... that's only *eight* days away!"

"I'll have all your finest clothes ready, my lord" Fletcher assured him.

"I don't give a damn about *clothes* ... it's Childe Harold ... where's the manuscript ... fetch me the manuscript."

Fletcher brought the manuscript. "You won't mind me saying so, will you, my lord, but I think you've made a spelling mistake on the front page."

Byron took the script in his hand while looking at Fletcher in a way that made the valet feel very uncomfortable.

"I know I've not got so much learning as you, my lord, but I know my letters and I know a spelling mistake when I see one."

"So tell me where you see one?"

Fletcher pointed. "There. Childe. It shouldn't be spelt with an e at the end."

"In this case, Fletcher, it *should* have an 'e' at the end, because although Childe Harold is not yet twenty-one, he is the son of a knight, and therefore a candidate for knighthood, so the 'e' denotes his aristocratic rank."

Gretta Curran Browne

Fletcher stared in wonder. "Well I never!"

"Never what?"

"Knew that."

Byron impatiently waved Fletcher away and sat down at his desk to read the manuscript ... but what was the point? He knew every word by heart, and it was too late to change it now, even if he wanted to. And besides, he had other things to deal with.

Old Joe Murray had sent him two letters complaining about the fraught situation at Newstead Abbey which he could no longer deal with, and all due to one of the maids, Susan Vaughan, who was upsetting all the household staff with her "*uppity ways and airs and graces*" which she flaunted in the faces of the others, because she knew she was "*favoured by his lordship.*"

"*And one particular I must mention,*" Joe wrote, "*she has wounded young Robert Rushton something sorely, and that I do not like nor approve of, because he is a good lad, and I dunno the cause of his upset.*"

There were two other letters from Newstead: Byron picked up the first, which was in Susan's hand.

My dearest, Dearest Friend,

Your affectionate letter I received with the greatest pleasure, nothing on earth gives me that pleasure as anything from your dear hands. You tell me not to think myself forgotten if I don't hear from you often. I hope you will not make it very long or I think I shall die almost at the thought of not hearing from you whom I so much Love'

It is impossible for me to express what I Feel and how I miss you. I am quite lost without you. I hope

99

you will be able to come to Newstead sooner than you expect. I have not any hopes of happiness only in receiving your letters. I have given you every proof of my affection, I only fear your love for me will not be as lasting as mine will be for you.

My dearest friend, your very kind <u>present</u> arrived here safe. Ever since you left, everything you gave me I value more than Life, and even my own Existence I'd sooner forfeit than part with any of those things you were Kind enough to give me. The locket is beautiful, indeed far more handsome than anything I could expect, but I am very angry with myself for being so stupid, I have spent hours over it but cannot open it, so I will leave it until my dear Lord Byron comes for without him there is nothing right in my eyes.

Her endearments went on and on and on, and he had to smile as he thought of Susan with her passionate eyes. They were good friends as well as lovers, so he was not prepared to hear a word against her, not from Joe Murray nor anyone else.

And then he saw a small reference to Joe Murray's complaints about her.

I am very distant with all in the house except Bessy because I cannot help but see their frowns. I am very suspicious of <u>Robert</u>, and nor can I get a correct answer from him ...

He frowned himself as he read through all the long passages that followed, because they were full of complaints about young Robert Rushton, which surprised him.

Susan's letter was so long he put it aside to finish later, and picked up the next letter, from Robert Rushton; read it, and immediately answered it:

To Rt. Rushton
Newstead Abbey, Notts.

8, St James Street.

Though I have no objection to your refusal to carry letters to Mealey's, you will take care that the letters are taken by Spero at the proper time. I have also to observe that Susan is to be treated with civility, and not <u>insulted</u> by any person over whom I have the smallest control, or indeed anyone whatever, while I have the power to protect her.

I am truly sorry to have any subject of complaint against you. I have too good an opinion of you to think I shall have an occasion to repeat it. I see no occasion for any communication between you and the women. If a common sense of decency cannot prevent you from conducting yourself towards them with rudeness, I should at least think that your <u>own</u> <u>interest</u> & a regard for a master who has <u>never</u> treated you with unkindness, will have some weight.

BYRON

Fletcher came into the room holding two jackets, one in dark blue and the other in black merino.

"Would his lordship like to wear the dark blue for his publication day of Child*ee* Harold, or is it still the black?"

Byron put down the pen and looked curiously at his valet. "Do you know anything about all this, Fletcher? This trouble between certain members of the staff at Newstead?"

Fletcher's face reddened with embarrassment. "Of course it's the black. What was I thinking? In respect to your mother you must wear the colour black for a full year after her death."

Byron's eyes flashed. "You *do* know something. So why have you not told me?"

Fletcher's gaze was fixed on the black jacket. "It's not my business to be talking about."

"If it relates to Newstead then it is *my* business. Or am I to expect *no* loyalty from you, Fletcher?"

"No loyalty?" Fletcher was flabbergasted with indignation. "You have *all* my loyalty, Lord Byron, and you have done since you were sixteen and me no more than twenty-two – *all* my loyalty! Did I not suffer through Spain and Greece and Turkey with you, riding over the roughest mountains in the world, and nearly got shot by bandits before I was nearly drowned in a Turkish ship?"

"Why don't you just tell me about Newstead?" Byron suggested. "Young Rushton has evidently upset Susan."

"No – it was *her* who upset Robert – her and that other maid, Lucinda. My wife Sally told me all about it. Shocking it was, but no one has dared to tell Nanny Smith or Joe Murray about it. Oh, there'd be *ructions* if Joe Murray knew!"

"So why don't you tell me," Byron suggested, "just between the two of us."

Fletcher shrugged. "You'll be upset if I tell you. Even more upset than Nanny Smith or Joe Murray would be."

It was like trying to scrape ink off a stone, but Byron knew he was getting there, slowly.

"Put those clothes down and take a seat. Surely whatever it is cannot be so bad?"

"Oh, it is, my lord, very bad." Fletcher put the jackets down and sat in a chair. "And I know it's going to hurt you if I tell you, my lord, and I don't want to do that, hurt you."

"You won't hurt *me*," Byron said confidently, unprepared for what Fletcher was about to tell him.

"It was last month ... in January, on the anniversary of your natal day," Fletcher said hesitantly. "Susan Vaughan said a party should be held to celebrate his lordship's twenty-fourth year, even though you was not there to enjoy it. But she said it was *her* natal day too."

Byron nodded. "Susan and I share the same birth date, except she is four years younger."

"She stole bottle after bottle of your champagne from the cellar, and then later that night ... oh, it's too bad, no, I can't tell you, my lord ... not only because of Susan but because of your fondness for young Rushton."

Byron half smiled in disbelief. "Don't tell me Susan got Rushton drunk?"

"Well ... you know that Robert and his father are Bible-reading Methodists and they never touch liquor, you know that."

"I do."

"They got *themselves* drunk, Susan and Lucinda, and then they got Robert drunk too, and then they carnally molested him – having their fun and using him like a plaything. When my Sally came across Robert he was beside himself with anger and shame. And now he hates Susan Vaughan, because she was the one who started it, who physically *seduced* him, but Robert has told no one about it except my Sally, and now Susan keeps picking on Robert, telling him to keep his mouth shut, and trying to get him dismissed from his employment at Newstead for fear of *you* finding out."

Byron's expression was cynically suspicious. None of this sounded like Susan.

"I don't believe it. I don't believe you. This a story made up against Susan by your wife."

"Made up by my Sally!" Fletcher jumped to his feet at such an outrageous suggestion. "My Sally is a good honest woman, and I can *prove* it. Not a word of a lie, I can *prove* it!

"Then prove it," Byron said tersely.

Fletcher disappeared and returned a few minutes later holding a folded piece of paper.

"This letter was found by Nanny Smith one day when she was making the beds. It was under Susan's pillow, and Nanny thought it was a letter to you and she admits she could not stop herself from reading it, and then she sees it was not a letter to you, but to some other man."

Byron took the unfinished letter and began to read it, and saw that it was definitely in Susan's hand and containing many of her usual words and phrases; and no, this letter full of saucy flirtation was definitely *not* to him, as she referred to "*my lord will be coming home soon.*"

He looked at Fletcher. "How did the letter come into your hands?"

"Nanny Smith showed it to my wife. 'Mrs Fletcher,' said she, 'I think my Lord Byron should see this, but I don't want to be blamed for sending it to him or for showing it to Joe Murray, but Susan's deceit should be exposed'. So my Sally said she would give the letter to me, for *me* to decide what to do about it. Me being so close to you and all."

"When was this?"

"Nigh on a month ago."

"And you are only showing it to me now?"

Fletcher nodded, mortified by it all. "Like I said, I didn't want to hurt you, because I know you and her have long been fond of each other. And if you want my opinion, my lord, I think that letter full of teasing and love-talk was written to no other than Robert Rushton, because Susan has always had a fancy for Robert when you are not around, then ignores him when you are at Newstead. And now that she's had him, she wants to get rid of him."

After a long silence ... Byron said: "Fletcher, tell me, in all your time at Newstead, and our travels as far as Gibraltar with young Rushton and Joe Murray, did you ever hear Robert tell lies or say anything bad about anyone?"

"No, never."

"Nor I ... in truth I cannot remember ever hearing him say a bad word against any other human being, which convinces me now that he would not maliciously assert an untruth."

After another long silence, Byron said quietly, "Thank you, Fletcher, now leave me be."

When Fletcher had left the room, Byron picked up Susan's letter to him and continued reading it.

I wish you was here with me, but I must content myself until I can See you at Newstead. Oh,

Newstead, I love it for the sake of its owner, no tongue can tell how I love you, I love you so much and so intensely that I am almost ready to hate any other person that comes into my Sight. I do love my mother, it is true, but I love you better, oh better than all the world —

He put down the letter, not wishing to read any more. Instead he picked up his pen and wrote to Joe Murray, ordering the immediate dismissal of Susan Vaughan and Lucinda Taylor, but all care should be taken of Robert Rushton.

He then wrote a second letter:

To Miss Susan Vaughan
Newstead Abbey, Notts.

I write to bid you farewell and not to reproach you. I will not deny that I have been attached to you, and I am now heartily ashamed of my weakness. You may also enjoy the satisfaction of having deceived me most completely, and rendered me for the present sufficiently wretched. From the first, I told you that the continuance of our connection depended upon your own conduct.

All is over. I have little to condemn on my own part but my credulity. You threw yourself in my way, I received you, loved you, and now I part from you with some regret, & without resentment.

I wish you well, but do not forget that your own

misconduct has bereaved you of a friend, of whom nothing else could have deprived you. Do not attempt explanation, it is useless, and you cannot deny your own handwriting.

Return to your relations, you shall be provided with the means, but he who now addresses you for the last time, you will never see again.

BYRON

He was spared from any further thoughts on the matter by the arrival of John Hobhouse, his face a study in astonishment.

"I have just seen an advertisement in the *Morning Post* for your Childe Harold's Pilgrimage. Your publisher is being a bit overly-optimistic, isn't he?"

"How so?"

"Byron, he is pricing it at *two pounds!* That's a ridiculous amount to charge. Why, that's almost half the amount of income that any regular gentlemen has for an entire *week*, so why would he pay that amount to read a poem, albeit an epic one in length."

Byron's expression was as doubtful as Hobby's. "And he's printing it in quarto too, which is a cursed hard size to sell. Even *Shakespeare's* poems didn't sell in quarto size."

Hobhouse frowned. "Which poem by Shakespeare was published in quarto?"

"Venus and Adonis."

"I fear," said Hobhouse with a vexed sigh, "that John Murray's greed by charging this exorbitant price is about to ruin you, Byron, and finish you off as a poet before you even begin."

PART TWO

Childe Harold's Pilgrimage

"His youth, the beauty of his countenance, and its constant play of lights and shadows – the gentleness of his voice and manner to women, and his occasional haughtiness to men – the effect was electric. His fame did not have to wait for any of the ordinary gradations, but seemed to spring up, like the palace of a fairy tale, in a night."

Thomas Moore.

Chapter Eleven

~ ~ ~

Few members of the *beau monde* – the very richest and most fashionable of London's high society – knew anything at all about George Gordon Lord Byron. Not until his controversial speech in the House of Lords did he intrude upon anyone's notice.

And now an epic poem written by Lord Byron had been published, *Childe Harold's Pilgrimage*, also controversial, in that no one could decide if the hero was good or bad – or a little bit of both.

Of one thing only, *all* were certain – Harold was no youthful angel, but a youth who had grown world-weary and tired of revelry and vice.

His house, his home, his heritage, his lands,

The laughing dames in whom he did delight,

Whose large blue eyes, fair locks, and snowy hands,

Might shake the saintship of an anchorite,

And long had fed his youthful appetite.

And what of Lord Byron himself? What other English poet would write so movingly about war-torn Spain and then so *voluptuously* about Spain's daughters?

Match me, ye climes! which poets love to laud;

Match me the harems of the land! where now

I strike my strain, far distant, to applaud

Beauties that even a cynic must avow.

Match me those Houries, whom ye scarce allow

To taste the gale lest Love should ride the wind.

Young ladies swooned in their drawing-rooms and needed smelling salts to restore them after such *wicked* words that filled them with delightful curiosity and led to heated whispers – "*To taste the gale lest Love should ride the wind?*"

Even the young men slyly smiled at such lines, yet their smiles vanished and their emotions surfaced when Byron passionately wrote of the *sons* of war-torn Spain:

Such be the sons of Spain, and strange her fate!

They fight for freedom who were never free ...

Although many saw this part as Byron's political cry on behalf of *all* young men, in England as well as Europe who – in the name of their King – were being forced to fight and fall in a savage and bloody war while their King and his politicians slept safely in their beds.

And must they fall? The young, the proud, the brave,

To swell one bloated Chief's unwholesome reign?

John Murray had expected the book to be at least a moderate success, because Byron had already laid the groundwork for his fame and impressed readers throughout the country with his satire *English Bards* three years earlier.

Hoping to sell the first edition of 1000 copies within the first month, Murray had sent some early proofs to various newspapers and a few established poets for their reviews.

When they came in, the early reviews absolutely

A Strange World

astounded him, especially as it was the magazines he feared most – famous for their savagery of new poets – who now did not hold back in their praise.

The Satirist declared — 'Childe Harold contains many passages which would do honour to any poet, of any period, in any country.'

Monthly Review — "We are disposed to think that no writer in our language has been so successful as Lord Byron in the management of this structure of verse, perhaps not even Spencer himself."

The Literary Panorama — "Childe Harold's Pilgrimage' is a poem in which narrative, feeling, description, sentiment, satire, tenderness and contemplation are happily blended: it is adorned with beautiful imagery, expressed in harmonious and animated verse."

From the established *poets* – the review by *Samuel Rogers* was the most amusing:

"Lord Byron sent me an early copy before publication, and I read it to my sister. *'This,'* I said, *'in spite of all its beauty, will never please the public. They will dislike the dissolute character of the hero.'*
I then left my copy by mistake with two old maids I know in Buckinghamshire, who wrote and told me they could not stop crying (with laughter) over the passage about Harold's *'laughing dames'* that had *'long fed his youthful appetite'.*"

The first edition sold out in three days. John Murray hurriedly rushed through a second printing of 5,000 copies, but this time in the smaller size requested by Byron – in *octavo* and not quarto. The second printing sold out within a week and John Murray was quick to order a third printing.

The Scottish poet, Walter Scott wrote – "*This poem has electrified the mass of readers, and has at once placed upon Lord Byron's head the garland for which other men of genius have toiled long, and which they have gained late.*"

Those lines by Scott, with their faint hint of jealousy, John Murray read with great interest, knowing that Walter Scott, although ever a kind-hearted gentleman, was probably now very worried that Lord Byron's immediate success, and the greater depth and verve of his narrative poetry might oust Walter Scott from his own position at the top of the poetic pile.

John Murray hoped so, because he had *banked* everything on Lord Byron – Byron was his greatest hope, his greatest business investment, and his greatest financial risk – one that he had taken willingly and without reservation as soon as he had clapped eyes on that young man, after reading his manuscript laced with genius.

On Byron *everything* now depended – not only his own solvency, but also his dream of getting out of the tradesmen area of Fleet Street and moving into a more salubrious area of London, such as *Mayfair* – an area where sophisticated men like Lord Byron and Walter Scott were more accustomed to frequenting when in London, and a far more suitable place for John Murray to put his bookselling business behind him, and build up his new *publishing* company.

And once Byron's success was out there for all to see, other good authors such as Walter Scott and Miss Jane Austen would perhaps start paying closer attention to

Byron's *publisher,* and with more interest.

Only one other established poet was not prepared to approve of Lord Byron or his poetry, because he had never forgiven Byron for lampooning him in his *English Bards and Scotch Reviewers* – William Wordsworth.

Wordsworth declined to review Childe Harold's Pilgrimage, insisting that Byron's style was not *English,* and his morals were even less so.

"And I believe there is insanity in that family, the Byron family," Wordsworth added spitefully to his circle. "So I think we can reasonably conclude that Lord Byron is probably a little mad."

PART THREE

Lady Caroline Lamb

~~~

"*His beauty drew every eye upon him when he entered a room. No picture is like him.*"

Walter Scott

Chapter Twelve

~ ~ ~

Lady Caroline Lamb was the granddaughter of Earl Spencer of Althorp, the daughter of Lord Bessborough, and the niece of the Duchess of Devonshire. She was also a young lady of the highest importance in the restricted circles of the *Haut Ton*. All her life Caroline had wanted for nothing, and everything she ever wished for had always been given to her.

Petite, slim and blonde, and utterly self-willed, she had grown up unaware that there was any other class of people between those of the serving class and the aristocracy. The Prince of Wales' Royal household was as well known to her as the servants down in the kitchen of her own home at Melbourne House.

At nineteen, her mother had planned for her to marry the Prince of Wales, but as Caroline thought the prince to be too old and physically unattractive, she had chosen instead to marry William Lamb, the son of Lord Melbourne; and although she still loved her "dear William" during the daylight hours, she still thought him to be very coarse and quite repulsive in bed, confiding to her mother that her honeymoon had been an absolute shock – a dreadful *nightmare* of rough suffering.

Happiest now in the company of her animals; washing her dogs or riding her horses, Caroline also had an inquisitive mind and loved to read good books that took her far away from the gilded world in which she lived – but not for long. Reading about other people and the world in which *they* lived was very novel in its way, but that was as far as she wanted to travel away from her own luxurious world and all its comforts – through the pages of a *story* in a book.

And now, at twenty-seven, as much as she loved good literature, her main passion was politics and the principles of the Whig Party, and the only men who attracted her notice in any way were those who possessed a good intellect, something which her own husband did not have to any great degree.

Reclining along the window seat in her own private bedroom in Melbourne House, propped up with cushions, she was reading Childe Harold's Pilgrimage and thought it exotic and strange and *revolutionary*. No male poet had ever dared to use such bold words before, or speak of things that were *unspeakable* in normal conversations, such as young men associating with professional courtesans — although nine out of every ten young gentlemen did — before they eventually married and metamorphosed into respectable pillars of society.

Yet the author of Childe Harold spoke about it as if it was nothing more than fact and nothing to be hypocritical about, especially in a world where most of those young men were going off to war and possible death, which accounted for the flash of fiery spirits and the seeking of comfort in a woman's love, if only for a night.

The real world was dark, dangerous and bloody, and the boldness of the author in writing so graphically, and at times so beautifully, about that wider world, filled Caroline with a strong excitement.

Unaware of the rain pouring down outside, she had travelled through every verse with the author, through war-torn Portugal and beautiful Spain, and then the rugged hills of savage Albania where Childe Harold left behind all signs of the Cross, and saw before his eyes the rise of the Moslem crescent and heard the chanting calls to prayer from the muezzins of the sunset minarets —

"There is no God but God! — to prayer — lo! God is great!"
Now Harold felt himself at length alone,
And bade to Christian tongues a long adieu;
Now he adventured on a shore unknown,
Which all admire, but many dread to view:

His breast was armed against fate, his wants were few;
Peril he sought not, but never shrank to meet,
The scene was savage, but the scene was new;
This made the ceaseless toil of travel sweet,
Beat back keen winter's blast, and welcomed summer's heat."

Enthralled that there should be such a place and people as this, so foreign and so strange, Caroline realised this was *more* than just a poem – but a tremendous drama told in verse.

She read on, her eyes fixed down, her hand briefly raising to wave away the maid who came with her tray of afternoon tea, reading on and on ... and then down she went with him, into Greece, his beloved Greece, the land of heroes, finishing with his beautiful song, *"Maid of Athens "*

Caroline was sad when the first two cantos of Childe Harold's journey came to an end, and especially his voice – there was something about the author's *voice* that truly fascinated her.

She turned over the last page of the *Pilgrimage*, wanting to read more – and there *was* more – the author's notes. For some reason Lord Byron had written pages of notes at the back of the book to explain in greater detail various aspects about each of the countries Childe Harold had travelled through, not about the scenery or the landscapes, but the *people*.

She began to read the notes, and there was that *voice* again, more clearly now, not as Childe Harold but as Lord Byron, speaking directly to the reader, speaking directly to *her* – voicing his opinions just as clearly as if he was sitting opposite her:

"The Greeks will never be independent; they will never be sovereigns as heretofore; but they may be subjects without being slaves.

At present, like the Catholics in Ireland and the Jews throughout the world, and such other cudgelled people, the Greeks suffer all the moral and physical ills that can afflict humanity. Their life is a struggle against truth; they are vicious in their own defence. They are so unused to kindness, that when they occasionally meet with it they look upon it with suspicion, as a beaten dog often snaps at your fingers if you attempt to caress him. "They are ungrateful, notoriously, abominably ungrateful!"– this is the general cry. Now, in the name of Nemesis! for what are they to be grateful? Where is the human being that ever conferred a benefit on Greeks or Greek? They are to be grateful to the Turks for their fetters, and to the French for their broken promises; they are to be grateful to the artist who engraves their ruins, and to the antiquary who carries them away; to the traveller whose servant flogs them, and to the scribbler whose journal abuses them! This is the amount of their obligations for gratitude to foreigners!

The English have at last begun to compassionate their black people, and under a less bigoted government may one day probably release their Irish Catholic brethren: but the intervention of foreigners alone can emancipate the Greeks, who, otherwise, appear to have as small a chance of redemption from the Turks, as the Jews from mankind in general."

"I have to meet him!" Caroline jumped to her feet, her heart beating as fast as it was capable of beating. "I *have* to meet him!"

She looked down at the book in her hands: now here was a young man with his own mind and who seemed to have the privilege of possessing his own *personality* – something most of the male members of the *ton* lacked: the young set copied everything Beau Brummell wore, did, or said; while the older ones fashioned their clothes and opinions to match those of the Prince Regent.

After reading the reviews and deducing that the poet Samuel Rogers was a friend of his, she sent a messenger summoning Rogers to Melbourne House and demanded to meet Lord Byron.

Knowing now of Byron's love of privacy and his reserve when meeting strangers, Rogers decided the kindest thing to do, would be to immediately kill off Lady Caroline's desire to meet him.

"Lord Byron, you know, is a very ugly fellow in appearance. He walks with a slight limp, and I believe I once saw him biting his nails. You would not like him at all, Lady Caroline, very few women do."

But Caroline had never in her life been denied anything she desired, and her interest in Byron was not his looks, but his intellect.

"I don't care if he is as ugly as Æsop," she insisted. "I *want* to meet him."

Chapter Thirteen

~~~

It was Lady Westmoreland's last Ball before her Easter break in Cheltenham.

In Melbourne House, Caroline was still dressing when Lady Melbourne came up the stairs to collect her.

"Caroline, it's after nine. Must you *always* be late for every function?"

Caroline was dabbing perfume behind her ears. "I hate being early or even *on time* for anything. It gives the impression that one has nothing better to do all day than wait eagerly in anticipation of attending someone else's party."

Lady Melbourne sighed in exasperation. She utterly loathed her daughter-in-law and wished to God that her son had never married her.

She sat herself down on a chair and waved her fan in the way she always did when she was irritated with Caroline. "Everyone who is anyone will be there. They say that even Lord Byron will definitely be there tonight."

Caroline made a small scoffing sound. "They said the same about Lord Holland's Ball, Lady Jersey's Ball, Lady Oxford's dinner party, and yet the poet did not appear. It seems he ignores all invitations from anyone he doesn't know."

Caroline looked at herself in the mirror: her hair was cut short at the back into the nape of her neck in the new style, with a mass of soft blonde curls at the front falling around her face and ears.

"I once thought Lord Byron was interesting and

wanted to meet him," she said, "but now I can only conclude that he is not only strange, but very rude."

"There is a rumour going round," said Lady Melbourne, "that Mr Wordsworth says Lord Byron is a little *mad.*"

Caroline looked at her mother-in-law. "Oh, then he *must* be a little mad, if Mr Wordsworth says so. It takes one to know one, and we all know that Wordsworth is more than a little upside-down at times."

"I suspect that Mr Wordsworth must have a very bad temper, or at least a liver complaint," said Lady Melbourne. "Did you know that he has now fallen out with his poet friend, Coleridge?"

"No, I didn't know, and I don't care – both are bald-headed bores. The next time we have a Ball here and we need a handsome poet to amuse us, I shall invite Walter Scott ... I loved his 'Lady Of The Lake'."

Lady Melbourne glared as she watched her daughter-in-law pulling on a pair of long white gloves.

"Walter Scott? What you seem to be forgetting, Caroline, is that Lord Byron is one of *us* – one of our own. It has been a long time, perhaps never, since the aristocracy produced a *poet* of such brilliance."

Caroline inspected herself one last time. "I'm told he is very ugly."

"*All* poets are ugly," Lady Melbourne retorted. "Now, are we finally *ready?*"

"We are," Caroline said agreeably, and then with a demure face added contritely: "I am truly sorry for keeping you waiting so long, Lady M."

Lady Melbourne stood and led the way out of the room, with Caroline tripping meekly behind her, while sticking her tongue out hatefully at her mother-in-law's back.

~ ~ ~

Thomas Moore had dressed very carefully for his dinner with Lord Byron, although Tommy usually dressed well, but tonight he was even more particular; as one must be when dining with a *Lord*.

It had taken Tommy at least half an hour to wrap his silk cream stock around his neck until it reached just under the chin, reminding him of the poem written by some London dandy:

My neckcloth, of course, forms my principal care,

For by that we criterions of elegance swear,

And cost me each morning some hours of flurry

To make it appear to be tied in a hurry.

Lord Byron appeared to be in no hurry at all when Moore arrived at his rooms in St James Street, not even fully dressed, still inserting some gold links into the cuffs of his white shirt, while his valet stood behind him holding a white waistcoat.

The shirt immediately caught Tommy's attention. "Is that shirt made of *Irish* linen?"

"Aye, Irish linen it is, Mr Moore," Fletcher answered. "On behalf of his lordship I am forced to order bales of Irish linen for the tailors to cut up for his lordship's shirts and bedsheets and pillowcases. Plain cotton would *never* do, not for his lordship."

"But the *front* of the shirt is not linen, is it?"

"Oh no, his lordship always insists that the fronts of his shirts and the *sleeves* be made in French Cambric, softer, see, and easier for the tailors to twist the little frills on the cuffs for evening wear."

"So," Tommy asked Byron, "where —"

"Though for his *day* shirts," Fletcher went on, "his lordship usually has the fronts done in a soft muslin that's woven up in Macclesfield – *English* muslin – like what I'm wearing now. He always has some shirts made up for me as well."

"Indeed." Moore replied, and then started his sentence again. "So," he asked Byron, "where are we dining tonight?"

Byron slipped on his white waistcoat and looked at Fletcher, waiting for him to give the answer.

Fletcher stared back at him, puzzled. "What?"

"Well, you have answered every question so far, so now answer Mr Moore again and tell him where we are dining tonight?"

"I dunno."

"At Lady Westmoreland's Ball."

"Are we?" Tommy's heart almost stopped at the thought of mingling with so many of the *aristocracy*. "I thought we were dining at Wattier's tonight."

Byron gave him an apologetic look. "You don't mind, do you? I have received so many invitations to Balls and Banquets and have accepted none of them, but today I received a personal note from Lord Holland asking me to attend Lady Westmoreland's tonight, and as he is the leader of the Whig Party, I feel I must comply."

"And you are taking *me*?"

"If you will come? I have no wish to attend on my own. It will probably be very stiff and formal, but we can leave early if you wish, and dine at Wattier's later."

"I don't mind accompanying you at all!" Tommy's heart was beating so fast he could hardly think. "Will the Prince of Wales be there?"

"He might be."

"And ... will we be able to *speak* to him?"

"No, that would be breaking all royal protocol. One is not allowed to speak to the Prince Regent unless he speaks to you first."

And with all the clamour of Childe Harold's Pilgrimage, Tommy was *sure* the Prince Regent would probably wish to exchange a few words with the poet himself. "Don't worry," he assured Byron, "I will stay very close to your side. You will have my full support."

Byron smiled. "I'm not taking you as my nanny. Once inside you may wander wherever you wish."

Tommy walked over to anxiously inspect his appearance in the wall mirror. Fortunately he had donned his best evening suit of dark green brocade and white breeches, but his hair ... oh goodness, his *hair*!"

"May I borrow some of your powder?" he asked Byron. "I cannot go to a Ball with my hair undressed."

"Powder?" Byron glanced at Fletcher and smiled his amusement. "Do we have any powder, Fletcher?"

"No, my lord," then to Moore – "His lordship never wears powder in his hair."

"No?" Tommy was surprised. "No powder – not even when attending a Ball? Why not?"

"More to the point, *why?* My hair is clean and black so why should I spend an hour dirtying it up by powdering it white. For what *sane* reason?"

Tommy couldn't think of one.

Byron disappeared into his dressing-room to finish dressing, and when he came out again, Tommy stared at him, and suddenly felt colourfully *overdressed* in comparison.

Byron was dressed all in black, full-leg trousers and evening tail-coat, but everything else was snow white, the shirt, the waistcoat, and Byron was *not* wearing a neckcloth rolled up under his chin.

Only then did Tommy notice that Byron's shirt was made with a larger and softer collar, which sat neatly and *open* on his neck with a thin black cord holding a square red ruby hanging just under the collar.

"No neckcloth?" he asked.

"No," Byron replied. "Neckcloths and stocks always remind me of an event with my late and dear friend, Charles Matthews, and since his tragic death last year I don't wear them anymore."

"Not even for Balls or Banquets?"

"Not even for the House of Lords," said Byron, "but the ermine collar on that red robe covers everything."

Tommy was looking at the whiteness of Byron' shirt – a sure sign of *wealth;* no common man could afford to wear a white shirt, except perhaps on a Sunday; not in smoky London he couldn't. Tommy's own shirt was his best buff one, the same shade as his waistcoat and neckcloth.

"How do you keep your shirts so white?" he asked Byron, who shrugged and moved past him, taking his cloak from Fletcher and throwing it casually around his shoulders as if going out to nowhere more special than a regular dining house.

"It's the way the shirts are washed," said Fletcher, proud to be able to pass on such exclusive information. "All men of the *high* society send their shirts out to the country to be laundered, so's they can be hung up to dry in *clean* country air. His lordship has always been very particular about his own cleanliness, right down to his skin – no colognes or perfumes for him. So for his shirts to be as clean and as white as he likes them, I always send them out to a laundry in the countryside of Islington. And then there's –"

"Moore, does all your conversation have to be so damned *domestic?*" Byron cut in impatiently. "If you want to dine at Wattier's later, we will have to leave for Lady Westmoreland's *now.*"

~ ~ ~

Once the carriage had come to a halt outside the porticos of Lady Westmoreland's mansion, Thomas Moore could feel the colour flooding from his face and leaving it as white as Byron's shirt, due to a sudden fit of nerves.

Byron noticed. "Is something wrong?"

Thomas Moore nodded. "This reminds me of my first day at Trinity College in Dublin. I was sixteen, terrified, and felt as sick as a dog."

"Why?"

"Because I was an Irish Catholic, about to walk inside an Irish *Protestant* bastion. How my parents managed to get me in there, I still don't know, but it was the only university to be educated in at the time."

"Were your parents wealthy?"

"No, not wealthy, quite the opposite," Moore admitted. "Two hard-working people who owned a grocer's shop, and we lived in the apartment above it."

A footman arrived and opened the carriage door but Byron curtly stopped him. "No, no, we are not ready to get out yet, so pray shut the door again."

Somewhat surprised, the white-wigged footman did so, and Byron turned back to Moore. "We will go in when you are ready, or not at all if you prefer."

"Thank you, but I *do* want to go in. I just need a moment to collect myself."

Byron relaxed back on the seat as if they had all the time in the world.

"You and I are more similar than I realised," he said. "Until the age of ten I also lived in an apartment above a shop, although it was much grander than a grocer's shop, it was a *perfume* shop, in Broad Street, in Aberdeen."

"In Scotland?"

"Yes, I am half a Scot, didn't you know?"

"No." Thomas Moore was very surprised. "But you know, now that you tell me so – I *thought* I detected the odd lilt in your voice here and there."

"That's mainly due to the influence over the years of my mother. She was full of *bonnies* and *braes* and *hoots* and, unlike myself, all her years in England never diminished her Scottish accent. But then, unlike myself, she had not been educated from an early age at *Harrow*."

Thomas Moore was smiling, more relaxed and less nervous.

"Come on, Tommy," Byron said, reaching to open the carriage door. "The haut ton don't like to be kept waiting, so let us throw off our cares and embark on this *Ship of Fools* together."

Chapter Fourteen

~ ~ ~

Inside Lady Westmoreland's crowded ballroom, under the glowing and glittering lights of the chandeliers, the younger members of the *bon ton* who lived only to sing and dance and fill their lives with pleasure, had found a favourite new song to swoon and sway to.

All knew every word of the song, but while the orchestra's singer stood and sang alone, the guests only joined in when it came to the last line of each verse – which all had learned by heart – although none knew what that last line meant:

"Maid of Athens, ere we part

Give, oh, give me back my heart!

Or, since that has left my breast,

Keep it now, and take the rest!

Hear my vows before I go

Zoë mou sas agapo.

By that lip I long to taste;

By that zone-encircled waist;

By all the token-flowers that tell

What words can never speak so well;

By love's alternate joy and woe

Zoë mou sas agapo

Maid of Athens, I am gone:

Think of me, sweet! when alone.

Though I fly to Istanbul,
Athens holds my heart and soul:
Can I cease to love thee? No!
Zoë mou sas agapo!"

All singing ceased abruptly when the announcement was heard — "The Right Honourable George Lord Byron and Mr Thomas Moore."

"What?"

None could believe it — the reclusive author of *Childe Harold* and *Maid of Athens* was actually *here,* come to join them?

As the crowd surged towards the top of the ballroom, the last tremors of Thomas Moore's earlier bout of nerves completely vanished, because not one pair of eyes was looking at him — all were staring at Lord Byron, and loving what they saw, especially the glowing females.

Moore was not a bit surprised; the reaction of the crowd was no different to the reaction of himself and Rogers and Campbell when they had first laid eyes on Lord Byron on that dinner-night of the "returned letter"

Even to have *known* beforehand that he was taller than average and stunningly handsome, would not have prepared one, on getting a nearer view, for the beauty of his features, and the charm of his smile and voice.

And now, added to that, was the attraction of his known other qualities — his vast mental powers as a political commentator, and his poetical genius. Surely anyone would forgive him the deformity of one foot and a slight limp in his walk when compared to all that?

Shoved aside as he was by the crowd, Tommy moved away and went in search of a drink ... and perhaps even the Prince Regent ... hoping the stand-in monarch truly *was* here tonight ... somewhere within these vast gilded rooms? Perhaps he could introduce himself as a *friend* of Lord Byron, and if the prince was friendly enough in return, perhaps he could even ask the prince to be the *godfather* of his child soon to be born?

Tommy smiled to himself as he allowed his imagination to run away with him ... wouldn't that be a sour lemon in the mouths of all those haughty Prods back in Dublin who *still* looked down on him for being a Catholic.

Up in the picture-gallery, Lady Caroline Lamb was being rebuked by her grandmother, Countess Spencer, over the scantiness of her dress.

"It's the new *Greek* style!" Caroline insisted. "It's the new rage in fashion since we all read Childe Harold's Pilgrimage. Now all our hairstyles are Greek, our dresses are Greek, and even our *songs* are Greek."

The Countess was still staring at the dress of gold muslin, a scanty high-waisted, low-bosomed, sleeveless garment.

"No stays, no underwear, just one clinging dress. It's indecent, Caroline."

"But I am wearing *gloves,*" Caroline said, holding out her white-gloved arms.

Countess Spencer shook her head with exasperation. "Now I understand why your mother-in-law finds you so difficult. Dear Caro, I do love you, but *why* are you always so wayward?"

"Because I am always so bored with life."

"You might be less bored if you dressed more respectably."

Caroline sighed her boredom. "Grandmama," she said impatiently, "the days when *you* were the belle of the ball in your one hundred petticoats and huge wigs, are gone. The fashion has changed overnight, and the gowns that you used to wear are now completely *old-*fashioned, suitable only for *old* ladies."

"William should have more control over you. Why is he not here tonight?"

"He *is* here. Tucked away somewhere with Lord Holland, agitating himself with politics. That's all he cares about, you know – politics. Yet *all* his opinions come straight from the mouth of Lord Holland."

Caroline suddenly laughed: she was standing by the rail looking down onto one of the corridors and saw Annabella Milbanke walking hastily. "There is dear cousin Annabella, looking more like a maidservant than an heiress in her prim frock ... what a frump!"

"I always find myself thinking there is something very sly about that young Milbanke woman," said Countess Spencer. "I find it extremely hard to like her."

"Then pity me for having to live in the same house as her," said Caroline. "Oh ... Grandmama, come and look ... there is Lady What's-her-name all bunched up in pink brocade and a ton of pearls. Would you prefer me to dress like *that*?"

"Countess Spencer ... Lady Caroline ..." both women turned as Lady Westmoreland came rushing into the picture-gallery.

Caroline immediately smiled because she was so very fond of Lady Westmoreland. "What has you so puffed, dear?"

"Lord Byron, I really must introduce you both to him."

Caroline stared. "Introduce us! You mean ... he is *here*?"

"Of course he is here. How could I introduce you to

him if he was *not* here? And you, too, Countess?"

Countess Spencer waved her away. "I believe I will make my way down to the supper room and find myself some hot soup, but take Caroline with you ... although when you *do* introduce her to anyone, please do not reveal that she is any relation of min*e* – not in *that* dress!"

Caroline laughed as she tripped beside Lady Westmoreland towards the stairs. "What is he like? Childe Harold? Is he as ugly as Mr Rogers says?"

Lady Westmoreland paused and stared at her. "Caroline, he is *not* Childe Harold, he is Lord Byron. And he is not ugly, but rather romantic-looking."

"Even with his limp?"

"His limp? Has he a limp? I'm certain I did not notice one."

"So," Caroline decided, "either Mr Rogers was lying to me – the rogue – or *your* eyesight is truly as bad as you always say it is."

"My eyesight is poor, Caroline, and you should not mock it."

"I mock everything and everyone," Caroline said with a smile. "It keeps me sane."

The smile was wiped clean off Caroline's face when Lady Westmoreland pointed out Lord Byron to her in the ballroom ... a tall handsome young man with black hair who was surrounded by young ladies, their heads all nodding excitedly and their bare white shoulders crushed against each other.

His own shoulder was leaning against the wall and his head was slightly bent as he listened to what some of the young ladies were busily chattering.

And then he suddenly looked up, although his head remained bent, looking around and meeting her eyes in what she could only describe as a sort of under-look, his eyes flickering over her clinging dress and then up to her face again.

She stopped dead in her tracks as she stared at him: the attraction was instant and physical and sexual, something she had never once felt before.

She turned and fled – out of the ballroom and out of the house, pushing her way through the white-wigged footmen to escape as quickly as possible, leaving Lady Westmoreland standing behind her at a loss to understand her actions.

Finally it was Lady Melbourne who came to Lady Westmoreland's aid, and then explained to both her and Lord Byron:

"My daughter-in-law can be a little eccentric at times. She probably remembered that she had neglected to wash one of her dogs, and has rushed back to do it."

Outside Caroline had fled into her carriage with a rapid order up to the driver to take her straight home, without a care as to how her husband would get home without his carriage. She didn't care about *him*—she couldn't remember now what he even looked like!

The only face she could see now was that of Lord Byron... Byron ... Byron ... Byron ... such a wonderful name, so much better than *Lamb* ... or Ponsonby or Spencer or Granville or Melbourne or any other name in the world!

Inside the great white marble hall of Melbourne House, Caroline paused and tried to collect herself as the footman stared at her, surprised she was back so early, and alone.

"This damned house is too big," she whispered, looking around her. The ground floor with all of its many huge rooms was now the residence of her in-laws,

Lord and Lady Melbourne, while the whole of the first floor had been given over to herself and William on their marriage. And above that – servants' quarters probably; she didn't know and she didn't care.

She quickly made her way up the stairs and along the corridors to her own boudoir, picked up *Childe Harold's Pilgrimage,* sank down on her window-seat and began to read it again, including every word of the Preface, which all sounded so different now – now that she had *seen* the young man who had written it:

"Amongst the many objections to the very indifferent character of the 'vagrant Childe Harold' it has been stated that he is very unKnightly, as the times of the Knights were times of love, honour, and so forth. Now it so happens that those 'good old times', were the most profligate of all possible centuries. Those who have any doubts on this subject may consult St Palaye, passim, *and more particularly, vol. ii, page 69.*

The vows of chivalry and chastity then were no better kept than any other vows whatsoever, and the songs of the Troubadours were not more decent, and certainly were much less refined than the songs of Ovid. So much for chivalry. Burke need not have regretted that its days are over.

I now leave Childe Harold to live his day, such as he is; it would have been more agreeable, and certainly more easy, to have drawn an amiable character, to varnish over his faults, to make him do more and express less, but he never was intended as an example."

Caroline's hands were hot with a strange fever, her forehead burned like fire. This was all so strange, so very strange. She felt like she had been struck by lightning. Ever since that moment, that *meeting of eyes* in the ballroom, her whole mind had been changed. Never once, never before, had she looked at a man and felt such instant desire, or any desire at all. Flirting and romancing were fun and a joy – but *desire* was an absolute stranger.

Her maid entered the room, offering to help her undress, but she waved her out irritably. "Out, out, it's not as if I have any stays or corsets to undo, is it?"

"No, m'lady."

She threw down the book and looked out at the night sky, murky and dark. Of course, she knew the reason for all this hotness in her hands and her brow and other less visible places ... his attraction was *sexual*.

Oh, yes, the nonchalant way he had stood with his shoulder leaning against the wall, and that under-look he had given her ... Oh, yes ... Lord Byron was literally dripping with red-hot *sex* appeal, every bit of him, especially when those blue eyes of his had flickered over her dress, as if he *knew* at a glance that she was naked underneath.

But then ... but then ... even in Childe Harold he had made no secret of the fact that in his youth he had often frequented the salons of courtesans who had *'long fed his youthful appetite.'*

She picked up *Childe Harold* again and flicked through the preface at random ...

'Harold is a child of the imagination. It has been

suggested to me by friends, on whose opinion I set a high value, that in this fictitious character, I may incur the suspicion of it being autobiographical. In some very trivial particulars, there might be grounds for such a notion; but in the main points, I should hope, none whatever.'

And yet, Caroline wondered, was it not a mystery that with *one look* he had opened her own eyes to the incoherence of her own life and the boredom of her existence?

Or was it only in the Preface and End-Notes in *Childe Harold* that he had done that? That straight and direct way of his when speaking to the reader? The man was a true conversationalist, even when only speaking in print!

Yet William – her husband never wasted much of his time in conversation with *women*, apart from the usual polite and light addresses demanded by etiquette. No, when it came to women, William Lamb was more interested in *beating* them, all for the purpose of sexual arousal of course – not that *she* had ever been aroused. How could she be? It was gross.

She thought back to those shocking and horrid three weeks of her honeymoon, when William had not only conjugalised her, but had also sodomised her – she had been sore for weeks!

And then ... and then ... when all that had palled on him, blaming her continual crying for his lack of arousal, he had gone to his portmanteau and taken out some illicit sketches to look at, and made her look at them too ... sketches of women caning naked young children, telling her he was a firm believer in the caning of children, especially young *girl* children who were usually the naughtiest children of all ... "*and on their cheeky little bare bottoms, one, two three ...*" he had said, imitating the whack of a cane.

Caroline ran a hand irritably through her blonde curls ... And this man, her husband, intended that one day in the future he would become England's *Honourable Prime Minister!*

Childe Harold was a saint in comparison.

Chapter Fifteen

~ ~ ~

Elizabeth, the Duchess of Devonshire, was sitting in her home at Devonshire House in London, writing a letter to her son, Augustus Foster.

"The subject of conversation, of curiosity, of enthusiasm, is not Spain or Portugal, the War or Warriors or Patriots, but Lord Byron!

This poem (Childe Harold's Pilgrimage) is on every table, and himself courted, visited, flattered, and praised wherever he appears. He is handsome, he has amusing conversation, and, in short, he is really the only topic of almost every conversation – the men jealous of him, the women of each other."

But then, one never really could say *exactly* what Lord Byron was like, due to his chameleon-like nature, which changed with his moods and his temperament; sometimes extremely reserved and sensitive, and other times hilariously funny, displaying a droll and dry humour with a genius for slipping in the *perfect* comic line.

During a soirée at Holland House, Lady Holland, although still only forty-one years old, was suffering from the sharp pain of arthritis in her hip and was forced to lay supine on a couch and miss all the fun and chatter ... until Lord Byron saw her alone and chose to miss it all also, spending most of the evening sitting with her, teasingly flattering her, and making her laugh so much that she enjoyed a wonderful night after all. So much so, that this rich and sophisticated daughter of an American planter wrote to one of her friends a few days later, admitting that she was now completely 'Byronised' — "*He is such a lovable person. I can still see him sitting there, with the light upon him, looking so beautiful.*"

Yet Lady Morgan, the Irish poetess, came to a different conclusion after meeting him at a function, and wrote to a friend — "*Lord Byron, the author of the delightful Childe Harold (which has more force, fire and thought than anything I have read for an age) is cold, silent, and reserved in his manners.*

Soon after his attendance at Holland House, Robert Dallas, Byron's literary agent, called upon him at his rooms one morning and found Byron in a state of fury and frustration.

"Look at all this! What am I supposed to do with all this! And I *will* get the staff from St Dunstan's church and immolate John Murray, because he is the man responsible for all this!"

Dallas looked around the drawing-room and saw huge piles of letters and invitation cards on every surface. "Oh no, my lord," he said slowly, "I believe *you* are the man responsible for all this."

"Me? What did *I* do? All I did was write a poem. Of course it is Murray's fault. He is the one who has manipulated all this, and *he* is the publisher who keeps turning it out by the thousands."

And no one was more pleased than Dallas himself: he was now back in the black at the bank; and John Murray was cock-a-hoop over the brilliant success of Childe Harold."

Byron looked around him. "I cannot *move* due to my rooms being constantly loaded with letters from critics, poets, authors and other hopefuls of fame as well as people from all different walks of life. And the letters from the women, oh God, the *women* ... all so lavish with their rapture and begging me to meet them somewhere in secret."

He snapped up a letter. "Here is one from..." he peered at the small neat handwriting of the address ... "Miss Sarah Agnes Bamber from Alphington, near Exeter – and she says ... *'Lord Byron, I have just finished a perusal of your incomparable work, and an impulse irresistible impels me to acknowledge your Pen has called forth the most exquisite feelings I have ever experienced ...'*"

He looked at Dallas – "and then she says she wants to know if we can *meet* somewhere!"

Dallas shrugged, endeavouring to hide his delight. "A fanciful young lady, that's all."

"And then there's this one – well there are *hundreds* like this one, all are more or less the same — *'I am a woman,'* he read, *"certainly a young woman, and I trust not a disagreeable one, and upon perusing Childe Harold and its accompanying poems, I became, as it were, animated by a new soul, alive to wholly novel sensations and activated by feelings till then unknown."*

He looked at Dallas. "And she also wants us to meet somewhere."

Dallas could not think of a word to say in consolation.

Byron could not understand it, this fame thing. "And if we *did* meet, why do these women not consider the fact that I might be the ugliest being on earth, with big ears and no teeth and God knows what else??"

"Oh, they know you don't look like that, "Dallas said reassuringly without properly thinking, "because of the sketch of you on the front cover."

"What sketch of me?"

"Oh ... did Mr Murray not tell you?" Dallas stuttered. "On th-the third edition, he had a sketch of you put on the cover of the new edition."

Byron stared for a long moment, and then erupted: "And *where* did he get the sketch of me? I gave him no sketch. I do not *possess* any sketch of myself, so where did he get it?"

"I b-believe it was in his office, one day when you were both discussing business ... apparently, there was a man ... an artist ... at the window ... making a drawing of your face."

"That deceitful, back-shop, Paternoster Row manipulator. I hope he *dies* in Grubb Street. And you may tell him I hope it will be soon. Do you think he has any idea of what he has done to me?"

"He has been helping to make your work a success."

"No, no, no – he has been helping to make *himself* rich – and you also*!* Both of you have been fattening yourselves while *I* am left to pay the cost."

"What cost, Lord Byron? Mr Murray is paying for everything out of his own pocket."

"And getting ten times as much *back* into his pocket, while I have to suffer all this ... " Byron picked up another handful of letters. "See, apart from the *women*, all these dinner and party invitations from the Jerseys, the Cowpers, the Abercrombies, the Melbournes, the Johnsons —" He stopped and looked again. "*Who* are the Johnsons?"

Dallas said: "Lord Byron, all these people, the Jerseys, the Cowpers, the Melbournes and so on, are all from the highest echelons of London society. All the richest doors have been widely opened to you with the warmest welcome. But until the publication of 'Childe Harold's Pilgrimage' by Mr Murray, you were hitherto an unknown young aristocrat."

"Was I indeed? So tell me, Mr Dallas, if I was to accept all these invitations, where would I find the time to do any more writing?"

"More writing?" Dallas became alert. "Are you doing any more writing? Something new?"

Byron sat down in a chair and closed his eyes tiredly for a moment. This truly was a *Ship of Fools!*

"Mr Dallas," he said quietly, "I write because I need to write. In the same way a perpetual drinker needs to keep topping up and refreshing himself from the bottle. It is something I have always done, and something I will always do. So I cannot be a social butterfly every day and night. And I cannot cope with all these letters crowding up my living and writing space."

"Then I will speak to Mr Murray right away," Dallas assured him. "I will tell him that no more letters from anonymous readers sent to his business establishment are to be forwarded on to you, and that they are to be kept at his establishment."

"Thank you."

"And this *new* piece you are writing? What is it? I am sure Mr Murray will be delighted to know about it."

Byron looked steadily at his literary agent. "You may tell John Murray, that he will know all about it, *after* I have immolated him onto a wooden fence in Grubb Street."

Dallas smiled weakly. "Surely not."

"On second thoughts," said Byron, sitting up as he remembered, "I will tell him myself. I am meeting him for dinner at six."

"Before or after his immolation?"

"Before, because I intend to *immolate* him with my words on this occasion. St Dunstan's staff can wait until another time, until he commits a worse crime than those he has already committed against me. That man is just *too* ambitious to become a publisher of note, moreso even than an ambitious politician."

"He is an excellent businessman though, you must admit. Can you at least tell me the *title* of your new work?"

Byron shrugged. "No. When you have done what you have vowed to do, and all the crazy letters stop piling in to my home address, then I will tell you."

"Crazy letters?" Dallas made a sympathetic face. "These women are ... admirers ... so it's wrong to be unkind."

Byron had forgotten that Dallas was also a *Reverend* in his local church, full of Christian pity.

"Mad, then?" He lifted an open letter that he had been reading before Dallas arrived, and read aloud: *"You must excuse this madness. I beg you to instantly destroy what was intended for your eyes only."*

He looked at Dallas. "Even she says it's madness, and it is."

Dallas was shaking his head again, still unable to comprehend it all. Byron's rapid celebrity was like no other England had ever seen at any time in the past. Almost overnight, it seemed, he had risen from being an obscure minor aristocrat, to a poet of rare splendour, and a literary star.

~~~

John Murray knew Byron was annoyed with him, because when the waiter arrived with the menu, he refused to order any dinner.

John Murray waited until the waiter had left them to peruse, then said: "Not eating? Nothing at all?"

Byron shook his head. "No, this is one of my starvation days."

"Are you not hungry?"

"Of course I'm hungry. I've spent most of my life feeling hungry, but I cannot put on weight, else I suffer in other ways."

"Indeed? How so?"

Byron helped himself to a glass of champagne from the cold bucket. "Mr Murray, you know I have a limp in my right foot, but do you also know that my right *leg* from the mid-calf down, is much thinner and weaker than my left leg. Consequently, if I was to get as fat as a fool and put too much weight on my right leg, the pain is very unpleasant, so I am forced to be abstemious on a regular basis."

"Indeed?" John Murray was fascinated.

"So would you like to put a *sketch* of my right leg and foot on the cover of my next book?"

"The reason these particulars fascinate me," said John Murray, ignoring the question, "is because Walter Scott suffers from the same condition, a bent foot and a thinner leg."

"Does he? Walter Scott?" Byron was shocked.

"So you see why I am so fascinated? Two brilliant poets with the same malady."

"Walter Scott, the author of 'Lady of the Lake'..." Suddenly Byron did not feel so alone in his affliction.

"I remember once having a conversation about it with Walter Scott," John Murray continued, "because he also is very abstemious in his diet, I presume for the same reason; although he is rather *obsessed* about finding out the cause. His family are all very healthy, you see, so since a boy he has never been able to understand why he was singled out for his disability. He has since told me that a doctor he spoke to is now sure his affliction is due to an infection they have discovered called *polio,* although I would not say you have the same condition, because Scott also suffers with severe pain in his spine, and you do not. Or do you?"

"No, all other parts of my body are very strong and without any pain at all. All I know is that mine is *not* a club foot, as people may say. And how did the doctor find out about this polio?"

"Oh, science, the wonders of science. Scientists are very strange people, you know? They search all over the world for answers and cures, and it seems the first clue to this condition was found in *Egypt,* of all places. Some antiquarians were studying the engravings on some of the walls of the ancient tomb of one of the Pharaohs, and as the Pharaohs in those times wore skirts down to the knees, it was clearly seen that this particular Pharaoh had one calf thinner than the other and a turned-in foot."

Byron was amazed. "I once heard a doctor telling my mother that it was all due to her vainly continuing to wear her tight corsets during her pregnancy, and that her *vanity* was the cause of my infirmity. Did Walter Scott say if he knew how this infection is caught by a child in the womb?"

"In his case, he believes it must have come from the midwife who attended his mother at her home in Scotland during the months beforehand. It's an infection that can be harboured unknown in the throat apparently, and all the harbourer has to do is breathe on another person and it can be passed on, often just to the child in the womb. There are three types of polio, Scott says, but I cannot remember what they are. You may have contracted only a very mild form, which affected only one limb."

Byron was feeling devastated. "My poor mother. In my childhood I always blamed her for my affliction, although she in turn always blamed *me* for coming out flawed."

He reached for more champagne. "How stupid we *both* were. Now I'm feeling the urge to get totally intoxicated, if only to drown away my feelings of guilt."

As the evening went on Byron got quite drunk, having eaten no food, although John Murray soon caught up with him, and by the end of the night both were laughing hilariously at every ridiculous thing the other said.

Out on the street, the night was warm and the oil lamps flared and flickered as they happily strolled along, ignoring every passing hackney cab and forgetting to hail one.

"I can walk home from here," Byron said, looking around him. "I live in St James."

"I do know that, Lord Byron."

Having drunk far too much champagne and his mind unguarded, John Murray smiled. "And I am depending on *you*, my dear sir, to get me out of Fleet Street and into a more salubrious area – such as St James. Just keep on writing the way you have been writing, and I will be joining you ..." he paused and pointed at the sky — "up there with the stars."

"Aha, that *reminds* me! The reason why I intended to immolate you tonight!"

John Murray laughed. "My dear Lord Byron, you are *always* threatening to immolate me. Here's an idea! Let us stroll now to St Dunstan's Church so I can take a look at that staff of his. If it is going to be my death-weapon in the future, I should at least say hello and make friends with it, maybe even break off the spike at its head, eh?"

"No, no, we must talk." Byron sat down on a wall. "Seriously, you and I, John Murray, we must talk."

"Very well." Murray sat down beside him, still gazing up at the sky. "Although not *too* seriously I hope."

"You see," Byron explained, "you are a back-shop, back-street bookseller from Grubb Street. You have learned all the manipulating tricks of your *selling* trade from Grubb Street. But I now ... I am a Cambridge scholar, a man of letters, and *you* are undermining everything I stand for."

"Which is?"

"My work. All these articles, and all your requests for me to sit for paintings or sketches ... if you encourage people to focus on *the man,* and not his work, then posterity will do the same."

The publisher could see that his author was quite serious.

"When Shakespeare died in 1616," said Byron, "he was personally so *unknown* to the men of his time that not one writer, nor one poet – picked up a pen to write a single word in tribute to him. Few knew anything about him. In those days he was just an actor and scribbler of the theatre, performing in the market place ... And yet still, even now what do we actually know about him – about Shakespeare the *man*?"

"Very little."

"Not enough to fill a page! Born and died in

Stratford-upon-Avon, had a wife and children, actor, playwright, nothing more, and that's all we know about the *man*. Yet the scope and genius of his *work* is now colossal and has long outlived his bones."

John Murray smiled. "So, you want to go down in history?"

"I want to be remembered – as a poet *worthy* of his fame, and not simply as a lord of rank, or for how I look, or for other ludicrous tittle-tattle about me."

"You cannot blame people for being interested in that aspect of you, not in these modern times. The world has changed since the days of Shakespeare. In those days, only one person in every hundred could read. Now it's one in every ten. And now, if readers like an author, they also like to know something about him."

"But surely not untrue *scandal*?" Byron declared. "Do you know, I read an article in a magazine the other day that said I had been educated abroad, they knew not where, but it was suspected I had *murdered* someone in that place, and I had returned to London to escape from all my *crimes*. And the reason why I was so reserved in public, was because I had some dark and mysterious secrets to hide."

John Murray's burst of laughter could be heard all the way down the dark street.

"Oh now, that was nothing to do with me or my colleagues, I assure you. We would not encourage such scurrilous gossip about you, quite the contrary. We *glory* in your rank and have no intention of besmirching it."

"I am capable of sin, who isn't? But I am not capable of anything so heinous as *murder*."

John Murray had stopped laughing. "I will make sure any nonsense like that about you is immediately met with legal action in the future. We cannot tolerate such libel against one of our authors."

"John Hanson has already started legal proceedings on my behalf," Byron said, "against a hack, one whom I *know,* and one whom I intend to relieve by law of every penny he possesses."

"Oh? And who is that?"

"Hewson Clarke. A failed poet who was a Fellow at King's College at the time I was at Cambridge, but now he spends most of his time writing lies and bam for scandal magazines."

"What did he say?"

Byron turned on the wall and looked directly at John Murray. "He said I was the illegitimate bastard son of John Byron, and that my mother spent most of her time at Newstead Abbey rolling around drunk."

John Murray was horrified. "Sue him you must!"

Byron nodded. "My attorney, John Hanson, has all the legal documents to prove my parents were legally married two years before my birth. And although my mother may be dead now, thankfully, because she was an avid reader of all magazines and something like that may well have *killed* her anyway, I will not allow anyone to speak of my mother in that way, not in any derisory way at all. So I hope my legal action will serve as a warning to other hacks in the future."

"Oh, dear, I am sorry," said John Murray, almost sober again, as was Byron.

"But apart from all that," said Byron, "all these letters sent to me by *women,* some are quite outrageous."

John Murray shrugged. "You alone must take responsibility for that."

"Why?"

"Well, you make it very clear that 'Childe Harold' was

a youth who was *'sore, sick at heart'* and the reason Harold went abroad was due to a girl he loved and lost."

"So?"

"*'And none did love him'*, you say. And as many believe the work to be autobiographical, all these women want to console you by offering you *their* love."

John Murray shrugged again. "Bags of those letters come to us every day for you. Byron *fanatics* we used to call them, but now we just refer to them as *fans.*"

"You will not forward any more of them to me."

"No. Robert Dallas came running round to me today with strict instructions about that. But now ... " Murray began to search in his pockets ... "as to why Childe Harold is such a success I brought along a review to show you, which sums it all up perfectly in my view ... or did I bring it? No, I must have left it behind."

Byron sighed tiredly. "Let's go home. You may stay in one of my rooms if you wish. My apartment is just around the corner."

"No, no, thank you, I will hail a cab. If I do not return home tonight my wife will be in a fret of worry."

Byron waited with him until a hackney cab came along and Murray hailed it.

"Oh, before I go," said John Murray. "Will you be writing *more* cantos about Childe Harold's adventures abroad? I'm sure the public would love to read them."

Byron smiled, shaking his head. "No, to get back the mood and write about Harold in his balmy climes I would need the sea and blue skies and the hot sun on my face, not sitting by an English coal fire."

"Oh, that's a pity. So what is your next work?"

"Something that *nobody* in their right mind could believe was me, nor anyone like me."

"Do you have a title?"

"Yes. The Giaour."

"The *Giaour*? Now what does that mean?"

"It's pronounced *The Jower*, an offensive form of Turkish slang. In English it means 'The Infidel."

John Murray's eyes brightened ... something else exotic from the East that no other English poet would write or even be *capable* of writing — but Lord Byron had gone there, seen it with his own eyes, and for a year at least he had even wandered through the East *alone*, with not even his friend Hobhouse for company. A brave thing for a young man to do, especially one of the soft and cosseted nobility, and *that's* what made Lord Byron so interesting to the public ... that and a few other things.

"We will have to make 'The Infidel' the sub-title, so our English readers know what it means."

"No need. It's clearly stated in the text what it means."

Murray climbed into the cab, but before closing the door — "I have enjoyed tonight, Lord Byron, with all it's various topics."

Byron nodded, closed the carriage door, and raised his hand. "Goodnight, sir."

~ ~ ~

When John Murray returned home, he saw the folded square of paper from *The Quarterly Review* lying on the hall table, where he had forgotten to slip it into his pocket in order to show it to Lord Byron.

He unfolded the paper and looked at it. The review was unsigned, of course, but he was almost positive that the critic George Ellis had written it.

"We believe that few books are so extensively read

and admired as those which contain the narrative of intelligent travellers. Indeed, the greater part of every community are confined to a very narrow space on the globe, and are naturally eager to contemplate, in description at least, that endless variety of new and curious objects which a visit to distant countries and climates is known to furnish.

By what accident has it happened then, that no English poet before Lord Byron has thought fit to employ his talents on a subject so obviously well suited to their display."

'Exactly ... 'thought John Murray. 'And when you add that to the intense *emotionalism* of Byron's poetry, his dry and subtle humour, and the immense *power* of his language ... what you end up with is ... a bestseller.'

Chapter Sixteen

~ ~ ~

Thomas Moore and Samuel Rogers were also suffering from Byron's fame in their own individual ways, and finally complained to his lordship about it.

"I am being *inundated* with invitations to every dinner party and soirée in town," Tommy said glumly, "and although all are wonderful opportunities for the social advancement of an Irish poet in England, I cannot accept any of them."

"Why not?" Byron asked.

"Because all end with the same proviso — *'And please bring your friend Lord Byron along with you'.*"

Samuel Rogers shrugged. "Do as I do, Tommy, and go along anyway, and simply say that Lord Byron was coming but was detained at the last minute."

He looked earnestly at Byron. "*My* difficulty is different to Moore's, and I must confess that I am getting tired of it, the constant *manoeuvres* of certain noble ladies to gain access to you through *me*."

"Which noble ladies?"

"Well, one of them is Lady Caroline Lamb, one of the 'first-raters' of the upper circle of society. She is very angry with me for something I said to her, all in jest, but now I would consider it a great *favour* if you could get me out of the stocks and come along with me one day and drop in to see her. It seems she owes you an apology."

"For what?"

"For refusing to be introduced to you at Lady Westmoreland's Ball."

Byron thought back. "Oh, I remember ... slender and blonde ... and likes washing dogs."

~ ~ ~

Caroline bent her head almost to the horse's neck as she rode at speed through the empty paths in Green Park and loved every minute of it. The fact that her slender body was dressed in boy's clothes and boots made it even more fun, because nobody would recognise her.

Not for her the sedate strolling through Hyde Park twirling a parasol like so many young ladies she knew, and all because it was the afternoon haunt of Beau Brummell and his set, although the Beau preferred to ride his horse through Hyde Park, slowly of course, so everyone could get a good look at him in his latest riding outfit. A born narcissist if ever there was one.

Returning to the stables at the rear of Melbourne House, she jumped nimbly down from her horse and entered the white marble hall through the back door, dripping with sweat. It had been a hard ride, but a good one.

Up the stairs to her own floor and walking along the circular landing, she was halted by one of the footmen who told her there were two guests awaiting her in her drawing-room, "Mr Samuel Rogers and Mr Thomas Moore."

Disappointed that Rogers had brought no one more interesting to see her, Caroline decided to show Rogers her dissatisfaction with him by refusing to change out of her sweaty riding clothes.

When she entered the drawing-room she was gracious enough with Thomas Moore, but then plonked herself down on the sofa beside Rogers saying, "You don't mind if I sit here with you in all my sweaty *filth*, do you?"

Rogers knew she was annoyed with him and quickly sought to remedy the matter. "You may do so if you wish, Lady Caroline, but I hardly think it will endear Lord Byron."

"Lord Byron?" Caroline sat up.

"Yes, he agreed to come today, but he has been detained by — "

"Oh, *Rogers*, not that nonsense again! How long do you think you will keep getting away with it?"

Rogers was all innocence. "I seek to get away with nothing, Lady Caroline. I *did* bring Lord Byron with me, but he has been detained —"

"By one of your *dogs*," Thomas Moore cut in quickly. "A large Irish Wolfhound that Lord Byron has stopped to have a friendly play with ... down in your garden."

Caroline let out a scream and jumped up and ran out of the room.

Thomas Moore looked wide-eyed at Samuel Rogers. "That's exactly what she did at Lady Westmoreland's Ball ... ran out of the room and almost pushed *me* over in her haste."

~ ~ ~

At the top of the stairs, a footman directed Lord Byron to Lady Caroline's drawing-room. He entered the room, ready to give his sincere apologies for delaying downstairs with the dog, but the lady was not there. He looked at Rogers and Moore.

"Is she out? Not at home? So why are you two waiting?"

"We were waiting for you," said Rogers.

"You could have come back down and saved me the trudge up all those stairs."

"If that had been the case, we would have done," said Thomas Moore, knowing that however Byron might be able to minimise his limp when walking, when it came to stairs he could only do it one step at a time.

"I believe," said Rogers, "that Lady Caroline has gone to wash after her ride in the park. She was not expecting us, so you must excuse her."

Byron really did not want to be here; he hated these social drop-ins with all their artificial conversations.

"Lady Caroline Lamb ..." he said. "You know her, Rogers, so what kind of person is she?"

"Oh ..." for once Rogers decided to be truthful and leave off the jesting.

"She is a wild, delicate, odd, delightful person. One really has to *know* her to actually like her, and then she is utterly fascinating. Her looks are not perfect, she could do with a bit more fat on her body, but she has one absolutely *divine* thing about her which —"

"Lord Byron ..."

Byron turned and saw her, dressed beautifully in a slender white dress, her blonde curls still wet from her bath.

She held out her hand to him, he took it his own and gave a small bow over it. "Lady Caroline."

She then spoke to him in the normal way of first acquaintances, and instantly Byron heard that other "absolutely *divine*" thing about her which Rogers had been about to mention – her voice.

Her voice was soft, low and caressing ... it softened him down as he listened to her ... hearing beauty and charm in its soft tone, which captivated him.

Samuel Rogers made another *faux pas* in his usual mischievous way.

"Lord Byron, you are very honoured. Lady Caroline

had come in very heated from riding and was sitting here in all her sweat and filth with us, but as soon as she knew *you* were here, she flew to beautify herself."

If Rogers had not mortified her with that statement, Caroline knew she might not have done what she did next; but *away* from Rogers she wanted to get as soon as possible.

"Will you allow me to introduce you to my son, Lord Byron?" she asked – and before Byron could reply, she had taken him by the hand and was pulling him towards the door, saying over her shoulder – "There's enchantment of every kind in those decanters on the sideboard, gentlemen, so help yourselves to as many drinks as you wish."

Byron glanced over his own shoulder at the two men, his expression bewildered – he had not expected *this!*

Yet when he met Lady Caroline's son a few minutes later, in a large and bright nursery further down the landing, all his discomfort vanished as he looked at the four-year-old boy ... a beautiful, innocent-eyed boy, named Augustus, who stared at him for one long moment, before he saw a spark of love in the child's eyes.

"Augustus, this is my new friend, Lord Byron," Caroline said softly, but the boy was already at Byron's feet, stretching up his hands to him.

"No, Augustus!" said the nursemaid, but Byron had already lifted him up into his arms and pretended to sniff his face in the way he would do with a small pup, and Augustus *sniffed, sniffed* back, before both smiled at each other.

Caroline suddenly felt excluded, and sent the nursemaid out of the room, quietly instructing her that they were not to be disturbed until Lord Byron had left the nursery.

When she had closed the door behind the nursemaid, and turned around, Caroline saw that Lord Byron had sat down in one the armchairs, with Augustus snuggling inside his arms.

"Oh, Lord Byron, I'm so sorry, I did not intend ..." She moved to take the boy away, but Augustus shook his head, pressing his face against Byron's chest, as if he, too, had found a new friend, and wanted to stay with him.

At a loss as what to do next, Caroline finally sat down on a small chair next to them, and looked apologetically at Byron.

"I'm so sorry," she said again. "I just wanted you to say hello to him, nothing more."

Byron could feel the boy's body relaxing, and bent his head to look at his face, and saw the eyes of the child were closing.

Caroline saw the eyes closing too, and gave a small bewildered sigh.

"It puzzles me," she said quietly, "why Augustus is always so much more sleepier than other children. And why he is still so *baby-ish* in his ways, even though he is now four years old."

Byron stared at her ... unable to believe that she had not yet seen what he had instantly seen ... the boy was mentally feeble. It was clearly visible in the blank innocence of the child's eyes. And even if he had not seen the eyes, the boy's head was slightly too large for his small body."

"You do not know ..." *No, and it was not his place to say it ...* "how pleased I am to have met him. He is a sweet-natured boy."

"Yes, sweet." Caroline nodded. "Everyone tells me

that Augustus is so sweet ... and he truly is an angel child, my own darling boy ... but I do wish he would *play* more and sleep less."

"How regularly does he see his doctor?"

"About what? Augustus is rarely ill."

"About his sleepiness."

"Oh, William took him to his own doctor to check him over, but they both assured me that Augustus would grow out of it."

Byron was looking at her, his heart full of pity for this poor woman who was either blinded by her mother's love for her precious child; or her husband and his doctor had duped her.

And Caroline was looking at Byron, thinking passionately ... *That beautiful face is my fate.*

"You are very kind," she said, "allowing yourself to be trapped in a chair by a sleeping child."

"I have an affinity with ... " *the damaged*, he nearly said, "with children."

"Do you? With children?

"Yes, just so long as they do their screaming very quietly."

Her face creased into a silent laugh, and from then on their conversation was very natural, although she did most of the talking in her soft voice.

"When I married William Lamb," she confided, "I went to him with great virtue and principles, which aught to have been cherished, and nobody but me can tell the almost childlike innocence and inexperience I had preserved until then. All at once this was thrown away and William himself seemed unconscious of what he had done. William taught me to disregard all the forms and restraints I had laid so much stress on. He called me prudish, said I was strait-laced, and amused himself with instructing me in things I need never have known."

Byron was not sure if he should be listening to all this, and Caroline was not sure why she was telling it to him.

"Do you not get on with your husband?" he asked.

"Oh, yes, William and I get on very well, " Caroline said with a slight smirk. "We understand each other perfectly. Just the other night I was trying to teach one of the maids the Ten Commandments, and I kept getting them mixed up. So I went to William and asked him, 'What is the *eighth* Commandment?' and without looking up from his newspaper he answered – 'Thou shalt not bother '."

A small knock came on the door and a maid stepped inside.

"M'lady, the two gentlemen in the drawing-room are requesting to leave. They wish to know if Lord Byron is ready to leave with them."

Byron glanced up at the nursery clock, surprised to see that he had been sitting here for almost an hour. "Yes, tell the gentlemen I shall be joining them shortly."

He stood up carefully and laid the sleeping boy down in the large armchair, speaking very quietly as he bade Lady Caroline goodbye.

He was halfway down the stairs with Rogers and Moore when she ran after him. "When will I see you again, Lord Byron?"

Byron was at a loss how to answer, so Thomas Moore answered for him. "We are all invited to Lady Jersey's Ball on Friday evening. Will you be there, Lady Caroline?"

Caroline smiled at Thomas Moore as if she would love to kiss him in gratitude. "Of course I'll be there."

~ ~ ~

Lady Jersey's Ball on Friday evening was a fancy-dress affair.

Lord Byron arrived in a smiling and swashbuckling mood, accompanied by two friends, whom Caroline was later to discover were Scrope Davies and John Hobhouse, and these three were immediately followed by Samuel Rogers and Thomas Moore – all five dressed as French Musketeers.

In an instant Caroline was at Byron's side, taking his arm and pulling him away from his friends. "Come, I have something to show you."

He scooped up a glass of champagne from one of the footmen's silver trays and then allowed her to pull him on and away from the crowd. "You are very cheerful," she said. "Have you started already?"

Byron grinned. "I have indeed. Scrope Davies always like to share a magnum of champagne before we set off anywhere."

She led him up to the minstrel's gallery overlooking the ballroom.

"So?" he asked. "What are you so eager to show me?"

"My costume," she said, giving a twirl. "Can you guess who I'm supposed to be?"

He took a step back and looked her over from head to toe. She was wearing a wig of long blonde tresses down to her waist, a blue pearl-studded headband around her forehead; a white clinging Greek-style dress with trumpet-style sleeves to her wrists, the skirt shorter at the front, showing her feet in white sandals with white laces criss-crossed up her ankles.

"Calypso," he said.

Her eyes widened. "How did you know so quickly? I

thought I would have to tell you!"

"I knew because I also have seen the famous painting of Calypso, many times."

"Oh, bother! But do you *like* it?"

He smiled slightly. "You are not *round* enough to be a Greek nymph."

"No? Why? Are all Greek nymphs fat?"

"No, but they have a roundness ..." his hands moved in a cupped waving way to demonstrate a fuller bosom, which shocked her.

"You *have* been drinking too much champagne, Lord Byron! Perhaps I should try and catch up with you!" She beckoned to a footman holding a tray of full glasses at the end of the gallery. "Leave the full tray here," she said, scooping up a glass and downing it in one."

Byron leaned his forearms on the wooden rail and looked down at the ballroom. "I should go down now and pay my respects to our hostess, before all the dancing starts."

"This is what I always do at these balls and parties," Caroline said lightly. "I always head straight up to the picture or minstrel's gallery so I can get a good view of everyone as they come in. It's great fun to watch. And *you* always look so uncomfortable down there amongst the milling throng, so I thought I would show you a way of escaping it."

"I only ever *feel* uncomfortable when the ladies try and get me to dance with them."

Caroline smiled as she looked down. "There's Lord and Lady Holland, an odd couple, don't you think? But glamorous, yes, very glamorous."

He looked at her. "In what way are they odd?"

"Well, in so many ways. He has been fighting for years against slavery, absolutely detests the whole abomination of it, while at the same time she owns a slave plantation in the West Indies. And she can be a frightful woman."

"Can she?" Byron frowned. "I found her very agreeable."

"Ah yes, I *heard* about you and she, all evening together on her sofa; but she has a reputation, you know, a very risqué reputation. Well, she has two reputations actually, but I will tell you about the first one first. Do you enjoy gossip?"

Byron grinned. "If it gives me information and helps me to know people better, then I *loves* gossip I do."

"Oh, you *are* almost drunk, and I'm still sober." She lifted two more glasses of champagne and handed one to him. "Drink up, your lordship, and may I say how absolutely dazzling you look as a French Musketeer. Is that pure velvet?"

Byron glanced down at the wine-coloured sleeve of his tunic. "Oh pray don't engage me in a conversation about *fabric,* I get enough of that from Tom Moore and Beau Brummell. Tell me about the Hollands."

"Well, he is a few years younger than her, and *she* was already married to Sir Godfrey Webster when she met Lord Holland, which led to them having a very passionate affair, until her husband divorced her on the grounds of adultery, naming Lord Holland as co-respondent. Society was absolutely shocked when she brazenly married Lord Holland only *two days* after her divorce. So now there are ladies, especially from the Tory establishment, who would not condescend to step inside Holland House or even walk past it. She is seen as a man-eater, so you can imagine what people are saying about *you* and her now, after your long *tête-à-tête* together on her sofa."

Byron shrugged carelessly. "I don't care what others say, I like her."

"Ah, but you have not been exposed to the worst of her, which is her other reputation – for being terrifying in her *rudeness,* which I believe is not really her fault but due to her being the daughter of an American."

Byron helped himself to another full glass, "I did not find her rude at all, and I like Americans. I like all revolutionaries. I wish we had a few more revolutionaries in Britain."

Caroline put up her hand. "No *politics*, not tonight, please."

Byron's eyes were on a fairly ordinary-looking girl, in a very plain dress, who was sitting at the side of the ballroom beside another woman. "That young lady down there," he said, pointing. "Is she a governess, or a lady's companion of some sort?"

Caroline looked ... "No! She is my cousin-in-law, Annabella Milbanke, and she is an heiress to a fortune."

"An heiress?" Byron couldn't believe it. "So why is she dressed like Cinderella *before* the Ball?"

Caroline couldn't help laughing at the question. "Because she claims to be very religious and prides herself on being a young lady of *Virtue* and not fashion."

Byron made a mock-fearful face, but within minutes Caroline had him laughing again as she told him about some of the rude antics of Lady Holland.

"I'm not laughing at Lady Holland," he said, "but the reactions of the *men.*"

Caroline nodded. "Gentlemen, all of them, and to find themselves invited to dinner and treated in such a way! And then there was Sidney Smith – when Lady Holland ordered *him* to ring the bell for a servant, he asked her if she would like him to sweep the floor as well. And Count d'Orsay got so tired of picking up her fan, that at his fifth descent he suggested it might be better if he just stayed under the table."

Byron found it all very funny.

"But," said Caroline, "when it was *his* turn, William Lamb did not find it at all funny. When Lady Holland ordered him to move his seat at dinner, and then ordered him again into another seat, he stood up and replied ..." she mimicked her husband's voice, 'I'll be *damned* if I will dine with you at all,' and walked out of the house."

Down in the ballroom, Annabella Milbanke kept glancing up at Lord Byron and Lady Caroline talking and laughing together.

"Do you not think it very rude," she said to Lady Melbourne, "that Caroline should have pounced on Lord Byron in that manner and whisked him away?"

Lady Melbourne sighed wearily as she waved her fan. "I am exhausted in my efforts to try and understand Caroline. She is not even a law unto herself anymore, but completely *lawless* to everything but her own amusement."

Out in the garden, as they lounged on chairs drinking champagne, John Hobhouse was saying much the same thing about Byron to Scrope Davies.

"What you do not understand, Scrope, is that 'Childe Harold's Pilgrimage' is full of in-jokes about me, which the reader could not know nor understand, but I know – and I also *know* that Byron put them in solely for his own amusement and to rib me."

Scrope was grinning. If Byron put some in-jokes into Childe Harold, then he wanted to be *in* on them. "Such as, Hobby? Are you sure you're not imagining it?"

"Of course I'm not imagining it. Why do you think I

hate parts of that poem?"

"I know you dismissed it as soon as you read it. Byron told me you did not approve of it."

"Because of all the secret *in*-jokes."

"Then tell me, Hobby, don't string it out."

Hobby lowered his voice and leaned closer across the garden table.

"When we were in Spain, in Cadiz, Byron had a three-day romance with a Spanish girl, leaving me on my own with nothing much to do. So I thought, if that's what he's doing, then I'll do the same, so I went to a whore ... and got the clap."

Scrope stared at him. "You mean ... a local whore, a *common* whore, and not a courtesan?"

"Oh, good grief, Scrope! I was in a foreign country and I did not speak the language. How was I to know better, and she looked clean enough. But I was sore for about two months afterwards, and Byron *pretended* to sympathise with me. Well ... in fact he *did* sympathise with me, taking me to a Spanish doctor for the remedy, and even administering some Sal Volatile for my headaches when I felt so ill ... but there was *one* time when he had the Sal Volatile in his hand that I was *sure* I saw an amused grin on his face."

"Perhaps whatever you were saying in your agony he thought was amusing. You know how he always sees the ridiculous in everything. And now you've learned your lesson, Hobby, not to go near any common whores. If you must, stick to the high class courtesans."

"But then, in Childe Harold's Pilgrimage," Hobby went on, "and all for his own secret amusement."

"*What* for his own secret amusement, what?"

"All that raving about Spain. *'Oh, lovely Spain, renowned, romantic land.'* And then going on about

'*Spain's maids ... formed for all the witching arts of love."*

Scrope was confused. "I see no in-joke there. If anyone, he was probably speaking about the Spanish girl he had been with."

"No, Scrope, no." Hobby was quite certain. "No one but Byron knew how much I hated Cadiz after that. Yet what did he write — "*Fair is proud Seville ... but CADIZ calls forth a sweeter praise. Ah, Vice! how soft are thy voluptuous ways!"*

Scrope tried not to laugh as Hobby nodded with even more certainty.

"It was treachery on his part, Scrope, nothing less than treachery. And then he goes on even more ... '*Fair Cadiz, rising o'er the sea ... Adieu, fair Cadiz! yea, a long adieu!"*

"You hate it so much, yet you remember *every word*!" Scrope Davies was laughing outright now; because he knew Byron well enough to be certain that the in-joke was all in Hobby's imagination.

Lady Jersey came out to the torch-lit garden, smiling with pleasure.

"Well, this is a nice sight for a hostess. Everywhere I look tonight I see people happy and laughing."

~ ~ ~

In the ballroom Lord Byron and Caroline Lamb were now absolutely intoxicated with champagne and had descended to the ballroom, and because Byron could not join her in a dance Caroline stayed with him at the side of the floor, her back to the dancers. Her hands were on Byron's arms as both swayed to the music, while above them the candles in the chandeliers flickered and dimmed.

"Oh! I'm so happy I could run away with you!" Caroline gushed joyously, unconsciously leaning into him. "You have made me feel so *young* again!"

"It's nothing to do with me and all due to night fever," Byron said, "and the music, and the champagne, and all these flickering lights."

Caroline looked at him with curious, glazed eyes. "What *is* night fever? Never heard of it."

He smiled wickedly. "Ah, well ... *night fever* is something I learned all about in Spain and Greece, but it's not suitable for the cold English temperament and climate. By the way, how *young* are you feeling?"

"About ten years younger than twenty-seven! How young are you?"

"Twenty-four."

"Caroline ... *Caroline* ..." Lady Melbourne appeared at Caroline's side, outraged. "Everyone is staring at you. We are l*eaving* now!"

She dragged a protesting Caroline away only seconds before Hobby and Scrope Davies joined Byron who was still smiling, and now that Caroline was gone, he put his hands on Hobby's shoulders and swayed with him instead.

"Stop that swaying, Byron," Hobby snapped. "I'm not your dancing bear. And *you* are making an ass of yourself."

"Don't care. You know me, Hobby, I always sway to music, ever since I learned I would never be able to dance to it."

Scrope said quickly, "You get one side of him, Hobby, and I'll take the other, and let's get him outside before everyone sees just how *mindlessly* intoxicated he actually is."

Outside, while waiting for a carriage, Byron was still

smiling and looking wickedly at Hobby. "This hot sultry night ... what does it remind you of, Hobby? Do you remember Spain ... or even better ... do *you* remember CADIZ?"

"Oh good grief – stop that laughing you two!" Hobby snapped, "You see now, Scrope, I *told* you he put those lines into Childe Harold deliberately just to rib *me!*"

Chapter Seventeen

~ ~ ~

Since his maiden speech in February, Lord Byron had returned to the House of Lords seven times, listening very carefully to the debates, although all the mumbling and long pauses to look at notes, had, on two occasions, sent him drifting off to sleep.

And now he was back in the House of Lords, facing his peers, ready to deliver his second speech to the House.

The Whigs in Opposition had lost their *last* major fight against the Government by only one vote, although few of the machine-breakers had been hanged as a result. Most magistrates were opting for the lesser sentence of transportation to the Antipodes, despite Lord Byron's statement that transportation was as bad as the death penalty for a man with a family.

Lord Holland was now determined that they would not lose *this* fight, for the emancipation of the Catholics in Ireland. A subject that Lord Byron was personally very passionate about, so who better to make the opening speech?

The Government benches were packed, all eyes on the young Lord who was only twenty-four, although since they had last seen him here in the Upper Chamber, he had become famous throughout the country as a *poet*.

"He had better not get *poetical* with us," Lord Liverpool said to his neighbour, Lord Castlereagh. "If he does, hiss him down."

Byron stood for a long moment, his eyes ranging over

every one the twenty-six bishops who had been brought here to vote against the Catholic Bill, and then he looked directly at Lord Liverpool, the greatest opponent to Catholic Relief.

"My lords ... much has been said, within and without the doors of Church and State; and although those words have too often been prostituted for party purposes, yet all, I presume, are the advocates of the Church of Christ and the State of Great Britain. But surely *not* for a State of exclusion and despotism, and *not* for an intolerant Church.

"Yet still our churchmen, not only refuse to the Catholics their spiritual grace, but all temporal blessings whatsoever. It was a statement by the great Lord Peterborough, that he was for a parliamentary King, a parliamentary Constitution, but *not* for a parliamentary God. The interval of a century has not weakened the force of that remark."

The bishops on the government benches were already whispering to each other.

"The opponents of the Catholics," Byron said, "may be divided into two classes. Those who assert that the Catholics have too much already, and those who allege that the lower orders, at least, have nothing more to require.

"The last paradox is sufficiently refuted, in that it might as equally be said that our black servants do *not* desire to be emancipated either. And that the Catholics are contented, or at least they *ought* to be, we are told. So I shall, now proceed to touch upon a few of those circumstances which so marvellously contribute to their exceeding contentment."

In his seat, Lord Holland bowed his head and smiled at Byron's exquisite sarcasm.

"Have the Irish Catholics the full benefit of trial by jury?" Lord Byron asked his peers. "No, they have not, nor can they ever have such a benefit until they are permitted the privilege of serving as sheriffs and under-sheriffs. Of this a striking example occurred at the last Enniskillen assizes. A yeoman was arraigned for the murder of a Catholic named Macvournagh. In court, three respectable and uncontradicted witnesses stated that they saw the accused load his gun, take aim and fire and kill the said Macvournagh. This was properly commented on by the judge; but to the astonishment of the bar, and the indignation of the court, the Protestant jury *acquitted* the accused.

"So glaring was their prejudice, that Mr Justice Osborne felt it his duty to bind over the acquitted, although not *absolved* assassin, into custody, thus for a time taking away his licence to kill Catholics."

"Well, he's done his homework," Lord Holland murmured to his neighbour, although now he could see the twenty-six bishops on the government benches beginning to stir like a pack of awakening feral wolves, getting ready to snap.

"Every schoolboy, any footboy – such as those who have held and hold a commission in our service – any footboy who can exchange his shoulder-knot for a soldier's uniform may perform all this and more against the Catholics, by virtue of that very authority delegated to him by his *Sovereign*. Such is law, such is justice, for the happy, free, contented Catholic."

Standing in the gallery, John Hobhouse was feeling very pleased. It was *he* who had spent long hours in discussion with Byron about the situation in Ireland. It was *he* who had brought the case of the murder of Macvournagh in the Enniskillen assizes to Byron's attention, even to giving Byron a copy of the court record of the trial, but all else, every other word Byron now uttered, was his own.

Hobhouse's mind wandered back to his time in Ireland and his six-month stint in the militia, writing to Byron about his fellow officers ... *'All Protestants, all most gentlemanly, but all very violent against the Catholics.'*

And Byron had written back in a worried tone: "*Do leave Ireland, Hobby, I fear your Catholics will find work for you, but surely YOU won't fight against them, will you?*"

Hobby had not, he had left Ireland, and now his eyes and attention returned to the floor of the chamber and Byron:

"It was said by someone in a former debate – if the

Catholics are emancipated, why not the Jews? If this sentiment was dictated by compassion for the Jews, it might deserve attention, but as a sneer against the Catholics what is it but the language of Shylock in *Merchant of Venice*, transferred from his daughter's marriage to that now of Catholic emancipation, because the sentiment is the same —

> 'Would that any of the tribe of Barabbas
> should have her, rather than a Christian.'"

"He's getting poetical, quoting Shakespeare now and bringing in the damned Jews!!" Lord Liverpool whispered to Lord Castlereagh. "Hiss him down!"

When the low wave of hisses began in the Government benches, Lord Byron laughed, and pointed to the line of Bishops, giving them another quote – from Horace,

"Caput *insanable* tribus anticyris!"

The Whig party loved it. Especially when Byron now pointed to the politicians —

"*There* are your true *Protest*-ants. *They* are the ones who *protest* against Catholic Petitions, Protestant Petitions, *and all* Petitions. They are against *all* redress, all reason, humanity, justice and even common sense! *There* are the persons who reverse the fable of the mountain that brought forth a mouse – yet *they* are the mice that believe themselves at war with the mountain."

Amidst the uproar and laughter from the Whig benches,

the Whig leader, Lord Holland, turned to his neighbour and remarked quietly, "You see, that is the quandary with Lord Byron ... one never knows what he is going to say next. And as he refuses to be censored to the party line, it's like having a *revolutionary* in our midst." He chuckled. "And Lord Liverpool looks like the top of his head is about to blow off."

When silence had been restored, Lord Byron continued calmly:

"To return to the Catholics. Have we nothing to be gained by their emancipation? What *talents* have been lost by this selfish system of exclusion?

"At this moment, the only triumphs obtained through long years of our Napoleonic war, have been achieved by an *Irish* general. It is true he is not a Catholic, and had he been so, we should have been deprived of his talents. Yet I presume no one will assert that his *religion* would have impaired his talents – though if he *had* been an Irish *Catholic,* then he would never have been allowed to command an army. And in consequence, it is Great Britain that would have lost a powerful military commander, General Arthur Wellesley, now known as the Duke of Wellington."

The Government benches were stunned into silence, for it was impossible to deny that the man known as "England's Greatest Soldier" was in fact *Irish.*

"And at this moment he is fighting battles for the *Catholics* abroad," Byron continued. "And your lordships will doubtless provide even more new honours for the Saviour of Portugal. It is strange to note that if Catholic Spain, faithful Portugal, or the no less Catholic King of Sicily stand in need of succour – *away* goes a British fleet and an army, an ambassador, and a subsidy to pay very dearly for our Popish allies – but let four million of our *fellow-subjects* in *Ireland* pray for relief, and they must be treated as aliens."

A number of the Whigs vigorously clapped their applause, but Lord Byron's focus was fixed firmly on Lord Liverpool.

"Allow me to ask? Are you not at this moment fighting for the emancipation of Ferdinand, the Bourbon King of Naples, who is certainly a fool? And have you more regard for a foreign Sovereign than your own fellow-subjects, who are not fools, for they know your interests better than you know your own. And they also know that the fetters of the mind are more galling than those of the body."

Lord Liverpool was glaring at him, at the sheer *audacity* of him.

"Upon the consequences of your *not* acceding to the claims of the Irish Catholic Petitioners, I shall not expand upon those consequences, for you know them, and will feel them, and your children's children will know them and feel them when you have passed away.

And it will be *Adieu* to that so-called Union with Ireland – a Union that insists on its people *never* uniting – a Union that gave a death-blow to the independence of Ireland, and may in time be the cause of her hatred and eternal separation from this country."

Standing in the gallery, Hobhouse and Thomas Moore then heard what they recognised as the true *Byronic* power of language.

"If the union of Great Britain and Ireland *must* be called a Union, then it is the union of the shark and its prey. The shark swallows up its victim and thus they become one and indivisible. Thus has Great Britain swallowed up the Parliament and Constitution and independence of Ireland, and refuses to disgorge even a single privilege, even though it might provide relief for Britain's swollen and distempered body politic, which is so dissatisfactory to the British people, so destructive to the British name, and even more destructive to the best interests of the British nation."

Byron bowed and sat down.

Lord Liverpool sat in his seat, his eyes staring straight ahead in thought, for now he had discovered something new and important about Lord Byron. He may be a poet, and he may be only twenty-four, but his mind and his language marked him as a new and powerful *political* force, and even worse – he stood firmly with the Opposition against the Government.

He would have to be stopped, of course, no question.

A way would have to be found to discredit or disgrace him. There was always a way. And who better to aid in that task but the Press. All newspapers were under Government control, all editors did as they were instructed, and the more famous Byron became as a poet with the public, the greater the interest in his private life. A few rumours of salacious scandals were always a good start in the business of ruin.

Still, there was no rush. To do anything now would be too obvious, especially to the Whigs. One must always bide time in these things, until the iron became hot enough to burn and scorch.

~ ~ ~

On leaving the chamber, Lord Sligo, one of Byron's close friends from Harrow, sidled up to him with his usual lop-sided grin.

"So, Byron, the vote is tomorrow night, and I see you and I have been paired again."

"Which will ensure that your Tory vote cancels out my Whig vote."

Sligo nodded. "Dreadful, isn't it?"

Byron smiled, due to the fact that he liked Lord Sligo enormously. Not only were they old schoolfellows, but when Sligo had arrived in Athens the previous summer, the two of them had enjoyed a month of fun in high foolery with some of the young ladies.

"Of course," Sligo suggested, "it need not be,"

"No, not if you were to vote with the opposition and help to give the poor downtrodden Irish Catholics their long-overdue emancipation."

"Vote with your lot?" Sligo stared. "Vote with the opposition? *Ooons!* — if I did that, Lord Liverpool would have me whipped! No, I have a much safer idea."

"Which is?"

Sligo put and hand to the side of his face, gently manipulating his jaw. "Tomorrow night, my friend, I fear I might find myself in the grip of the most damnable toothache that will prevent me from attending to register my vote."

And true to his word, the following night Lord Sligo did not show to cast his vote, due to a severe abscess in his mouth.

The vote came out equal on both sides – a stalemate. A second motion would have to be called at a later date. And Byron knew that if Lord Liverpool and Lord Castlereagh had their way, that "later date" might not be for *years*.

Chapter Eighteen

~~~

If – by some magical power – Byron been able to foresee the future and the outcome of it all, he would never have allowed himself to get involved in any kind of relationship with Lady Caroline Lamb; not even the merest form of trivial friendship, nor the coolest of acquaintances.

Samuel Rogers was sitting in his drawing-room with Moore and Campbell and feeling very guilty about it all.

"I wish I had never taken him there – to Melbourne House. From the first moment she set eyes on Byron, she has absolutely *besieged* him!"

Thomas Moore nodded. "I have seen her do it."

"And now, whenever they have a quarrel," Rogers continued, "more often than not I have come home at night to find her walking in my garden waiting for me, solely to beg that *I* would reconcile them."

Moore was shaking his head in bafflement. "Byron showed me the first letter he received from her, in which she told him that if he was ever in want of money, all her jewels were at his service." He looked at his two friends. "Now, is that not a *strange* thing to write?"

"Very strange," Campbell agreed. "Why would Byron need money or her jewels? Perhaps she thinks his devotion can be bought?"

"And whenever she meets Byron at a party," Rogers continued, "she always makes sure to return home from the party in *his* carriage and accompanied solely by him."

"I can testify to that," said Tom Moore. "Many a time

she has pushed me out of the way to do it. And that's usually *after* I have been pushed aside by other females rushing out to get a last look at him – the romantic author of *Maid of Athens*."

"And such is the insanity of her passion for Byron," Rogers continued, "that when she is not invited to a party where she knows he is going to be, she has often stood outside all night and waited for him in the street until the party was over."

Rogers sipped his drink. "I remember one night, after a party at Devonshire House to which she had not been invited – at around two in the morning when a lot of us were leaving, I saw her, yes, *saw* her, talking to Byron with half of her body thrust into the carriage which he had just entered."

"And it's not just the women," Campbell put in. "I'm embarrassed to say that some of our young dandies are acting no better. One morning last week Lord Byron and I were in Baillie's Coffee House, and before we had even finished our coffee he was surrounded by them, all offering him their cards and seeking to make his friendship. It discomfited him tremendously and we were forced to make our get-away through the back door, aided by the proprietor."

Rogers sniffed. "Well, what else can one expect from dandies? Nothing more than over-rich Bond Street layabouts with nothing to do all day but amuse themselves wasting time. It's the shameless behaviour of Lady Caroline Lamb that I find so absolutely shocking. She may wear the title of a *lady*, but she is certainly not behaving like one. In fact, I am quite convinced she has lost command of her senses."

And she was not the only one, thought Thomas Moore, for he had been in Byron's company too often of late and had seen the madness and unparalleled *mania* of it all. The dignity of his bearing, the romance of his aristocratic title, the public interest in his travels wandering in strange and brutal lands, and much of it alone, which showed not only great bravery, but also combined to lend an irresistible charm to his appearance and excited an obsessive curiosity in his personality. Young and handsome and possibly *wicked*, he had literally set the women crazy.

After a silence, Thomas Moore heaved a deep sigh. "All this gives me great pain," he said quietly. "I'm beginning to fear that Byron's fame will be dearly bought."

~~~

The following morning a pre-arranged meeting was held at Melbourne House to discuss the problem of Caroline. Her grandmother, Countess Spencer, and her mother, Lady Bessborough, attended the meeting; both expressing their deepening anxiety to Lady Melbourne.

"Now, about Lord Byron," said Countess Spencer. "I don't know what to think or how to judge him. And it really is pointless trying to discuss him with Caroline, because she has accustomed herself to representing things her *own* way. So much so, that now I can never depend on what she says as being anywhere near the truth."

"Oh yes, she is quite a skilful liar," Lady Melbourne replied in a cool way, "especially in all matters relating to Lord Byron."

"Is it true," asked Caroline's mother, "that he allowed her to travel with him, unchaperoned, to Holland House last week? Just the two of them, on their own in the carriage?"

"No, no," Countess Spencer insisted. "Caroline would never defy convention in such an outrageous way!"

She looked at Lady Melbourne. "What does William say about all this? He is her lawful *husband* after all."

Lady Melbourne sighed, shaking her head. "William is the same now as he was as a boy. He always finds some excuse for *not* doing what he prefers to avoid. He has chosen to simply ignore all Caroline's antics, because he is quite certain that her passion for Lord Byron will soon burn itself out."

"And Lord Byron himself, pray? What say you of him?"

"I can only speak of what I have observed at the various social gatherings," Lady Melbourne replied. "And it seems to me that all the passion, if you can call it that, is very one-sided, as he appears to me to spend most of his time determined to elude her."

"Yet she is still writing to him," said Caroline's mother anxiously. "It is dreadful, but I hope he is determined enough to make all her letters useless."

Chapter Nineteen

~ ~ ~

Byron had spent the afternoon sparring with "Gentleman John Jackson", the renowned boxer, more commonly known as "*The Bruiser.*"

From as far back as his Harrow days, during every school holiday, Byron had religiously gone down to London to take boxing lessons from Jackson, as well as fencing lessons from Henry Angelo, because these were the only two physical sports his right foot would allow, if he wanted to remain strong and healthy when the weather was too cold for swimming.

The fact that these two gentlemen were a part of the *demi-monde* did not snag Byron in any way. He enjoyed visiting the outer edges of London's underworld and listening to how the people there talked when voicing their opinions; it was a refreshing change.

Although, in his college days, when he had invited both men up to Cambridge to continue his tuition in fighting skills, the Mayor of Cambridge had been outraged to learn that "*two pugilists*" had been brought up from the metropolis to use one of the main rooms of the Town Hall as a boxing ring, and withdrew his permission.

Byron had been equally outraged.

"*We will humble this impertinent Bourgeois yet,*" he had later written to Henry Angelo, who could read letters a lot better than John Jackson.

Now Jackson and Angelo were his long-time chums, and visiting one to box, and the other to fence, was one of his favourite pastimes.

Fletcher had his bath filled when he returned to St James Street.

"I had your bath ready for the *exact* time that you said you would be back," Fletcher grumbled, "but that was two hours ago, and now it's all gone cold."

Byron shrugged. "Then I'll get into it cold. It was a hard spar with Jackson this afternoon and I was still sweating through an even harder dinner with Tom Cribb afterwards So *out*, Fletcher, out of the room and throw in the soap."

"Oh, and, my lord ... I've put all today's letters from *you-know-who* on your desk."

Byron frowned. "So how do *you* know the letters are from *I-know-who*, Fletcher? I presume they are still sealed?"

"I only know because her messenger delivered them, every hour or so, destroying my peace, and with me having to sign a note in return to prove they had been handed in here safely."

Byron stood silent; Caroline Lamb now wrote to him perhaps ten times a day, and he was at a loss to know what to do about it.

Later, refreshed and clean, he looked at the bunch of letters on his desk, and decided to ignore them ... for now, at least.

Instead he sat down and opened his new journal, because Francis Hodgson had advised him, after he had told Hodgson about his difficulty in sleeping – often dreaming about his mother as if she was still alive, bossing and bawling and possessively chasing him everywhere—that the solution to all this dreaming was to end the day by emptying all his thoughts into a journal.

"*Even the slightest thing, no matter how mundane,*

write it down, and that will clear your active mind and help you to sleep," Hodgson had advised, and Hodgson was usually right about such things.

He lifted his pen and began to write:

Just returned from dinner with Jackson (the Emperor of Pugilism) and another of the select, Tom Cribb, the reigning champion for the past two years, but not this year. I drank more than I like, but I have no headache. Cribb, very facetious. He don't like his situation, wants to fight again, and pray he may ...

It was no good, no distraction ... he had to open her letters and send some reply, otherwise there would be hell to pay ... and yet still he hesitated, so weary was he of Caroline's constant attention, and her obsessive need of his attention.

He had been delighted with her at first; she was bold and independent, so rare in a woman, and she was small, slim, and perfectly formed; and that *voice* of hers, which had once so completely captivated him ...

He sighed irritably – now her voice grated on his nerves, not because it had lost any of its lushness, but because of the affected and ridiculous way so many of the ladies of the London aristocracy spoke – saying *"yallah"* instead of yellow, and a china teapot was a *"chaney"* teapot, and *"cow-cumb-ah"* instead of cucumber. Now, it was not for him to criticise – they could speak however they wished and he respected it – but to have one of them constantly whispering endearments *into his ear* in that plum-duff accent ...

He opened the first letter and read:

"My dearest Byron – You have been very generous

and kind IF you have not betrayed me – and I do not think you_have.

My remaining in town and seeing you is sacrificing the last chance I have. I expose myself to every eye, to every observation. You think me weak and selfish, you think I do not struggle to withstand my own feelings; but indeed it is exacting more than human nature can bear, and when I went out last night, which was of itself an effort, and when I heard your name announced, the moment after I heard nothing more, but seemed in a dream. I felt so ill I could not have struggled longer. Lady Cahir said, 'You are ill; shall we go away?' which I was very glad to accept. But we could not get through, and so I fear it caused you pain to see me intrude again.

I never see you without wishing to cry. If any painter could paint me that face as it is, I would give anything I possess on earth — no one has yet given the countenance and complexion as it is. I only could if I knew how to draw and paint because one must feel it to give it the real expression.

Pray do not be angry with me, and —"

He put the letter down, unwilling to read any further, more angry with himself than at her, although she was beginning to infuriate him in so many ways, and he could think of no way to find a solution to it all ... He would like to have spoken to Hobhouse about it, to get his advice, but Hobby was so very *chaste* these days, and hated any reference to the opposite sex or anything carnal.

No ... even before Cadiz, Hobby had always suffered great difficulty with women, because he usually found it simply *impossible* to understand them. The light trip and airy nonsense of some of their conversations truly puzzled him.

"Why can't they just SAY what they want to say, instead of all that flitter-gibbeting around it?"

Also, despite being an avowed atheist, Hobby was a firm stickler for respectability and all the rules of *English* convention, so a relationship between a single man and a married woman would be shocking to him, very shocking indeed.

"So what to do, what to *do*?"

He picked up another letter from Caroline at random and opened it, hoping it would be more rational.

'Write, write, write, write, write! I will add nothing more until you WRITE back to me!'

He sighed, picked up his pen and began to write in his journal, seeking an escape from the madness of it all by a fixed concentration on the mundane things of the day just lived.

So I sparred with Jackson and then dined with him and Tom Cribb. Tom has been in action at sea and is now only three and thirty. A great man! has a wife and a mistress and he conversations well — apart from some sad omissions and misapplications of the words.

Tom is an old friend of mine; I have seen some of

his best battles in my nonage. He is now a publican, and, I fear, a sinner; — for Mrs Cribb is on alimony, and when he first introduced me to the woman he is now living with, and having his own opinion of my morals, he passed her off as his legal spouse.

Talking of her later, he said to me, "she is the truest of women" — from which I immediately inferred she could NOT be his wife, and so it turned out.

These eulogies don't belong to matrimony — for, if true, a man don't think it necessary to say so; and if not true, the less he says the better. Cribb is the only man except Webster that I ever heard harangue upon his wife's virtues; and I listened to both with great credence and patience, and stuffed my handkerchief into my mouth when I found yawning irresistible — By the by, I am yawning now.

~~~

Thomas Moore was as punctual as he always was when meeting Byron for dinner in a small restaurant off the Strand the following evening. It was an exclusive little place, away from the main thoroughfares, and it had the kind of privacy that Byron not only liked, but needed.

Byron greeted him as friendly as ever. He truly liked Thomas Moore, because as well as being a good conversationalist, Moore was also a very good listener. Almost ten years older than him, a happily married man, and now the father of a daughter, Moore had lived through some rough times and he knew how to be discreet and keep a friend's secrets.

Byron frowned as he watched Tommy beginning to tuck into his slab of fried steak.

Tommy looked up and saw the expression on Byron's face. "Is something wrong?"

"Moore, do you not find eating *meat* makes you ferocious?"

Tommy laughed. "Just because it comes from an animal don't mean it turns you into an animal."

Byron was not convinced, and changed the subject; although he waited until the coffee and brandy had been brought before he brought up the subject of Lady Caroline Lamb.

Thomas Moore listened silently, not interrupting, as Byron knew he wouldn't, and when Byron stopped speaking and looked at him questioningly, Moore said, "So at the start, it was all platonic on both sides?"

"Yes ... at least on *my* side it was. Although I did like her, very much."

"And when did this platonic friendship turn into an obsession with her?"

"I don't believe it was ever truly platonic, not even on my side," Byron said, "but one of her main attractions for me was that she was so *literary,* so well-read, and always wanting to read more and more books. Up until then I thought that all a woman needed to keep her happily occupied was a mirror and a box of sweets."

Tom Moore laughed. "You're jesting"

Byron smiled. "Yes, jesting. Although that's what Hobby always used to say when we were first at

Cambridge. He had no experience of females then, none at all, but I knew different, because by then I had already met ... " Byron paused ... and then found himself telling Thomas Moore all about the love of his life, Mary Ann Chaworth ...

He spoke in great detail, as if he had seen her only yesterday, and as Thomas Moore listened, he realised that Caroline Lamb was not the only one who was plagued by an obsessive form of love.

After a thought-filled silence ... Byron said, "I love dogs, all dogs, they are my favourite animal, and I cannot resist petting any dog I meet. And I love women, all women, and I could make love to any one of them if she wished it ... but it's all no more than *affection* to me, the utmost I can feel now is affection, although these days so many, so carelessly, usually call that love."

Moore listened.

"But I have only ever truly *loved* one dog, and that was my Boatswain, and I have only ever truly *loved* one girl, and that was my Mary. To me, Mary was ... my Morning Star ... my Evening Star ... "

After a silence he went on with half-smile, "Why do I still always say *my* Mary? Yet she should have been mine. Our union would have healed feuds in which blood had been shed by our ancestors – it would have joined lands broad and rich, it would have joined at least one loving heart and two persons not ill-matched in years – she was only two years my elder, and – and – and – what has been the result?"

Moore saw a look of extreme sadness in his eyes, those very light blue eyes which wore always so expressive of his thoughts.

"I adored everything about her. And I often find myself thinking of her when I look at the faces of some of these society ladies and their very white faces."

He looked directly at Moore. "Have you noticed that, Tom? The way they dab white powder on their faces to make them look as pale as possible?"

Moore nodded. "Thankfully my Bessy does not wear any powder at all. Her beauty doesn't need the help of artwork."

"Nor my Mary. Her facial colouring is all natural. I remember remarking to Caroline Lamb how I found all that white face-powder so very unappealing and unfeminine, and she immediately stopped using it – but not without quipping that I obviously preferred the appearance of country milkmaids to refined society ladies."

A waiter arrived with a pot of fresh coffee, refilled their brandy glasses, and then vanished again.

"And yes," Byron said, "I do find a soft rosy hue in a girl's cheek far more appealing, especially if its natural. I can't stand those round red blobs of rouge."

Moore brought the subject back to Lady Caroline Lamb. "So when did your friendship with Lady Caroline change?"

"Caroline? ... Oh, when I gave her a flower, a white rose, and she took it as a declaration of my *love*, instead of my affection."

"In your rooms?"

"No, in the beginning, she would invite me to visit her at Melbourne House, in her private sitting-room, and we would discuss books, lend each other books, and then the books she wanted to read suddenly changed to titles such as *Les liasions dangereuses* and Jack Cazotte's *Le Diable amoreux* ... books that no gentleman would ever read in the presence of a lady, or allow to be seen on the shelf of his family library. And yet Caroline not only bought these books, but also begged me to *read* them to her, especially those parts which she claimed she did not understand. Now I can *read* French fluently, but my speaking of it is not so fluent, and she would laugh when I enunciated words wrongly, showing me that her understanding of written French was every bit as good as mine ... And then I saw it for what it was – a very *artful* form of seduction on her part ... and, well, under the influence of such literature ..."

"And now she is following you everywhere you go," said Moore.

"And now she has become just like my *mother!* Hounding me everywhere! Bombarding me with letters every day. And I can't allow the possibility of going through all that possessive insanity again. I did not expect it from Caroline Lamb, nor will I tolerate it from her."

Moore was puzzled. "What is her husband's reaction to it all? Her behaviour? Do you know?"

Byron shrugged. "Caroline says he was born with a streak of indifference down his spine."

Later, as they strolled back to St James's, Moore suggested a possible solution.

"Ignore her, and all her letters. Ignore everything, even the sight of her."

"I've been doing all that, but to no avail."

"Then write to her, in the strongest terms, even if you have to be cruel, and tell her that you no longer wish to have the suffocation of her relentless friendship."

Byron, as usual, was looking around up at the night sky. "I don't wish to be cruel to her, and I certainly don't want to continue as her friend, but in view of everything that has passed, and my own guilt in that, I could never be her enemy."

~ ~ ~

Lady Caroline Lamb now believed that everyone inside Melbourne House was her enemy. Lady Melbourne was outraged that her daughter-in-law's *indiscreet* behaviour was now becoming the only subject in the talk of the town.

"I heard someone say the other day," she remonstrated, "that whenever one goes to a party, one never has to pause and even *wonder* where Lord Byron may be located within the house, because all one has to do is to *look* to wherever Lady Caroline is staring, and follow the beam."

"Strange, then," Caroline retorted, "if I am such an object of derision, that so many have stopped wearing white face-powder since *I* stopped using it."

Lord Melbourne lowered his newspaper, was about to comment, and then changed his mind, knowing it did not do to interfere in women's gossip.

"It's a disgraceful way for a married woman to behave," said Lady Melbourne. "And especially one of your advancing years, Caroline. One should know better at twenty-seven."

Caroline gave her mother-in-law a demon look. "And how old were you when *you* —" she shot a half smile towards *Lord* Melbourne, and her mother-in-law recognised the threat.

"Leave the room, Caroline, please go back up to your own floor. We are entitled to some peace down here at the end of the day."

"Very well. Goodnight."

Caroline stood up and left the room like an obedient child, making a loud clip-clop sound of her shoes on the marble floor of the hall as she walked to the first step of the red-carpeted staircase, where she paused, took off her shoes, and crept back down the hall to stand with her back to the wall by the open door of Lady Melbourne's drawing-room and listened.

Lord Melbourne was speaking. "So what does William have to say about it?"

"William thinks her infatuation with Lord Byron is merely a temporary fancy and should be ignored," replied Lady Melbourne. "And he has no intention of ending his marriage over a fancy. Especially now that he is hoping to be re-elected into Parliament."

"Good show, good boy, at least he knows where his true duty lies – with his King and Country."

Caroline smirked as she listened, wondering if Lord Melbourne would want William to be so dutiful to the reigning Prince Regent, the future King, if he knew that for over five years his wife had regularly gotten into bed with His Highness and begotten their youngest son from him?

She was about to turn away when she suddenly heard Annabella Milbanke speak up – that quiet dormouse full of virtue who sat there doing her embroidery and listening to all conversations in her sly and superior manner, rarely speaking a word unless it was to criticise someone, and then in that awful flat *Durham* accent of hers.

"I must confess, I do not understand this mania that Caroline has for Lord Byron," she said in a condescending tone. "And so many other ladies of the Ton are scrambling for his attention and suffering from the same mania. It really is rather pathetic."

"*Mania?*" said Lady Melbourne. "Oh, Bell, I would not go so far as to call it a mania."

"I would," replied Annabella. "In fact, I have already given it a name —Byromania."

Lady Melbourne laughed. "Nonsense."

"Nor do I understand," Annabella continued, "what Lord Byron finds in Caroline to be so enamoured with. Someone said he admires her voice. Pray tell me why? Because all I hear when I listen to Caroline is her *ba-ba-ba-ing* like a sheep."

Lady Melbourne laughed again. "No, Bell, that is unfair. Whatever faults Caroline has, and I agree she has many, her voice is one of her main attributes, perhaps her *only* attribute."

Caroline was so hurt by their criticism she fled down the hall and out to the garden, tears slipping down her cheeks. Oh, those hateful, *hateful* Milbankes!

She could not believe that those two Northern Durham *bumpkins* should mock her – a true aristocrat, niece of the Duchess of Devonshire, and a granddaughter of Earl Spencer! Why, Lady Melbourne herself had once been plain Elizabeth Milbanke, and Annabella was the daughter of her brother, Sir Ralph Milbanke, he of *Dur-um* trade. They owned coal collieries up there in Durham which brought them in an income of forty-thousand pounds a year, although they paid their miners in weekly pennies.

No wonder her own family had been so shocked, and her dear mother had almost collapsed, when she told them she had been proposed to and had accepted William Lamb, daughter of Elizabeth *Milbanke* Lamb.

"But they are all so *coarse,* all those Milbanke-Lamb boys!" her mother had said. "And not one of them with decent table manners – all that *barking* in laughter at each other across the table when people are trying to eat. And that awful mother of theirs!"

Since then, the Ponsonbys and Spencers had created their own secret nickname for Lady Melbourne – *The Thorn*. And Annabella was just as bad.

Caroline sat down in a dark corner of the garden on the grass and began to cry silently. All she wanted now was to get away from them all and go to Byron, live with Byron, beg him to elope to somewhere on the Continent with her.

Her love for Byron could conquer anything, *thwart* anyone. There was no one else in the world like Byron. From the start he had fascinated her, but since he had made love to her and she had seen the beautiful symmetry of his naked body, it was as if she had become possessed by some obsessive erotic delirium.

She pulled at a blade of grass by her foot ... It was true, so true, when Nature picked up her pen to draw Byron; she had created a work of art. And the fact that Nature had dropped her pen and stabbed Byron in the right foot, well that was Nature's crime, not his.

She stood up and walked slowly back inside the house, just in time to see Annabella heading towards her room on the ground floor.

'No doubt to end the day reading her Bible as usual', Caroline thought bitterly. *'And after being so hurtful about another human being. Damned hypocrite!'*

Caroline had no intention of allowing an upstart like Annabella Milbanke to get away with mocking her; although she would not respond in a coarse *Dur-um* way. (Oh, the way that girl said "*Me Mam*" and "*Me Dad*" was truly frightful!)

No, she would do it in the more refined way of the *London* aristocracy; and hopefully teach Annabelle Milbanke not only some polite manners, but also force her to examine her own Christian soul.

Up in her boudoir, she sat down at her escritoire, and wrote a letter to Annabella Milbanke, ostensibly from Annabella's "*older and more experienced cousin-in-law*" who was merely seeking to give the younger girl some well-meant advice about life down here in London.

It is more the pity that you have come to London, for everything that enters this fair City is tainted more or less—your danger will not arise from Balls, roués Coxcombs and Gossips – but beware of what comes across to you in the shape of Genius.

Avoid friendships with women – you are a little inclined to have a certain Frankness of manner – never let them make you their confidante & when you hear them killing the character of another, answer them coldly – there is no wit in this species of conversation – & a word, a look, a mockery, or a very trifling addition to the truth, may make a world of difference & blast a good name for ever – & never give in to speaking what is false about another, for no good will come of it. Leave your white lies & innuendos & black deceits to others. Parrots can talk well – therefore as I said before in your friendships look ever – not to sentiments but to Conduct.

~ ~ ~

Inside her bedroom, Annabella Milbanke was not reading her Bible; she was sitting at her dressing table in her plain white nightgown, brushing her long brown hair, engrossed in her thoughts – so engrossed that she did not notice a letter being slipped under her door.

Annabella was thinking of Lord Byron, as she so often did of late. She saw him not as others did, as some idol to be adored, but as a fallen angel who had sinned much and needed to be saved.

Her certainty that he was a sinner would allow no doubts in her mind, for he had admitted it himself by bragging about his sins in Childe Harold' ... *Ah, Vice! how soft are thy voluptuous ways!"*

She pitied him, and yet there was a part of her that was fascinated by him, simply because she was certain he was an angel, albeit a fallen one. He had been graced with too many blessings in his looks and his amazing talents, both poetical and political, and there was a 'softness' in his voice that was quite heavenly in its kindness.

But then there was his limp, his damaged foot, the mark of Lucifer who had been thrown out of Heaven, and he the most beautiful angel of all, the one God had loved best. Yet he had transgressed and thought he was above all need of virtue ... *Ah, Vice! how soft are thy voluptuous ways!"*

She had said her prayers, requesting forgiveness for Byron, and beseeching that she should be the one chosen to save him and bring him back to God. What a victory that would be, and for one so young as her, as yet only nineteen ... she frowned ... but soon to be twenty, and once in the twenties the years quickly progressed toward middle age ...

Yet she knew she would achieve nothing if she behaved as other females did, harmless things, who fluttered around him like colourful butterflies.

She was not so foolish. Whenever she was in the same room as Lord Byron she always put on a manner of reserved silence and disinterest just to intrigue him. The fact that he had not yet observed her indifference to him, nor showed any signs of being intrigued by her, did not deter her from her goal.

She was a very clever mathematician, more enamoured by the magic of numbers and their equations than any poetry or prose. *Parallelograms* and their geometrical opposite sides were her poetry. So a steady calculation of events as they happened, and a careful and measured response to all things, would achieve her goal at the right time and in the right place.

She brushed her hair some more, still thoughtful. Although numbers and equations were not her only perfection, she could be a dab hand at poetry too, in those times when she had nothing better to do.

She moved over to her small desk, picked up her pen and wrote in her journal —

Woman! How truly called 'A harmless thing!'
So meekly smarting with the venom'd sting.
Forgiving saints! — ye bow before the rod.
And kiss the ground on which your censor trod.
Reforming Byron with his magic sway
Compels all hearts to love him and obey.

Still in a scathing mood about all these silly women and Byron's peculiar impact upon them, turning them all into juvenile idiots, she dipped her pen in the ink and wrote a letter to her mother with "*all* the gossip" about life in London, yet managed to cover only one subject —

'Lady C has seized on him, notwithstanding the reluctance he manifests to be shackled by her, and

when he is present Caroline ba-ba-ba's to him till she makes me sick.

All the women are absurdly courting him and trying to deserve the lash of his wit. I thought <u>inoffensiveness</u> was the most secure conduct, as I am not desirous of a place in his poems. I have made no offering at the shrine of Childe Harold, though I shall not refuse his acquaintance if it comes my way.'

Carefully blotting her letter, folding it in a very precise way, and then sealing it, she stood up and, as she moved towards her bed, Annabella's eyes finally saw the letter that had been slipped under her door.

She picked it up, opened it, saw it was from cousin Caroline, and then stood and read it ... and read it again, an amazed expression on her face.

"*How very remarkable,*" she muttered, thinking the advice in the letter to be absolute rubbish, and wondered why Caroline had felt the need to write it? Such a nitwit.

Scrunching the letter up into a ball, she threw it dismissively across the room into her waste-paper basket.

Chapter Twenty

~ ~ ~

The following afternoon, Fletcher opened the door and was handed a letter from a messenger.

"Mr Fletcher?"

"Yes."

"It's for you," the man said, "for Lord Byron's valet, Mr Fletcher."

"Aye, that's me."

Fletcher was highly flattered when he opened the perfumed sheet of vellum decorated in blue sea-shells, and addressed personally to *him* ... although he was not so pleased when he read the letter ...

FLETCHER — Will you come and see me here some evening at 9, and no one will know of it. You may say you bring a letter and await the answer. I will send for you to come in, for I wish to speak with you.

I also want you to take the little foreign page I shall send over to you this evening straight in to see Lord Byron. Do not tell his Lordship before-hand, but when the page comes with flowers, show him in. You will see he is quite a child.

Lady C. L.

Well now, Fletcher had no worries about that, showing the lad and his flowers in – his lordship was always getting flowers sent to him by some person or another – but if Lady Caroline thought he would go over to Melbourne House one night to see her and talk to her behind his lordship's back, then she had another think coming.

He could lose his job for doing that, and he didn't want to risk losing his employment with Lord Byron. And *fondness* would not save him. They had all been shocked at the speed in which his lordship had dismissed Susan Vaughan, and he had been very fond of her. So go over to Melbourne House and talk to Lady Caroline behind Lord Byron's back? — No fault, no fear.

~ ~ ~

Hobhouse was running late. He had arranged to call in and collect Byron at seven, and then both would go on together to join some more friends up in Harrow for a social dinner.

Reaching St James's Street, he found the street door of Byron's building wide open, and then up the stairs to see the apartment door wide open and heard the sounds of a rumpus going on.

As soon as he entered the lobby Fletcher came rushing up to him in a state. "It was not my fault, Mr Hobhouse! I thought he was a *lad*. She said she was sending a *page* with some flowers and to show him straight in!"

Hobby entered the drawing-room to see Byron distractedly rushing towards the dressing-room leading to his bedroom and being chased by the page who was dressed in a scarlet hussar jacket, white pantaloons and a feathered fancy hat, calling out –*"Byron, please!"*

At the same moment that Hobby heard her voice, her hat fell off and he saw her blonde curls – "Lady Caroline!"

From then on it was all a wild confusion. *"You drew me to you like a magnet and now you shove me away!"* she was sobbing frantically. *"Are there others now? You were not so cold before!"*

Byron saw Hobby and immediately tried to calm himself. "Hobby, will *you* speak to her? She won't listen to me. Tell her I cannot have her sneaking into my rooms in this way!"

Caroline ignored Hobhouse as if he was not there, her stare full of disbelief and fixed on Byron. "You will *not* elope with me?"

"*No!*"

"So you do *not* love me?" Caroline wildly looked around her, and seeing Byron's dress-sword lying on a chair grabbed it up – "Then there will be blood spilt!"

Hobby dashed forward and placed himself in front of his friend. "It shall not be Byron's blood."

Caroline raised the sword high in both hands as if about to plunge it down into her chest. "It shall be *mine* then!"

"*God!*" Byron pushed Hobby aside and managed to wrestle the sword out of Caroline's hands.

Fletcher was at the apartment door dealing with some people from downstairs who had come up to know what all the ruckus was about — "Surely Lord Byron does not have a young *lady* in there?"

Hobby was horrified by the madness of it all, and flashed furiously at Byron, "Despite those clothes they all now know that the page is a *female*. This is a disgrace! Lady Caroline, do you not realise that you are ruining Lord Byron's reputation as well as your own?"

"She's a *servant*," Fletcher was saying to the neighbours at the apartment door, at a loss for any other excuse. "A bad servant, and she's upset and screaming because Lord Byron is dismissing her."

"She doesn't *sound* like a servant."

Fletcher nodded and cursed Lady Caroline's upper-class voice. "That's why Lord Byron is dismissing her – notions of grandeur above her station. Now please go back to your abodes, she's quiet now and she'll be gone soon – back to Bedlam."

What happened next was all very distressing for Hobhouse, who joined with Byron in urging Lady Caroline to don the dress and bonnet which Fletcher brought in belonging to his wife, and once Caroline had done so, Hobhouse took her downstairs and put her inside the first hackney cab that came along, sobbing every step of the way:

"I *know* he loves me ... you will speak to him, Hobhouse, and pray assure him that my being married is no obstacle ... I can get a divorce in the same way that Lady Holland did ... I know he loves me ..."

Hobhouse saw the carriage off and returned upstairs where he asked Byron: "What the deuce has been going on between you two? I can understand you not wishing to elope with her like a peasant boy and a milkmaid running off together, but *do* you love her?"

Byron looked back at his friend with an expression of extreme weariness. "I am coming very close to *hating* that woman."

~~~

Later that evening when Hobhouse had left him, Byron remembered something that had been bothering him, and asked Fletcher: "By the by, those clothes belonging to your wife that you gave to Lady Caroline ... so where is Sally? I have not seen her for days."

Fletcher's face reddened. "Oh, you know, my lord, these country girls ... so used to all that peace and slow living and fresh country air ... they just can't settle to this noisy London life."

"So where is she?"

"Gone back to Newstead."

"Indeed? Gone back to Newstead?" Byron said archly. "So she is still in my employ then? Even though she is no longer here to clean my rooms or cook my food?"

"Well now, that's not really a problem, is it, my lord, because you always dine out?"

"So who cooks my breakfast?"

"I do."

"You, Fletcher, *you* cook my breakfast?"

Fletcher shifted uneasily on his feet, certain that his lordship was picking on him, and still blaming him for allowing Lady Caroline into the apartment.

"It's not a hard thing to do, my lord, to cook your breakfast, seeing as all you have is tea and crackers, and the occasional boiled egg."

"And who cleans my rooms?"

"I have a cleaning woman who comes in to do that, every day. Mrs Mule. A very respectable housekeeper type of woman she is, like Nanny Smith ... although it's me that lights all the fires in the morning, and anything else that needs seeing to."

"And Sally ... your wife ... she was quite happy to leave you here on your own?"

"Oh, very happy, my lord," Fletcher assured him. "Happy enough to be back in her old home at Newstead again with the prospect of seeing me whenever I go back to the country with you on visits."

"Do you not miss her?"

"Miss her? My wife?" Fletcher frowned in a puzzled way. "No, my lord, why would I? A man has his work to do and his woman has to wait. That's the way it's always been ... for us servant class anyway. And, Sally, well ... she has always had more fondness in her heart for

Newstead Abbey than she has ever had for me."

Byron stood looking around him in bewildered thought, wondering just *when* his world had turned upside down, and everyone in it had gone crazy?

Chapter Twenty-One

~ ~ ~

The obsession of Caroline Lamb and her persecution of Byron continued, writing love-letters to him every day and attending every Ball, soirée and party which she knew he had also been invited to – always attempting to get into his carriage at the end of the evening – and always blocked from doing so by Hobhouse, Samuel Rogers or Thomas Moore, who kept a close eye on her.

On those occasions when Byron did not appear at the Ball, soirée or party, Caroline spent most of her time warning all the other young ladies to protect their virtue by having nothing to do with Lord Byron, because — *"He is mad, bad, and dangerous to know."*

Hobhouse was outraged that she should be spreading such scandal. "Good grief! — swords being lifted and threats of blood being spilt! *She* is the one who is mad, bad and *dangerous* to know!"

~ ~ ~

Byron was unpacking a box of books he had ordered from Hatchards: new editions of old editions by Pope and Spenser, as well as a copy of *Corinne* by the French writer Germaine de Staël. She was one of the few female writers he enjoyed reading, and now he wanted to re-read her book on *Jean-Jack Rousseau,* his original copy having been half eaten at Newstead by his old wolf-dog, Woolly.

He moved over to his desk and sat reading, turning the pages with all the pleasure of a book-lover, lost in the world of Rousseau and disagreeing with him too often on many points of his philosophy.

He lifted his head, pausing to think, and while doing so his eyes noticed a book on the far corner of his desk, a book that was not his ... a book which he knew to be the favourite of Caroline Lamb.

He picked up the book, opened it – startled to see a message written on the flyleaf, dated the previous day, and written in Caroline's familiar handwriting —

Remember me?

Shocked and furious, he found Fletcher who protested earnestly that he did not know how she could have got into the apartment ... and Byron could see that Fletcher truly did not know.

"All I can think is that she must have been watching this place," Fletcher said, "and when she saw me going out to give Leander his walk, she maybe got in by speaking falsely to Mrs Mule the cleaning woman."

And so it turned out. "She was a *lady* true enough," said Mrs Mule. "A very polite lady, and she said all she wanted was to drop in a book for his lordship."

Byron asked: "And how long did she stay?"

"I don't rightly know, now that you ask. I was busy polishing the silver in the kitchen and humming away to myself, as I always do, and then Mr Fletcher came back and him and me had a cup of tea together."

Furious, Byron left Fletcher giving loud warning to Mrs Mule to *never* to let anyone inside the apartment again, while he returned to his desk and rapidly dashed off a reply to Caroline Lamb —

Remember thee — nay, doubt it not —"
Thy husband too may think on thee!
By neither canst thou be forgot,
Thou false to him — thou fiend to me!

But he did not, could not, send it to her. To be cruel or viciously sarcastic to a woman he had once made love with was not what any decent gentleman would or should do.

Yet, he could not help thinking that even his own possessive mother would not have been capable of the clever deviousness of Lady Caroline Lamb.

And worse was to come.

During one of his visits to John Murray, he asked to see the miniature painting he had sat for which Murray wanted to put on the cover of *The Giaour*.

"You already have the painting," Murray said.

"Me? No. Why would I ask to see it, if I already have it?"

"Now that *is* strange," said John Murray, "because I received a letter from you, about a week ago, asking me to give the painting to a page whom you were sending in later that afternoon to collect it."

Seeing the look of disbelief on Byron's face, Murray searched through his papers and found the letter. "Here it is. Is that your handwriting?"

It was – a perfect forgery of his handwriting. And he did not have to wonder just who had copied his handwriting so flawlessly. He knew it was Caroline Lamb, and told Murray so, half-laughing in amazement as he did so.

John Murray was not amused. "But this is downright *burglary*. Shall I inform the police?"

"No, no," Byron said quickly. "She is a lady, after all, and the embarrassment of being charged ... can you get another copy from the artist?"

"Yes, I believe so. He will have his original drawings."

"Then get a copy, and say no more. Invoice the extra cost to me."

"But really, to *steal* a painting by the deceit of forgery!" John Murray was still astounded. "And if she is doing all you say, even insinuating herself by false pretences into your private apartment when you are not at home, then there should be a *law* against that kind of thing."

Hobhouse agreed with John Murray when he heard about it. "You're too soft with women, Byron. You always have been, letting them get away with the most appalling things, right back to your *mother.*"

Byron looked at him — and realising that Byron was still wearing black in bereavement, Hobhouse immediately apologised.

"I'm sorry, I should not have included your late mother in that."

~ ~ ~

Caroline was in a constant state of either heartbreak or fury, unable to understand why Byron was now so cold with her, or why everyone in her circle was so cross with her. All now appeared to be very much on *Byron's* side.

Had she not known these people for ever? And had they only known *him* for such a very short time? Yet Lady Holland would not hear a single word against Byron, nor would Lady Cowper nor Lady Jersey; and, of course, every single one of the *men* sympathised with him deeply, so much so that Lord Holland warned that if she did not improve her behaviour whenever Lord Byron attended one of his functions, then all welcome to Holland House would be withdrawn from her.

And now even her husband was furious with her.

"Could you not have been more *discreet* in your infidelity?" William demanded. "Instead of acting like a pubescent fourteen-year-old? Now we, yes *we,* Caroline, have *not* been invited to the Duchess of Devonshire's annual Grand Ball at Devonshire House. Now *I* am being ostracised as well you."

"Oh, that is so very unfair," Caroline commiserated. "What reason have they for not inviting *you*?"

"Because you are my *wife,* and so must be included in the invitation, and they will not risk you hounding and harrying Lord Byron again. *He* is the main event at every function now. It's him people want to see at their parties – not me, and certainly not you!"

Caroline was not sure she understood. "William, is it my imagination, or do I detect some partiality for *Byron* in your voice."

William shrugged. "Caroline, the most important thing in a man's life is mainly his *work,* his career. And my career is that of a politician — a *Whig* politician, in opposition to this Tory Government."

"So? What has all that got to do with Lord Byron?"

William Lamb's frustration with his wife was reaching new heights.

"He also is a Whig, and he carries the vote of a *Whig,* and there is not one man of the Whig party – whether from the House of Commons or the House of Lords – who has heard Lord Byron address the Upper House on important issues and not admired him!"

Caroline began to smile in her mischievous way. "So I'm not the only who loves Lord Byron, am I? I believe you love him too, William?"

"*I detest him!*" William turned on her in a rage. "He has Lord Holland kissing his hand and kneeling at his feet! And if *you* don't cease this obsession of yours, I will divorce you, Caroline, and I will throw you out!

Caroline's smile now became smooth and more cynical. "Divorce me? Throw me out? Oh, I don't think so, William, because that would certainly ruin your precious political career, would it not?"

"No." William had given some previous thought to it. "No, because a divorce did not damage Lord Holland's political career, did it?"

"Because it was not *he* who got divorced," Caroline said calmly. "It was his American wife who was divorced, before she married Lord Holland." Caroline stood up. "I think I'll go up to the nursery now and see our child."

She walked smoothly across the drawing-room to the door, where she paused, and looked back at her husband.

"And what you also have to remember, William, is that Lord Holland is the nephew of the previous great Whig leader in Parliament, Charles James Fox ..." Her smile returned. "So he is of the famous Fox family, William, one of the *Foxes* ... while you are merely a Lamb."

~ ~ ~

Caroline did not go up to the nursery. She walked straight past it and every other room until she reached her boudoir. There she locked herself in and unlocked the drawer where she had placed her miniature painting of Byron, her face softening with love as she gazed at it.

She lay back on her bed, her hands holding up the painting as she gazed and gazed, murmuring to herself, "*My beloved ... why have you sent me from rapture to woe, from rapture to woe ...*

She closed her eyes, remembering that blissful night he had made love to her ... her groin tightened at the memory, she jerked upright, moving to sit on the side of the bed, clutching the miniature painting to her breast.

No, no, she would not give him up, because deep down she knew he *did* love her, he must do – had he not also achieved great pleasure that night?

Perhaps he should be *reminded* of that night of pleasure in some way?

~ ~ ~

The dream was a bad one, a close thing, never so close before. Byron awoke with a start, his breath fast and panting, his body trembling, exhausted from all the running.

Fletcher made him drink a cup of hot tea.

"Your favourite – green tea – the delivery came yesterday from the Fortnum & Mason store."

"Delivery?" Byron looked at Fletcher. "Fortnum and Mason is just around the corner."

"I know, but they don't charge for delivery and it saves my arms."

"From the weight of carrying a packet of tea?"

Byron closed his eyes again, his mind still struggling with the fright of the dream.

"And also," Fletcher said, "they expect a lord to have his orders *delivered* in their fancy boxes with their name on it. Same way they expect you to run up an account with them and not trouble yourself with the bother of handling dirty money. Not when they can just send you a big bill at the end of the month."

"Fletcher, go away. Far away. It's too early to listen to your prattle."

"It's past eleven, my lord."

"Is it? Oh well ... even more reason why you should stop your prattling and scram."

Byron got up from the side of the bed and limped over to his bedroom desk, his right leg still feeling sore from all the running in the dream. He opened the journal in which he had been writing the previous night.

Francis Hodgson had instructed him: "When you have an alarming dream, write it down as soon as you wake up."

I awoke from a dream! — Such a dream — but she did not overtake me! I wish the dead would rest. Ugh, how my blood chilled, and I could not awake — and — and — and — heighho!

~ ~ ~

Later that afternoon, Mrs Mule made her humming sound as she brought a small box into the room where Byron was again at his desk reading about Rousseau.

She kept on humming until Byron stopped reading and looked up.

"This small box has just come for you, me lord. Looks to me like a nice gift, so I brought it straight in."

"Thank you."

The wrapper was silver; the box inside was plain white. Curious, he opened it and saw a large rose-gold locket. He opened the lid of locket to see a small square of folded paper inside, it's front decorated with tiny love hearts in red ink.

Lifting it out and unfolding the paper, he saw a small clipping of fair hair with a tinge of blood on it ... jolting back in shock as his eyes saw the words on the note —

Caroline & Byron — I cut the hair too close and bled, but if shedding blood means love —

He dropped the paper from his hands, repulsed and disgusted – nauseated that she could have done something like this — sent him a clipping of her *pubic* hair.

What had made her *do* such a thing? And then he remembered ... it was straight out of the book *Le Diable amoreux.*

He jumped up and furiously threw the box and its contents into his waste-paper basket.

Then he went into his dressing room and washed his hands clean. Yes, clean ... and now he would wash his hands of her completely. No more taking the stance of a gentleman, not now that she was behaving no better than a whore.

His letter in response to her was brief and brutal.

Lady Caroline Lamb, — I am no longer your lover. And since your unfeminine persecution obliges me now to confess it — learn that I am attached to another, I love another, whose name it would be dishonourable to mention.

I shall ever continue your friend, if your Ladyship will permit me so to style myself. And as a first proof of my regard, I now offer you this advice – correct your vanity, which is ridiculous – exert your absurd caprices on others – and leave me alone.

BYRON

Chapter Twenty-Two

~ ~ ~

To avoid any further contact or chance meeting with Caroline Lamb, Byron moved into a new apartment at 4 Bennett Street, St James, and refused all invitations to dinners, parties and theatre, secluding himself away writing *The Giaour*.

His publisher, John Murray, was delighted at his first sight of these early drafts, thinking them to be "*wild and beautiful!*"

Murray knew these *Eastern Tales*, set mainly in the Levant, would be more exotic reading for those who knew no other country than their own.

Yet he also realised that all of Byron's poetry had one underlying *political* theme – that the world could never be peaceful or civilised so long as the people at the top had such entrenched power, while those below them had no powers at all.

The Ottoman law in the Levant that allowed females to be tied alive in a sack and thrown into the sea as punishment for a transgression or infidelity, was one of these examples, as told in *The Giaour*.

It was also a metaphor for how England treated her own individuals and the mass of its people – throwing men and women carelessly onto the scrap heap to starve, like the textile workers in Nottingham and now also in Lancashire and Yorkshire. The misery was spreading, while the huge machine of bloody war was still churning up young men by the thousands and spitting out their bones.

~ ~ ~

By the autumn of 1812, *Childe Harold's Pilgrimage* had sold multiple thousands of copies in edition after edition and Byron's name was now becoming famous throughout Europe and even in parts of America.

Byron had also washed his hands completely of the House of Lords, complaining to Hobhouse over dinner.

"It may well be different for you down in the House of Commons, *if* you ever get there in the future, Hobby, but for me, in the House of Lords ... I now know, as everyone knows, that not even Cicero himself, and probably the *Messiah,* could ever alter the vote of a single bishop."

Byron sat back in his chair, his expression gloomy. "And if you knew, Hobby, what a hopeless and lethargic den of dullness our old Hospital of Lords is during a debate, and what a mass of corruption in its patients, you may wonder – *not* that I very seldom speak – but that I ever attempted it at all. It's a complete waste of any man's time."

"No, no," Hobhouse could not agree. "It's your duty, Byron, in your privileged position, to exert every effort possible to at least *try* and bring about some change."

Byron looked at him in amazement. "In *this* country?"

"Of course in this country, where else?" Hobhouse huffed. "And why not?"

"I'll tell you why all political efforts for change are wasted here in England, and why nothing ever, *ever* gets done. Now listen, Hobby, listen well, because I am going to spell out the reasons for you, one by one."

Byron held up his hand and ticked off each finger. "We have a mad King who *can't,* and a Prince of Wales who *don't,* patriots who *shan't,* and politicians who *won't!* "

He held up his four fingers. "So there you have it, four things that are ruining all hope for change in this country – the mad, the bad, the useless, and the *base.*"

Hobby's expression was grumpy. "Do you always have to make your points in rhyme?"

Byron laughed. "There you go! A *typical* politician! When you have no response to a statement, change the subject by asking a new question."

"Well, I am going to change the subject now," Hobby shrugged, "because I think it's time we were heading off to the theatre."

They left the restaurant by the *back* door and made their way to a carriage waiting at the end of the lane.

"Oh, by the by ..." Byron turned to Hobhouse. "I told Tom Moore we would pick him up on the way. That's all right with you, is it?"

Hobhouse shrugged again. "If you must have him always tagging along beside you."

Hobhouse was thoroughly *sick* of Thomas Moore, a nice enough fellow, but he was now certain that Moore was trying to usurp his own position as Byron's best friend. He was also certain that Moore was using Byron's fame in an endeavour to enhance his own.

"Here's another 'by the by' for you," Hobhouse said as the carriage rolled off. "For a married man with a child, do you not think Moore goes *out* in the evenings rather a lot?"

Byron smiled. "That's probably why he likes to go out so much, *because* he is married – women can be the very devil."

Although, at St James, when Byron called for Moore and met his wife, Bessy, she seemed closer to an angel, fresh-faced, smiling eyes and apple-red cheeks, and she was truly ... rather beautiful. She insisted that Byron came inside to see their baby daughter, a sweet little cherub who had Tommy's twinkling blue eyes.

"Tommy, you are blessed!" Byron said as they walked back outside.

Tommy nodded. "And now that I have *two* females to support, my need to succeed is even greater than before."

They climbed into the carriage and as it moved off again, Hobhouse suddenly had a dreadful thought: "I say, there's no chance that Robert Coates will be on stage tonight, is there?"

Byron responded by shivering in an exaggerated way.

"Are you cold?" Moore asked.

"No, I'm shivering for Shakespeare – if that idiot Coates gets up on stage to mangle his words."

"No fear of that," Moore smiled. "John Kemble would not allow Coates to get even a *toe* inside any theatre where he was performing."

When they arrived at the theatre, there was a large crowd waiting outside.

"God damn!" exclaimed Hobhouse. "Some *idiot* must have told the papers that you had reserved a box tonight, Byron."

"Probably Kemble himself," quipped Tom Moore, "to ensure a full house."

Byron looked at Moore, "Which play is it tonight?"

"Richard the Third."

"Oh for goodness sake! Hobby, you wretch – you told me you were sure it was *Hamlet.*"

"I thought it was," Hobby said sincerely, although he could not help smiling, because no one could mimic a better *Richard the Third* than Byron. So much so that whenever he wanted to escape from tedious Balls or parties where he was being crowded to suffocation and needed Hobby to rescue him, he would write a secret note with his pencil, using his code-name in case the page-boy mistakenly delivered the note into the wrong hands. And all the notes usually contained the same words — *'Richard wants to leave.'*

The carriage doors were opened by two of the theatre's footmen so Byron was given no chance to change his mind. "Oh well," he said to his friends, "just push through as quickly as you can."

Hobhouse stepped down first, at Byron's front, with Moore staying behind to cover his back ... the roar of the crowd was deafening ... until Byron emerged from the carriage and all got their first glimpse of the famous poet whom some lady had said was "mad, bad, and dangerous to know."

And yet, as always, a sudden hush fell on the crowd when they saw him ... reserved and polite in his manner, and stunningly beautiful ... nothing mad or bad-looking or dangerous about him at all!

Some of the females surged forward, attempting to touch him — *"Byron! Byron! Byron!"*

Inside the theatre, upon entering the box, the seated audience were of a higher class and far more sedate and respectful in their manner. As soon as the whisper went around, and then Lord Byron appeared up in the box to take his seat, all rose to their feet and loudly clapped the superb author of *Childe Harold's Pilgrimage* and *Maid of Athens*.

Following a quick modest bow, Byron took his seat at the back of the box, in the shadows, while Thomas Moore sat at the very front, in the glow of all the candle-lights, his Irish face smiling happily and his blue eyes twinkling merrily at all the faces staring up at him.

Byron lowered his head and spoke to Moore in a low and amused voice, "See how famous you are, Tommy?"

Thomas Moore turned his head, grinning, "I'm not a fool, Byron, but I *am* hoping that someone from Ireland is down there. It only takes one – *one* gossip, and within a month the whole of Ireland will be told that not only Lord Byron – but Thomas Moore *himself* was clapped."

Still grinning, Moore winked, "And then all of Ireland will be referring to me proudly as *'one of our own'* – even the Protestants."

Throughout the play, conscious of all the eyes constantly glancing up at him and not at Kemble on the stage, Byron could neither concentrate nor enjoy; and during Act Four, as soon as he heard the Duchess of York declare from the stage – *'Bloody thou art, bloody will be thine end!'*—he nudged Hobhouse, "Let us slip out before the end and go somewhere more cheerful?"

"Where?"

"I am asked to attend at Lord Holland's tonight. Will you come with me now, or will you stay?"

"Thomas Moore turned his head and whispered to Byron, "I will come with you."

Hobhouse frowned irritably. "It was *me* he asked, Moore, not you."

"Both of you, quietly now, bend your heads and follow me out into the shadows of the corridor."

~ ~ ~

When the three friends reached Holland House, Lord Holland was very relieved to see Lord Byron.

"I'm so glad you could come, because I believe I forgot to tell you – our reception tonight is to welcome the French writer, Madame de Staël, and she has particularly requested to meet you, Lord Byron."

"Madame de Staël?" Byron now felt absolutely delighted that he had decided to leave the theatre early. "The pleasure will be all mine. Which room is she in?"

"Oh, she has not arrived yet, so go in and prepare yourself with some champagne. Good evening, Mr Hobhouse, Mr Moore, a pleasure to see you both again."

Moore was smiling at Byron as they moved through the lobby.

"Madame de Staël herself? And *requested* to meet you. You see now, Byron, how the meridian burst of your fame has changed everything for us poets? No longer are we considered to be mere scribblers; no, now we are being referred to as *writing blades!*"

Entering the main room, Byron saw Caroline Lamb speaking with a young dandy and laughing loudly at every word he said to her.

"She always does that when she sees you," Hobhouse said in a low voice. "It's her way of telling you that she couldn't care less."

"So?" asked Thomas Moore. "What did you think of Kemble?"

"Excellent," Byron nodded, "although, in my opinion, he's not as good an actor as Kean."

"So why do you say he is excellent then?"

"Because Kemble *is* excellent in his own way, but Kean is *glorious.* Kemble *acts,* but Kean *feels."* Byron smiled. "I love actors, and watching great actors like Kean in performance is almost a sensuous pleasure for me."

"Unless they're playing 'Richard the Third'," Hobby said in his dry way.

A moment later they heard "*Madame de Staël*" being announced and all turned to see a heavy woman in her forties wearing a loose robe and a white turban. She was speaking quickly to Lord Holland, who pointed to Byron.

"*Oh, mon Deu!*" she exclaimed in loud rapture. "*My Shilde Arold – 'e is 'ere! Bon!*"

She threw out her arms and rushed towards Byron with all the speed of a galloping war-horse.

Byron moved to bow over her hand but she threw *both* hands around his neck and kissed him on both cheeks. "*My 'Arold! My Byronn!* I love you both, and at last we meet, eh?"

"It is an honour, Madame de Staël," Byron replied, and it truly was, for she was not only a great writer, but she was also a revolutionary and had recently been exiled from France by Napoleon who was reputed to fear her.

She stepped back to take a longer look at his face, and then stood clapping her hands in delight. "*Beau!* Day say der is only one *Byronn,* and *oui* it is true – der ist no oder like 'im!"

Lord Holland arrived at her side to make the official introduction and she grabbed his arm. "Send all these people away – *phff, phff!* Milord Byronn and I want to 'ave a *petit* shat."

Lord Holland looked around at all the staring guests. "Madame, there is a room down the hall —"

"A room? Yez, yez, Milord Byronn and I will go to a *room* for our little shat."

She grabbed Byron's arm and pulled him down the hall in a very unladylike way, crying out joyously — "*Allah illa Allah! It is Shilde Arold who comes with Germaine de Staël! Enfin, enfin!*"

Byron quickly turned his head and looked nervously over his shoulder, calling — "Hobby?"

But Hobby could not save him, not from Madame de Staël who pulled him into a vacant room, sat him down on one of the little settees and plonked herself down beside him, her hand on his arm as if to prevent him escaping.

"Not since Jean-Jacques Rousseau!" she exclaimed, "'ave I admired so much a writer of genius!"

"That is very kind — "

"*Enfin seuls!*" she cried, speaking over him — "Now we have our little shat, eh?"

Byron listened patiently as she talked on and on, her torrent of words in broken-English flooding over his head and boggling him.

At first, when she had asked him a question, he foolishly thought she expected an answer, but as soon as he opened his mouth she answered her question herself to her own satisfaction; and for every other question that she asked him, she immediately supplied her own answer.

Byron began to relax. He was not a great talker himself, not with strangers, so he allowed her to talk on and on and found himself wishing that all women were as good at conversation as Madame de Staël; it would save men like himself a lot of unnecessary effort.

After a time, his mind began to drift, because her conversation with herself was now beginning to sound like an essay being read – one must listen to it, but never interrupt ... It was hard to believe that this was the great intellectual and revolutionary woman who had helped to write the French Constitution in her own Paris salon in 1791 ... how on earth did the *men* manage to get a word in?

His hand surreptitiously slipped into his breast pocket to find his pencil and small notebook...

"Your Monsieur Wordsworth, 'e is not a poet. *Non!* He is a *poetess. Psha!* He writes like an English lady. All English poets write like *femmes,* clouds, flowers, fine ink, so *gentee*l – but not my *Byronn* – he writes like a *man* and he writes in *blood!"*

Less than thirty minutes had passed before Hobby was handed a note by a page.

"Now you see," Hobby said wearily to Tom Moore, "that's *another* thing Byron is very skilled at – disappearing!"

"Oh?" Tom Moore leaned over and read the note in Hobby's hand. *"Richard has gone – out back door to carriage – join quick if you want lift."*

"Are you coming?" Hobby asked.

"No, no, I think I will stay a while longer." Tommy was enjoying himself, and meeting too many influential people to leave now. "I'll get a lift from someone else or take a hack."

Hobhouse made his way towards the back of the house so that he too could slip outside without Lord or Lady Holland noticing.

He saw Madame de Staël surrounded by a gaggle of females further down the hall and winced at her loud and excited voice which reached back to him:

"... So sharming! So eloquent! We talk together so long and I do not tire to hear him! And mon Deu!— those eyes! Un bel homme!"

Outside, Hobhouse quickened his steps until he reached the front of the house, and then abruptly stopped walking, startled, when he saw Byron's yellow carriage – the door was wide open and a female was leaning inside, her voice agitated and pleading ... a voice he instantly recognised ... yet he could hear no response from Byron.

"You broke my heart, Byron, yet still I love you."

Hobhouse walked slowly forward, and on reaching the carriage he said quietly, "Lady Caroline, please withdraw. Lord Byron and I must leave now."

She pulled back and stared at Hobhouse, and then meekly stepped back.

Hobhouse climbed inside the carriage and closed the door, sitting down opposite Byron. "What did you say to her?"

"Not a word."

A second later the carriage door was yanked open, and both men looked to it ... Caroline Lamb was staring at Byron, her eyes glistening with venom.

"You once told me of all the different ways that foreign women take their *revenge* on a man. One day, Byron, I will show you how an *English* woman does it."

Chapter Twenty-Three

~ ~ ~

John Murray was a very happy man these days. In August he had moved from his bookselling trade business at 32 Fleet Street, and bought a beautiful five-storey Townhouse in Mayfair at 50 Albermarle Street, which was now his home and the offices of his new *publishing* house.

He had taken out a number of mortgages in order to secure the property, but he had no doubt that all the mortgages would be swiftly repaid – and all thanks to that twenty-four-year old, wayward young man, Lord Byron.

Since the phenomenal success of *Childe Harold's Pilgrimage,* the writer Walter Scott had decided to give up poetry and not even try to compete with Byron in that field, choosing instead to write his first novel, which he had brought to John Murray for his appraisal.

Unlike other publishers, who merely sold those novels they believed would *sell* and bring them back a good profit, even if it was a pile of utter trash compiled into a book, John Murray was determined to make his publishing house one of the most respected and influential in the country.

And to achieve that, his first criterion was to publish nothing but books of quality. The originality of the work, and the *quality* of the writing, was all and everything. He would not expend his time and resources on any work that was amateurish or sub-standard. Why waste his time on books that would survive for a year and no longer? The books that *he* would now publish would survive for generations and beyond.

He had previously inherited his bookselling business in Fleet Street from his father, John Murray the First, and he had every intention of passing on his *publishing* business in Mayfair to his own young son, John Murray the Third.

Consequently, he had now signed a contract with Walter Scott for his first historical novel, *Waverley;* and he had also been visited in his Mayfair offices by the brother of Miss Jane Austen, to discuss a contract for her next novel, *Emma.*

He had been somewhat confused when Henry Austen had visited him. Of course he had read Miss Austen's first novel, *Sense and Sensibility*, which he had admired extremely, but — "I did believe, Mr Austen, that your sister had determined on *self-publishing* any books she may write in the future, as she did with her first book."

Henry Austen had shrugged, a slight smile on his face. "Yes, but that was before the extraordinary success of Lord Byron's *Childe Harold.* My sister Jane, sir, is a country girl who believes in speaking straight to the point, and she now insists that if *you* are a good enough publisher for Lord Byron, then you are certainly good enough for her."

"How kind." John Murray had smiled; but then Henry Austen had proved to be as practical and straight-to-the-point as his sister when he added, "Jane will of course expect the best percentage terms you can offer, and she will also expect to be paid promptly at all times."

"Of course. Has Miss Austen written anything else since *Sense and Sensibility?*

"Nothing that has achieved any success. My sister Jane, you know, has long been an admirer of Frances

Burney — "

"Oh, *Fanny* Burney, or Madame d'Arblay as she is rightly called. Yes, she is worth admiring, although she is getting quite old now; over sixty, at least."

"Indeed, but in her prime she had a great influence on my sister as a girl, and some years ago, oh, fifteen or sixteen years ago, Jane wrote a novel and sent it to Miss Burney's publisher, Thomas Cadell, but he declined to even read it, dismissed it after the first page. It gave Jane quite a bad bump, I can tell you."

"And the title?"

"*First Impressions.*"

"Ah, an early attempt."

"Yes, but it was really rather good, and Jane simply adored the characters in it, so rather than waste it, I sold it for her a few months ago, to Egertons."

"On a commission basis again?"

"No. An outright sale of the copyright for one hundred and ten pounds, which is rather a good price for a rejected novel that has been lying in a drawer for over a decade."

"Indeed."

"Although Jane has changed the title now, to *Pride and Prejudice.*"

"And this new novel?" John Murray had asked. "How far advanced is the manuscript?"

"Fairly advanced I would say, about half-way. However, Jane has given me the first four chapters of *Emma* for you to read, and she expects you to make your decision and offer your terms based on those four chapters.

John Murray was not too pleased about that, until he read the first four chapters of *Emma,* and oh my dear the *quality* of the writing was superb. Miss Jane Austen was as good in her female way, as Lord Byron was in his male way, two excellent authors, and now they were both *his* authors.

Although the *name* of one of those authors could *never* be revealed. Publishers and booksellers may gossip amongst themselves, and know who was publishing who – but as far as the public and Miss Austen were concerned – the author's identity must always remain a mystery. Consequently, all her published books so far, simply declared that the work was written – "By a Lady."

John Murray smiled at the timidity of the fairer sex.

He would comply, of course, with the stipulation of the lady in this case; but there was nothing like having a *named* author like Lord Byron to make a publisher successful, because then other authors worthy of becoming a *name* themselves, followed suit and sent letters of enquiry.

Only last week he had received a letter from an *American* writer named Washington Irving, who not only lived in Manhattan, but was also "*a great admirer of Byron*" – and who was now offering John Murray the publishing rights to his book *The Sketch Book of Geoffrey Crayon, Gent;* a compilation of stories which included a synopsis for another story which the author planned to include, entitled: *The Legend of Sleepy Hollow.*

Oh, yes, John Murray was very happy about many things these days – and even happier when that wayward twenty-four-year old author of his, Lord Byron, unexpectedly called in to see him the following day.

"So, Murray, what do you think?" Byron asked, showing John Murray his new walking-stick with a beautiful brass handle, shaped like a dog's head.

Byron was grinning his infectious grin. "Walking sticks are all the rage now. Every young gent is either twirling or casually leaning on one, even Brummell, so why not I?"

"Why not indeed?" Murray nodded his approval: after all, a walking stick would actually provide some *service* to Byron with the affliction of his foot, unlike others who used them solely as an item of fashion.

"Been strolling, have you?" Murray asked. "Taking your stick out for a walk?"

Byron laughed. "No, this morning I have been fencing with Henry Angelo. I'm here to collect a few copies of Childe Harold, if you would be so kind."

A member of staff came in to request John Murray's signature on a number of urgent letters. "You don't mind waiting, do you? " he asked Byron.

Byron shrugged, waving a hand for Murray to do whatever he had to do, his eyes travelling over the rows of books on the floor-to-ceiling bookshelves: all 'First Editions' that Murray had paid a high price for.

John Murray sat down at his desk, certain that Lord Byron would be happily occupied perusing the rows of classic books – his head shooting up and his eyes staring when he saw that Byron was not perusing the books, but *fencing* them with his walking-stick.

He continued to watch as Byron marked out a book he obviously did not like, then lunged towards it in a fencing motion, touching the title with the stick.

"You are very energetic today, Lord Byron ... and those books are all *first* editions."

"And surely the *last* for some of them," Byron replied. "Now *this* one by Hayley," he said, taking some steps back and then lunging his stick at it, "this one should carry a health warning on the cover – '*contents may nauseate'.*" He looked seriously at Murray. "Do you not agree?"

Murray was not prepared to disagree because, as happily married as he was – like most people eventually did – he had fallen in love with Byron, absolutely adored him.

"But *the stick,* Lord Byron," he admonished, "I don't think you should ... all those first editions costs me a small fortune ... and I would hate to see them damaged."

"Oh, my apologies," Byron said, and then made a great display of blowing on the spine of the books that his stick had touched, rubbing them down with his handkerchief with the concentration of a shoe-shine boy, blowing on them again, and then examining each book minutely with one eye to ensure that not one bit of street dust had soiled them, until John Murray and his colleague were both laughing at such clownish antics.

"So, you are very good at *mime* as well as rhyme," Murray said, "but in future, Lord Byron, my books —"

"Oh, I will bow down and genuflect on one knee to all your shelves of books when I arrive in future, Mr Murray. I will even stand and sing a hymn in homage to them if you wish. How about the Halleluiah?"

John Murray laughed. "I would simply prefer that you did not practice your *fencing* on them."

Byron twirled his stick in the air and pointed it at John Murray. "Then I won't."

~ ~ ~

After Byron had left, John Murray was still smiling. It was not only Byron's poetry that had been such a success, but also Byron himself. And the proof of that could be seen all over London, and now probably far beyond London, if one could actually *see* that far.

Byron was not only a member of the London world of high fashion, he had actually *changed* fashion – the style of the dandy had been thrown out and replaced by the look of the *poet*.

Some dandies still adhered to the old rules of course, spending hours winding yard after yard of cambric around their necks to stock up their chins, donning elaborate waistcoats, big hats and yellow kid gloves; but most of the younger ones were now opting for the low, soft collar with a thin cravat loosely tied beneath it to display the hollow of the throat.

To be a young gentleman of *fashion* these days, or to be deemed an intellectual or a poet on his way upwards to literary fame and riches – one now simply had to wear the *'Byron collar'* and when outdoors, the *'Byron cloak'*. And the white-powdering of hair for social functions was now a taboo for any man under forty. Powdered hair was considered to be not clean, not young, and not *Byronic*.

And then there was his famous *underlook* – his inimitable way of lounging against a wall and keeping his head slightly lowered while lifting his blue eyes to look at whoever had caught his interest across the room. Oh, the bad *imitations* were everywhere.

John Murray continued musing, tiredly now, because the new Byronic fashion was also inundating most of the manuscripts sent to him through the post. He read every unsolicited manuscript himself and most were an intolerable nuisance, because the hero was always a caricature of Byron – a dark and handsome young man affecting an air of romantic and haughty gloom, surrounded by a twilight of mystery and with the most seductive blue eyes that made every maiden swoon at his first glance – and all the manuscripts were the *same*, the *same*, the *same!*

All were based on Lord Byron, and all had the picture of their hero wrongly-drawn, because the Byron the public saw — reserved, dignified, and remote in manner was *not* the Byron of his friends – all of whom knew him to often be full of fun and wit and there was no end to the playful tricks he was capable of playing on them.

Before long ... Murray thought derisively ... many of these amateurish writers would not even bother to make attempts at characterization or any real plot, but simply take a stick of wood, dress it in a soft collar and a dark cloak; say that all the maidens knew him to be *mad, bad,* and *dangerous to know* — and then smugly believe they had produced the book's perfect romantic hero!

Intolerable! Absolutely *intolerable* for a publisher to find himself reading such trash.

And it was not only would-be *writers* who were now indulging in such nonsense. A few nights previously, he had attended a party where there were a number of elderly society ladies present, and all claiming to be very *literary* and ardent admirers of good poetry.

"And so when this gentleman called to see me," one lady had said, "and I was told he was also a *poet* – well, of course, I ordered that he be brought in to me immediately ... but as soon as I saw him, I deduced that yes, he *was* a gentleman, but definitely *not* a poet!"

"And how did you deduce that?" Murray had asked her in some bewilderment, "merely on the first sight of him."

"Oh, my dear, it was obvious immediately! He was wearing an old-fashioned stiff stock around his neck."

Chapter Twenty-Four

~ ~ ~

John Murray may have been happy with his young author, Lord Byron – but John Cam Hobhouse was not so happy, and now he was becoming very worried about his friend.

Since throwing off the possessive chains of Lady Caroline Lamb, Byron was now living a very fast personal life in different circles, moving from one to the other whenever it pleased him – from the circle of Scrope Davies and Beau Brummell and their fast gaming set in the nightclubs, to the less salubrious circles of Gentleman John Jackson and the illegal fight clubs.

Byron had always loved boxing, and could throw a hard punch himself when he needed to, but now Hobby knew that Byron was also putting up the money to finance these secret fighting matches in private venues where only the invited were allowed.

"If the police find out and make a raid, *you* will be the one arrested," Hobby warned him, but Byron merely shrugged.

"It's harmless, and it's the only way some men can make a living. Besides, they rarely get very hurt – the decisions are all made on points, Hobby, on *points,* same as any other sport."

"Oh, you and your points," Hobby said irritably. "And when you announce the winner, do you do that in *rhyme* as well?"

Byron laughed — he was stretched out on his sofa with his sleeping dog Leander lying beside him — "*I* don't announce the winner, the referee does. Although, Hobby, if there was ever a contest for the best *grumbler* in England, you would be crowned the champ."

"And then there is your womanising."

"My womanising?" Byron gently stroked the dog's head. "I've no idea what you are talking about, Hobby, no idea at all."

"Oh stop it, Byron! You are becoming more notorious for all your quick-change love affairs than for your politics or even your poetry."

"I've given up politics."

Hobhouse stared. "You can't have! You are even more political than I am."

"More political than *you*? Oh, I doubt that." Byron gently eased the sleeping dog aside and sat up. "Perhaps it would be more accurate if I said I have given up my membership of the Whig party."

"What? No!"

"Yes! And I want no argument about it." Byron stood up. "Let me get you a snifter of whisky to ease your shock."

Astounded, Hobhouse watched him move over to the drinks cabinet. "But I thought your loyalty was *devoted* to the Whig party."

"So call me capricious, because I've changed my mind."

"I'll call you a renegade!" Hobhouse took the glass Byron handed him. "I thought we were united in this, ever since Cambridge. And already you have done so much more than me – can do so much more than me – because *you* are a member of the House of Lords."

Byron shrugged. "Hobby, on a political level, the House of Lords holds no charm for me. There, a man may *think* one thing, but is forced to *say* the opposite in order to uphold the party line."

"Because that's how it's done!" Hobby countered. "One party gaining the vote over the other party."

"And too often the *truth* and the interests of the people are sacrificed merely to secure the triumph of one political party over another, one political faction over another. And always, *always*, one must not step over the party line. I could never be that tame."

Hobhouse knocked back his whisky. "Does Lord Holland know you have quit the Whigs? Have you told him?"

"Yes, and when I explained my reasons, he assured me of his continuing friendship, but agreed it was the wisest thing for me to do in the circumstances."

"What circumstances?" Hobhouse frowned. "Is there something I don't know?"

"No, and my views have not radically changed in any way. At heart I am still a liberal, still a Whig, but I cannot stand all the jarring debate and the in-party squabbles that serve no real purpose to anyone outside the Upper House."

After a silence Byron said, "It's better I do it this way, if only to protect the Whig party."

"Protect? How so?"

"I want to be a man who can think, speak, and act for himself. I don't want my opinions to be given to me second hand. I want to stand alone, be independent, and whatever I might say publicly – and things do need to be said publicly, *truthful* things – so whether it be my virtues or my vices or anything else, I don't want my own personal opinions to cast a shadow over the Whig party."

"Then you can stay in politics," Hobhouse insisted. "You can always stand and speak as an Independent in the House of Lords."

"Oh, Hobby ..." Byron flopped back down on the sofa. "If I speak in the House I am heard by two maybe three hundred people at most. A note of what I say may even be printed the following day in a few newspapers, but even then it's edited according to their political prejudices. And what good does it ever do? What change does it bring about? None whatsoever. Each article is like one chattering dunce following another chattering dunce down the same old road every morning, and nobody pays any serious attention to them any more."

Hobby could not deny it; most political articles in the papers were either manufactured or censored by the government.

"Nevertheless I think you should —"

"No, Hobby, *no!* If I want people to seriously *listen* to what I have to say, right or wrong, then I must separate myself from any political party and stay away from the House of Lords."

Hobhouse thought it was all rather ridiculous and returned home feeling very disappointed with Byron. His politics must have been all a sham, or just a novelty he had played with – else why give it all up now? And so easily? And if Byron didn't speak in the House of Lords who would hear him? And what newspaper would even mention him?"

Hobhouse mentally kicked himself a few weeks later when he realised he had forgotten something very important about Byron, something that Byron was now using to its fullest extent for political purposes – his *fame* as a poet.

Now that he was famous every newspaper sought interviews with Lord Byron, seeking his opinion on every day-to-day event that occurred, but especially his opinion on politics.

"Politics are not worth an opinion."

"And the Prince Regent?"

"Is doing *nothing* for the poorer people of this country, except sending their sons to war while he takes naps and eats five huge meals a day."

Within months, Byron's views of men and of events became as widely known as his celebrity, raising smiles of delight from the Whigs, cheers from the common people, and causing increasing alarm amongst the leaders of the country due to the boldness of his opinions and the cut of his sarcasm, accusing the ruling government of having one objective above all, and that was "*to keep the country in the dark while blowing their own trumpets under a blaze of fake glory.*"

Hobby's disappointment in Byron turned to pride, although he realised with envy that it was the independence of Lord Byron's station in society that allowed him his independence of mind and *speech*. Yet, even allowing him that, one had to admire him for saying aloud what others dare not even hint.

~ ~ ~

In the drawing-room of 8 St James Street, Byron and Leander were once again asleep on the sofa when Fletcher entered the room.

The dog opened one eye and watched Fletcher coming closer – raising his head with a short threatening bark when the valet touched his master's shoulder.

"My lord, wake up, you have a visitor."

"Who?"

"Lady Melbourne."

Byron had quickly brushed himself down and sent

Leander into his bedroom when Lady Melbourne was shown into the drawing-room, holding a hat box.

"Lord Byron, forgive me for calling without notice," she said graciously, "but as I was at the milliners .. so near to here ..."

Byron bowed over her hand and directed her to a seat on one of the sofas.

"I know, of course that it is not proper for a lady to visit a young gentleman in his private rooms," she went on, "but in view of my age ... and you *are* younger than my own sons."

"Indeed," said Byron, not knowing what else to say. Lady Melbourne was tall, full of grace and dignity, and although she was in her sixtieth year, she was still a very handsome and influential woman.

"Forgive me," she said again, "but I have come to speak with you on a matter regarding a member of my household."

Byron's weary expression made her smile. "I have not come to chide you about Lady Caroline, but to seek your help on another matter."

"How so?"

"Is Caroline still declaring her love for you?"

"No, she is now threatening her revenge."

Lady Melbourne smiled her amusement as she slowly removed her gloves. "Although," she added, "Caroline *can* be a very dangerous woman if she takes it into her head to be so. My advice to you is to humour her."

"No." Byron's agitation caused him to stand up again. "I don't want any further contact with her."

He looked at Lady Melbourne. "I have done everything to end it. You must know that?"

"Oh, everyone knows it. Everyone has *seen* how you try to avoid her at all costs. It is the only scandal on everyone's lips."

"I'm sorry to hear it. It was not my intention to be the cause of any scandal."

"Oh, *don't* be sorry," Lady Melbourne shrugged. "All dinner parties would be very dull affairs if there was no scandal for the diners to get excited about."

She placed her folded gloves on her lap. "Last night, for instance, I attended a dinner at the home of Lady Jersey who does *not* allow any scandal whatsoever at her table. Consequently, by the time the dessert was served, we were all finding it very hard to keep our eyes open, so boringly dull was the conversation passing back and forth."

Byron half-smiled and sat down again, unable to make head nor tail of this woman.

"So why do you need my help?"

"Oh, yes, I almost forgot ..." she pulled open the cords of her purse and took out some folded paper. "My niece, Annabella ... she has written some poetry and would like your opinion of her talent in that direction. She is far too shy to ask you herself, because unlike Caroline, Annabella is a perfect young lady in every respect."

Byron was so relieved he agreed. "I could read them tomorrow."

"Oh, thank you, but now *do* address your honest opinion back to me personally and not to Annabella. It would not be proper for you to contact her direct."

Fletcher arrived with the usual tray of tea, which Lady Melbourne graciously accepted and then fell into casual conversation about many things in general.

Byron began to find her fascinating, this still-handsome woman who had fascinated the Prince of Wales, Lord Egremont, and so many others. Her manner was so relaxed and unaffected, her voice and expression so incredibly passive and *kind* that he found himself thinking she would make the perfect *mother;* the type of kindly and understanding mother he had often wished for in his childhood and youth.

So he did not react with any antipathy when Lady Melbourne said helpfully, "You know, the one *certain* way you could end Caroline's persecution of you, is to consider marriage."

"Marriage?"

"Indeed." Lady Melbourne nodded. "It would also end all that nonsense from other women, as well as getting rid of those guttersnipe females that crowd around the gardens of whatever house they know you are within at nights. It would also help the rest of us to get away in our carriages more quickly."

"You exaggerate; it was merely a few females on *one* occasion," Byron laughed; but Lady Melbourne was very serious.

"And with your next poetic production it will get worse," she said. "Your fame is growing by the day. And then there is the impossible problem of Caroline ... I do advise you to think about it, Lord Byron. Marriage is not a stupid suggestion by any means."

"I know no person I would wish to marry," Byron said. "At least, not one who is single and available."

"There is my niece, Annabella," Lady Melbourne suggested. "You could both be poetic souls together. She is also an heiress to her uncle's fortune, so she would make a very good wife in many ways."

"And you would become my *aunt*?"

Lady Melbourne laughed. "And how delightful that would be for me – inheriting such a distinguished *nephew* as Lord Byron."

It was all a joke of course, and Byron was enjoying it,

until he realised that Lady Melbourne was not jesting at all, going on to reveal to him what a perfect and *virtuous* young lady Annabella Milbanke truly was.

"Others have sought her hand, all fortune-hunters of course, but she has refused them all."

"Then she would hardly accept me, considering we hardly know each other and there is no love on either side."

"Love?" Lady Melbourne was taken aback. "What has *love* got to do with it? A woman *may* occasionally marry for love, but a man in our society must surely be more prudent and judicious when choosing a suitable wife?"

Byron was still smiling at the ridiculousness of it all, replying quite honestly: "With all due respect, Lady Melbourne, I have no desire to become better acquainted with Miss Milbanke. She sounds too virtuous a young lady for a rebel spirit like me. I think I might like her better if she was a little *less* perfect."

'And so might we all,' thought Lady Melbourne, standing to leave.

"I do hope, Lord Byron, that you will be kind enough to visit us some day at Melbourne House. On the *ground floor*, of course, well away from Caroline. We take tea most days at three."

~ ~ ~

"Lady Melbourne is a fascinating woman," Byron told Hobhouse later. "Intelligent conversation, captivating manners. It's a long time since I have met a woman that I liked so much after only *one* interview."

Hobhouse cocked an eye. "And she's *sixty* you say?"

"She must be, maybe younger, maybe older, no matter her age, she is still fascinating. No wonder she had the Prince of Wales at her feet for years. She knows how to be *kind* to a man."

Hobhouse gave a grunt of disgust. "Byron you know I hate this kind of talk! I'm a man's man, and I thought you were too, but now wherever we go, we are constantly surrounded by clawing women!"

Byron laughed. "Is it my fault that I woke up one morning and found myself famous? All I did was write a poem."

"And have you now given up your poetry too – to spend more time in the company of women?"

"Women *are* poetry, Hobby, as you would know, if you gave them a little more attention."

"I give them *no* attention, because they are either too meek to say a word, or talk far too much and bore me silly. Have *you* ever heard a woman engage in a sensible conversation about politics?"

"No," Byron admitted, "but if that is all you talk to women about, politics, then you probably bore *them* silly."

Byron sat down, lounging back in thought. "You are right of course. Like most men, I feel more at ease in the company of men ... but there is something very *softening* about the presence of a woman, which always softens my own mood, and even if one is not in love with them, there is —"

"Oh I'm not standing for any more of this!" Hobby said, standing up. "You and Scrope Davies make an intolerable pair of womanisers. I'm off to Parliament to listen to the speeches. Lord Liverpool is getting worse by the day, and Lord Castlereagh – oh do *not* speak to me about that demon Castlereagh!"

"Hobby no, don't go ..." Byron stood up quickly. "Don't go yet, because I have something to show you."

"What? Some new poetry?"

At his desk, Byron lifted a large brown packet and removed a thick wad of papers. "Now these papers may interest *you,* Hobby. Will you take a look and them, and then tell me what you think?"

Hobhouse joined him at the desk and Byron pulled out the chair. "Sit down, Hobby, sit down, make yourself comfortable."

As soon as he had sat down and glanced over the first page of the bulk, Hobby looked up at Byron. "These papers are from your attorney, John Hanson."

"Yes."

"Business papers and legal documents."

"Yes, the very thing you love reading, Hobby, documents.*"*

"*Political* documents are my forte, not *your* business documents."

Yet even as he spoke Hobhouse knew there was little point in protesting, because he and Byron had been through this routine many times before.

Byron had a complete *aversion* to all business documents. In his poetry and private letters he could write rapidly, his pen flying over the paper as quickly as his thoughts, but he hated nothing more than writing formal official letters, or even *reading* them – a drudgery which he always put off from one week to the next, until he eventually persuaded Hobhouse to do it all for him.

And now here he was again, handing the task over, and *pretending*, despite all protestations to the contrary, that he knew Hobby *enjoyed* reading dry and antipoetic documents.

"You are a man of business, Hobby, and you are so good at it."

"*Political* business."

"Whereas I'm not even very good at *arithmetic,"* Byron insisted. "I know two and two make four, but my problem is that I keep trying to make them add up to five."

Hobby gave up, knowing that once Byron had taken any whim into his head, he listened not to contradiction, but went on laughing and jesting until he eventually triumphed and had Hobby smiling along with him.

Hobby finally allowed himself to be persuaded into reading over a mass of documents, dull and uninteresting – yet at the same time Hobby *did* like to know all of Byron's business.

"These documents are all about your coal mines in Rochdale," Hobby said a short time later. "Hanson is very worried about the latest situation."

Byron was on the sofa reading some of Coleridge's poetry. He looked over at Hobby. "Do you know, when I was ten years old, Hanson told me the business of Rochdale would all be sorted out within two or three years, and yet here he is, fourteen years later, *still* writing to me about it."

"The fault is not his. He was very successful in winning the court case to get the coal mines back for you after your great-uncle wrongfully sold them, but the delay is due to the other side lodging a protracted appeal in the Appellant Court."

"So, let them appeal. The mines were legally entailed to me. The old Baron had no legal right to sell them, and the High Court has already ruled on that."

"That is not the problem," said Hobhouse gravely. "The problem is that you are seriously in debt, and without the settlement of the Rochdale business, Hanson has no way of paying off those debts."

While Byron thought about this, Hobhouse sifted

through some more papers.

"Hanson is also querying some of your bank cheques, in particular one to a Mrs Falkland for five hundred pounds.

"Her husband had just been killed in a duel, leaving her and her children without a provider and penniless. What else was I to do but help her?"

"Is she a close friend?"

"No, I've never met her, but I knew him, a decent fellow who unfortunately ended up with a sword in his gut."

"And five hundred pounds will keep his widow in luxury for a number of years. Byron, you are such a *fool* with money. *Fifty* pounds would have been enough to keep the widow in comfort for at least a year."

Hobby sifted through more of the papers. "And all these cheques of £10 every month to a Mr T. Ashe? Who is he? Hanson is querying them."

Byron had to think. "Oh yes, now I remember. He is a writer who invested all his savings in publishing his *magnum opus*, but it failed to sell even one copy, leaving him destitute. So when he appealed to me, I agreed to support him at £10 a month until he gets back on his feet again."

Hobhouse went through each query in turn, finally discovering that Byron was the financial benefactor of quite a few people who had sought his help.

"Hanson is also querying the number of cheques you have sent to George Leigh, as well as some bank drafts to be paid directly to Mrs A. Leigh."

Byron sat up and stared, his whole manner changed. "Don't you *dare* to question how I may help my sister. She has three children and a hapless husband who unfairly fell foul of the Prince of Wales. And she is my sister, Hobby, my sister!"

"No, she is only your *half* sister, and it is not your responsibility to support her and her family as well as half of the families in England."

"None of that is any of *your* business."

"It is," Hobby glanced down at the papers, "because you have made it so."

After a silence, Byron sighed and shrugged. "Yes, you are right, Hobby, you always very kindly take care of business for me, so let us not quarrel about it."

"I have no wish to quarrel," Hobby replied. "Although I hope you will allow me to say that I do understand John Hanson's alarm."

After another silence, Byron sighed and said, "Enough of this business. Why don't we go to Brooks's for dinner and have some fun with Scrope Davies and Brummell afterwards."

"I'll gladly go with you for dinner, but I'm not going near any gaming tables."

"Neither shall I – at least not to play," Byron replied, "That is one entertainment I do *not* spend my money on these days – the vice of the dice."

Chapter Twenty-Five

~~~

The Duchess of Devonshire wrote again to her son Augustus:

> *"He continues to be the greatest attraction at all parties and suppers, when they can get him to attend. The ladies still spoil him, the gentlemen still jealous of him. There is talk that he is thinking of going back to Naxos, and if so, then the husbands may sleep in peace. I would not be surprised if Caroline were to try and go with him, she is so wild and imprudent."*

Caroline was determined to go to Lady Heathcote's Ball, without William, and was just as determined to get Byron's attention by wearing a clinging muslin dress which she had wetted down with water to make it cling even tighter. She knew she had a beautiful, perfectly-formed body, and her only wish was to remind him of it.

Byron was already there when Caroline arrived; deep in conversation and laughter with one of his literary friends, the pretty Bessy Rawdon.

Caroline sat on one of the sofas and watched them jealously, as did Annabella Milbanke.

"Byron is deliberately *flirting* with her," Caroline said.

"Lord Byron flirts with everyone," Annabella replied. "Your mistake, dear, was that you took it all too seriously."

Caroline wanted to slap her, but she controlled herself, faking a cheerful smile when Bessy Rawdon came and happily flopped down on the chair next to them.

"Oh, he's a devil that Lord Byron!" Bessy laughed. "Satan incarnate with all that talent, beauty, genius, wickedness and hypocrisy! You should have heard all the flattering things he said to me – so funny, even *he* was laughing when he said them. No wonder all the women adore him – and now even *I* adore him!"

Caroline abruptly stood up and walked out to the coolness of the garden. How *dare* he flirt with Bessy Rawdon! And how dare he flirt with *everyone*, as Annabella had said – and Annabella should know if he did or not, because *she* was always watching Byron like a hooded-eyed hawk.

Back in the ballroom Bessy Rawdon was back with Byron, laughing at his nonsense when he agreed with her that he was a devil.

"But don't judge me too harshly, because I come from a mad family. My father was a doomed gambler and my great-uncle, the last Lord Byron, was accused of being a murderer."

"A murderer?" Bessy's eyes popped in shock. "And was he a murderer?"

Byron nodded. "He definitely killed a man. And my father killed himself, so there's definitely madness in the Byron family – at least, that is what Mr Wordsworth is telling everybody, and Mr Wordsworth *may* be right."

"Oh, you're a devil!" Bessy Rawdon was laughing again, not believing a word of it. "I suppose you will be telling me next that you really *are* Childe Harold and *you* did all those bad things that he did."

"What bad things?"

Bessie flushed. "All the ... vice."

Byron smiled. "*Ah, vice!*" he quoted softly, "*how soft are thy voluptuous ways.*"

Bessy got in such a dither she almost tripped as she rushed away, causing Lady Jersey who was standing nearby with Hobhouse to say reprovingly – "Byron, you really are wicked! Now Miss Rawdon will believe that you truly are mad and bad and dangerous to know."

"And the woman who said that ridiculous thing about you is here tonight," Hobhouse observed. "Have you seen her yet, Byron? I noticed her earlier."

"She is *here* – Caroline Lamb?" In a flash, all Byron's mischievous merriment disappeared. "*Damn!*"

~ ~ ~

"Ah, my Lord Byron, you handsome young soul, show me up to the supper room, will you? I'm dashed hungry and all the other gents pretend not to see or hear me because I'm not young and beautiful anymore. Dashed bad manners I say!"

It was Lady Rancliffe, a little stout woman in her late seventies who was half blind but would never admit it, due to her childish passion for parties and party-food.

"Where is your stick?" Byron asked.

"My stick?" she looked at him with her rheumy old eyes. "Why on earth would *I* need a stick?"

"Why indeed?" Byron agreed, giving her his arm. "To the supper room we will go, my lady."

As soon as they entered the supper room, which was almost empty, Byron came face to face with Caroline Lamb.

"Lady Caroline," he said with polite civility, "I trust you are well?"

"Oh, I'm in a merry humour," she answered bitterly.

"I'm pleased to hear it."

Seeing Lady Rancliffe's back was turned and her attention focused on the array of food on the long table, Caroline suddenly picked up a large knife from the beef platter and said quietly to Byron, "I mean to use this."

"Against me, I presume?"

Byron looked at the knife, unconcerned. Caroline's amateur dramatics no longer shocked him. "If you mean to *act* the Roman's part tonight, Caroline, mind which way you strike your knife. Be it at your own heart, not mine."

After a long silence, staring at him whitely, Caroline mouthed the word "*Byron*" and then ran out of the room, still clutching the knife.

"You will stay with me, won't you, Lord Byron," said Lady Rancliffe, her back still turned "if only to help me find the red jelly. I simply *adore* red jelly, and I shall want lots of cream with it."

Byron searched the long tables until he found the bowl of jelly, a dish not usually served at adult supper parties.

"They must have known you were coming tonight, my lady, because here it is – red jelly in abundance and a large jug of cream beside it."

"Oh goody! Now serve me a nice big bowl will you, and then pour the cream *around* the red jelly, not on top of it."

Byron lifted the scoop and ladled an ample amount of red jelly onto a plate, making Lady Rancliffe's rheumy old eyes twinkle with childish delight.

"The cream must go *around* the jelly," she reminded him, watching carefully as he poured a circle of cream around the bowl with all the flourish and aplomb of an experienced waiter.

"Oh, you dear boy, thank you – although why there are no butlers in place to do it for me is a dashed mystery."

"It's too early for the serving of supper," he said, and indeed it was, as most of the guests had not long arrived.

"Now carry the plate over to one of the tables for me, will you? And then come back and escort me to my chair."

Byron had just seated her and placed the spoon into her hand when Lady Westmoreland rushed into the room, visibly distraught.

"Lady Caroline Lamb has stabbed herself and there's blood all over her gown!"

"What?"

She looked accusingly at Byron. "What on earth did you *say* to her to make her do such a thing?"

The entire house was in a commotion when Byron went downstairs to be told that Lady Caroline had been taken home by Lady Melbourne who had insisted that, after inspection, Caroline's injury was not dangerous.

"It was done deliberately and carefully," Hobby said, arriving at his side. "Just another of her menaces to get your attention. She looked furious when Lady Melbourne rushed her outside to the carriage."

Lady Westmoreland was still very distraught when addressing Byron again — "You *must* have said something to distress her. You know, between two people in your situation, a word or a look goes a great way."

Byron was beginning to lose his temper. "This really is insanity. If I am to be haunted with hysterics wherever I go, then *she* is not the only person to be pitied."

"But you saw her with the knife," said Lady Westmoreland. "So why did you not go after her?"

"I could *not* with any politeness leave Lady Rancliffe to drown herself in wine or water or be suffocated in a jelly dish without a spoon or a hand to help her," Byron exclaimed. "And If I had guessed Caroline to be serious, I would have done everything to pacify or prevent her."

Quite a few of the gentlemen were now taking Byron's side and making comments in his defence.

"She had no knife in her hand when I saw her, but she *did* have a small pair of scissors and was wounding herself, but not deeply. I don't believe she used the knife at all."

"I would not have believed," said Lord Holland, "that it was possible for any woman to carry her need for attention to such a pitch."

Byron had heard enough. He turned to leave the room and was quickly followed by Bessie Rawdon who had been so charmingly seduced by his flattering merriment earlier.

"Oh, Lord Byron, surely you are not leaving?" Bessie held out her copy of Childe Harold's Pilgrimage. "I was hoping to take this home tonight with your own signature on it."

Byron paused momentarily to give her what she later described as "a glare" and then quitted the room and the house without deigning to reply, leaving Bessie on the verge of bewildered tears.

~~~

Upon reaching his apartments with Hobhouse, who sought to advise him, Byron was still fuming at the unfairness of it.

"I said nothing to cause her to start cutting and maiming. I thought she was acting a part as usual, and when she held the knife and said 'I intend to use this,' I presumed she meant against *me*."

"Her cutting was very slight," said Hobhouse, "just enough to produce an adequate amount of blood to cause consternation and gain everyone's attention."

"I will have to leave England. That's the only solution. If I stay here I will be forever followed and persecuted by that woman."

"But all your *friends* are here," Hobhouse exclaimed. "And your publisher."

"All my life," Byron said, "I have detested scenes of any kind, ever since I suffered so many of them from my mother. And now I can endure no more trickery or scenes from Caroline Lamb. I swear, until the last hour of my life, I shall hate that woman."

Hobhouse left him then, after advising him to get some sleep and forget all about it. "This is what she wants, you know, to get into your mind, one way or another, good or bad. So don't give her the satisfaction of achieving that. Wipe your mind clean of her and go to bed."

Byron nodded his agreement. "But first, I must write a letter of apology to Bessie Rawdon.

~ ~ ~

More than an hour after Hobhouse's departure, Byron went out again and finally found his friends Scrope Davies and Beau Brummell at Brooks's club in St James.

"My dear fellow ..." Scrope Davies looked concerned, immediately putting a comforting hand on Byron's shoulder – but Beau Brummell was smiling with amusement.

"The gossip has reached us already," said Brummell. "In an attempt to disgrace you, Lady Caroline Lamb has made an absolute disgrace of *herself* tonight."

Scrope Davies did not find it at all amusing. "The woman must be deranged. Was Hobby there with you?"

Byron told them briefly what had happened, and then made it clear that he had come out solely to forget the entire damnable incident.

Scrope and Brummell agreed, ordering champagne and talking of other and more cheerful things until even Byron's mood had turned from serious to humorous; but then it was impossible to be anything but cheerful in the company of Beau Brummell. His jokes and comic dry wit were designed to defy the world at its worst, but he could also be very shrewd and knowledgeable on most serious topics.

Tonight, though, Brummell was determined to make someone pay for Caroline Lamb's attempt to bring Byron down in the eyes of others, and so chose as his target any male member of Brooks's who were known to be Lady Caroline's friends.

Although, wisely, Brummell always waited until Byron was away from the table or out of earshot before he made his own view on the gossip very clear.

One unsuspecting young gent came up to the table and spoke obsequiously to Brummell, who ignored his question and replied gravely – "My dear fellow, I advise you to leave here immediately and tomorrow – pray confine yourself to walking through the *back streets* of London until you eventually find a decent tailor."

The young man looked down at his clothes, dismayed, because Beau Brummell was not only a great designer of clothes, but also the most revered expert on male fashion in London.

"Perhaps," Brummell added pointedly, "your friend Lady Caroline Lamb can suggest one to you? She does, after all, have a *penchant* for wearing male clothes occasionally. Does she borrow yours?"

Another friend of Caroline's got the same treatment an hour later in the gaming room, congratulating Brummell on his win. "A fair few hundred guineas there, Beau. Lady Luck is at your elbow tonight."

"Oh, but my dear fellow, what is this on *your* elbow?" Brummell replied, touching the man's sleeve. "If you say it is one of *my* designs, then I really must protest!"

"But ..." the young man, whom Brummell knew to be hideously vain, was stupefied. "But ... this is my most *precious* coat. I always wear it on special occasions."

"Oh, is it a family heirloom then? Something you must wear whenever your mother is in town? So *is* your mother in town? Is that the special occasion?"

"No —"

"Or was it given to you as a gift by your friend Lady Caroline Lamb perhaps? That vindictive woman never did have much style."

Scrope Davies, who had overheard the conversation and did not approve, later relayed it to Byron, and then it was Byron who was protesting to Brummell.

"I told you I wanted the entire thing forgotten, so why are you deliberately offending her friends?"

"Not offending, but *warning* them," Brummell replied. "And it is essential to do so, because I know London society a lot better than you do, Byron. In London fashion is everything. And if you are not *in* fashion, then you are *out* of it, and it's goodbye to all further invitations."

"That's the trouble with London," Byron replied, "fashion has replaced *passion* in everyone's lives. Now a man is not judged by what he thinks or feels or does, but what he wears."

"Indeed," Brummell agreed. "If a man cannot control the quality of his clothes, then who would allow him to control their business or bank account or anything else?"

"So what has that got to do with the gossip about myself and Caroline lamb?"

"If the gossip is not nipped in the bud *now*," Brummell explained, "then the gossips will exaggerate the scandal to such an extent, that by tomorrow it will be all around town – possibly even in the newspapers – that it was *you*, Byron, who stabbed Caroline Lamb, and God knows what other fiction besides. But now the town gossips know that they will have *me* to contend with if they dare to tell a false lie against you."

Byron could not help smiling. Cold and heartlessly satirical as he sometimes could be, Beau Brummell was a true friend.

~ ~ ~

In the days that followed Byron discovered that Brummell had been right in his warning. The gossip was everywhere, causing a great sensation even in the newspapers, paragraphs after paragraphs speculating on what could have happened between Lord Byron and Lady Caroline Lamb at Lady Heathcote's Ball, resulting in the spilling of blood.

All the old Countesses in the country were, naturally, on poor Lady Caroline's side, convinced that *Childe Harold* had done something terrible to her – but then, "what could one expect from a misguided young nobleman who had spent so much time in the barbaric countries of the *East?*"

The Duchess of Beaufort wrote from her country residence to Lady Holland, begging for more information, because —

> *"These tales of horror strike me, I assure you, with terror, but in the country only imperfect reports reach us. You will, I hope, write and give us <u>every detail.</u>"*

Lady Holland did write, making it very clear that Lord Byron was an innocent bystander at the event, and indeed had not even been physically present in the room when Lady Caroline resorted to such foolish dramatics in her need to cause a spectacle around herself.

Immediately the tables turned and it was Lady Caroline who became a 'persona non grata" in high society; and Lord Byron — *"the unfortunate victim of a deluded woman's indecent passion for him,"* found himself bombarded with even more invitations to dinners and parties.

Chapter Twenty-Six

~ ~ ~

Having spent most of the previous night in the Cocoa
Tree Club and not getting to bed until dawn, Byron was
still asleep at noon when Fletcher woke him with a cup
of tea and a letter that had Lady Melbourne's seal on the
outside.

"You read it, Fletcher, and then just tell me in short
what it says. I'm not ready yet to receive any more bad
news from Melbourne House."

Fletcher slowly read the letter ... "Lady Melbourne
begs to inform your lordship that she intends to visit
you this afternoon at four o'clock and hopes you will be
at home to receive her. If you have other engagements
and will not be at home, she asks if you would be so
kind as to send her a note by messenger."

Byron shrugged bleakly. "More accusations from
Caroline Lamb, more unpleasantness."

Yet when Lady Melbourne arrived, her every word
and smile was full of kindness and sympathy, making it
very clear that she was on Byron's side in this matter.

"She is calm this morning," said Lady Melbourne,
"but her instability of mind is most worrying. She still
believes that she can win you over and get you to run
away with her."

Byron was at a loss. "So what am I to do? I have said
and unsaid and resaid all that I can say to her."

"Marry," said Lady Melbourne bluntly. "It was my
advice to you before, and it's my advice now. It's the
route that most men choose when needing to escape
from a bad and tiresome connection. And for you to

escape from Caroline and her mania about you, I assure you, it is the *only* escape."

Byron was even more at a loss. "But I don't even know anyone that has even *slightly* induced such a thought to enter my mind ... except, perhaps ... the very pretty Miss Bessy Rawdon who never fails to make me laugh when I tease her."

"A silly idiot," said Lady Melbourne dismissively, and then went on to speak of her niece, Annabelle Milbanke, an heiress, who was not only very intelligent, but also had the *sweetest* nature.

Byron had forgotten all about Lady Melbourne's niece, Miss Milbanke, who, in any event, seemed a bit too frosty in her manner for his taste.

"Some people *do* consider my niece to be rather prim," said Lady Melbourne, "but I assure you, she is not prim at all, just very shy. Within her own circle she can be very amusing."

Byron just looked at Lady Melbourne, not knowing how to answer her.

"And you know ... being married will not prevent you from having the occasional *amour* here and there," said Lady Melbourne with a confidential smile. "Not as long as you keep it discreet.*"

Byron could not help remembering that Lady Melbourne had been involved in her own share of affairs after her marriage, and only one of her three children was sired by her husband.

While she talked on he looked at her with a man's eyes and saw that she must indeed have been very beautiful in her prime. She would have to be, for the Prince of Wales to spend *five years* cheating on both his wife and mistress with her. And before that Lord Egremont ... and such was her charm that even now both men remained very fond and on good terms with her.

"Well, I suggest you at least think about it," advised Lady Melbourne, and immediately changed the subject from her niece back to Caroline.

"She has *no* discretion, not as far as you are concerned, and as yet William remains bound to her, but for how long? How much scandal can a man take from his wife? And if he once throws her off, then I dread to think of the persecution that will follow *you* thereafter."

Byron remained silent, feeling very guilty himself about William Lamb, especially as he was a fellow Whig. If he had been a Tory he might have felt less so.

Yet, in his confused guilt, he did not think Caroline should take all of the blame.

"I must take my own share of the blame in all this," he said. "In situations of this kind the man is, and always must be, the most to blame, and no less so in this instance. She was married, and I knew it, I seek no excuse, but if I had known —"

"How *could* you have known?" Lady Melbourne interrupted consolingly. "Now you must not blame yourself. You are still so very young, and she older and more experienced. And I saw myself how *relentlessly* she chased you, using all her wiles and ways on you."

This must be how she had comforted the Prince of Wales in all his distresses, Byron was thinking, feeling very much consoled himself.

"She has made *my* life a complete misery," Lady Melbourne confided. "From the day she married William. And now all these threats and hopes of you eloping with her. I cannot tell you how, of late, I have come to *hate* living in the same house as her."

Not knowing how to console her in return, Byron sought recourse in his usual flippancy. "So why don't you and I elope instead?" he suggested. "And then we would *both* be free of her."

After a moment of shock Lady Melbourne could not stop laughing, and seeing the smile on Byron's face, laughed even more.

"Now that really would cause a *scandal*," she said. "An absolute earthquake of a scandal! But, oh, my dear, even in jest, what an absolute *compliment* to myself ..."

She found her lace kerchief and dabbed at the tears of laughter in her eyes. "Would you mind if I told some of my lady friends? If only to make them envious? At my age, and you so young, it would be just marvellous."

Byron shrugged good-humouredly. "Be my guest. I am already the talk of the town."

"Yes, and we must put a stop to that," Lady Melbourne replied seriously, taking command of herself again.

"Now, Caroline's mother, Lady Bessborough, is going to her estate in Ireland for a few months, and I'm sure she will be very agreeable to my suggestion that she takes Caroline with her, if only to get her away from London and hopefully cure her of this madness of hers. I may even be able to persuade William to go with them."

She stood to leave. "I shall write a note to inform you of how things go."

"Thank you."

At the door, she hesitated. "Now you *will* give some thought to my niece, Annabella, won't you? If you were my son, I would be unable to make a more *perfect* choice for you."

Byron agreed that he would give it some thought,

without any intention of doing so.

Yet as the day went on he was inundated with letters from Caroline herself; the first informing him that she had decided to leave London to enter a convent and become a nun.

The second letter an hour later begged him to elope with her — "*to your beloved Greece. How happy we would be there, just the two of us in the sunshine, without any interference from anyone. I know you love me, it is others who have turned you against me ...*"

He ignored all the letters, only to receive yet another letter in the evening —

I will kneel and be torn from your feet before I will give you up. Yet you give us both up.

Byron could take no more. Infuriated and frustrated and driven by desperation, he went to his desk and impulsively dashed off a rash letter to Lady Melbourne, asking her to make his proposal of marriage to her niece, Miss Annabella Milbanke.

Chapter Twenty-Seven

~ ~ ~

Annabella went frigid with shock when her delighted aunt passed on the marriage proposal from Lord Byron.

"Well?" asked Lady Melbourne, seeking some reaction. "The handsome young poet whom almost every young lady in London wants to capture, has expressed his wish to marry you, Annabella, *you*! I had no idea he was so attracted to you!"

Neither had Annabella, and her shock showed on her face. She had yearned to be noticed by Lord Byron, but so far he had showed no interest whatsoever, yet now he was proposing *marriage* to her!

"I need to think about this," she said, and returned to the privacy of her room, where she sat down feeling a great deal of confusion, until she began to calculate the situation from every angle.

Why *her*, and why *now*?

Because he needed an escape from the clutches of Caroline.

Did he think she was that stupid – that she would be content to be the little wife in the background? Or in the *fore*ground, fending off the attentions of all bothersome females? That certainly must be his thinking, it must be, because he certainly did not love her – how could he, when he didn't even know her beyond the occasional hello and a polite sentence here and there at a party.

No, this was not how she dreamed it, not how she wanted it to be. For him to be *in love* with her, that's how she had dreamed it ... and perhaps now, she suddenly realised ... with this absurd proposal, he had taken the first unconscious step in bringing their union forward on a more proper basis.

If he were to be *in love* with her, she would be able to reform him, turn him away from his wicked vice and libertine ways, and become a true and decent Christian.

She took out a piece of paper and began to write very carefully, remembering so well a statement that she had often heard her own dear father say again and again ... "*A man always wants most, that which he cannot have.*"

Lady Melbourne sat alert when Annabella returned to the drawing-room, her eyes on the sheet of paper in Annabella's hand. "Ah, you've written your acceptance already." She smiled knowingly. "I always *knew* you had a particular fancy for Lord Byron."

"I have never had a particular fancy for anyone," Annabella said coldly. "So please pass on my rejection to Lord Byron with my apologies."

"What? Your are refusing him?"

"Yes."

"Why? He is the best catch in town! So why on earth *why?*"

Annabella handed over the sheet of paper. "Here are my reasons."

Lady Melbourne sat staring at the long list of necessary attributes that Annabella required in a husband ... "*Wealth. A title of rank. Handsome. Good manners ...*" she looked up, "But Lord Byron has all these attributes!"

"Read on," Annabella instructed.

Lady Melbourne read on ... "*Clean living. A virtuous mind. Religious principles ...* Annabella, you are looking for the *perfect* man, and no such a man exists!"

"Men can change, be reformed."

Lady Melbourne was at the end of her patience with
Annabella, wishing her brother Ralph had not sent his
daughter down from Durham to live under her roof. A
weed sent to live in a flower garden.

For such a *plain* girl, who really was not at all popular
in society, so often left to sit like a wallflower at Balls
and parties, and for a girl who really had only the
promise of her fortune to attract a man, Annabella
clearly had too high an opinion of herself. And the fact
that she was so terribly prim in her manner and dress,
made Lady Melbourne wonder why *any* man in London
society would propose to her, even with the temptation
of her fortune ... although she knew wealth was not the
reason why Lord Byron had proposed.

Lady Melbourne sat back, suddenly feeling very
pleased that her niece had rejected Lord Byron's
proposal, because now she did so *like* Byron, even more
than she had once liked her niece, but that was a long
time ago, before the priggish girl had come to live with
her. And liking Byron so much as she did now, she could
not in all sincerity wish Annabella on him.

She continued reading the list in her hand ... so
preposterous! Well, she had done her duty to help
Annabella find a suitable husband in London, but
tonight she would have to write to her brother in
Durham and inform him that all her efforts had been in
vain, because no man less than a *saint* would do for her
niece. She would also make some very broad hints that
perhaps a city such as London was not the right
environment for a girl like Annabella.

"So tell me," she said to Annabella, "why must I be
the one to give Lord Byron your refusal? Cannot you
write a letter to him yourself telling him so?"

"No, because he did not write a letter to me, did he?

He merely asked *you* to pass his proposal on to me. So I must respond likewise, by asking you to pass my refusal back to him."

Later that evening, Lady Melbourne was still grumbling about Annabella to her husband when Caroline approached the door of the drawing-room, hearing the previous few sentences.

Her face was stark white when she entered the room, staring with huge eyes at Lady Melbourne. "Byron ... *Byron* has proposed to Annabella?"

"Yes."

"That insufferable prude! Byron could never be happy with someone like her! He likes women who laugh and make him laugh —"

"Then no wonder he got rid of *you*," said Lord Melbourne angrily. "No man could tolerate the way you have been behaving. And how *my son* puts up with you is beyond my understanding. If I was William I would throw you out this instant."

Caroline was not too perturbed by the words of her father-in-law, she had heard it all before. It was the words that Lady Melbourne spoke next, quietly and seriously, that disturbed Caroline the most.

"But surely, Caroline, the fact that Lord Byron has expressed a wish to marry Annabella, must prove to you now that he has no intentions of ever eloping with *you*."

Caroline stood staring at her.

"But you do have your own husband," Lady Melbourne reminded her. "A good husband who has tolerated all your perversions and even forgiven you for such. And my advice to you now, Caroline, is to return to your husband with a good heart and do everything you can to repair your marriage, if only for the sake of your own *child*, dear sweet Augustus."

"My child?" Caroline replied. "Augustus? My own sweet boy ...?"She turned and fled out of the room.

Chapter Twenty-Eight

~ ~ ~

After more than a week of enjoying the company of his friends Scrope Davies and Beau Brummell, wining on champagne late into the night, Byron had forgotten all about his impulsive proposal to Lady Melbourne's niece, until he received a reply from her Ladyship regretting her niece's refusal.

Byron almost collapsed with relief. "I don't even know the girl," he told Hobhouse later that evening. "So only God knows why I was so stupid to do it ... other than ... in a moment of mad desperation, I must have been ready to do *anything* to free myself from Caroline Lamb."

"It was still a stupid thing to do."

"Yes," Byron agreed ruefully. "And I need not have been so rash, because Caroline's mother and husband have taken her off to the family estate in Ireland for a few months, so we can all breathe more easily again."

"Well let this be a lesson to you," Hobby advised. "In future, have nothing to do with any woman that is married."

"Never again," Byron agreed, and a week later he was at Lady Jersey's 'Autumn Ball' flirting happily with the very beautiful Lady Oxford who had whispered to him secretly that she was suffering "*a terrible love*" for him.

"Lady Oxford is *married.*" Hobhouse angrily pulled Byron aside in the supper room. "And you *know* she is married, so what are you doing?"

Byron popped a cherry into his mouth. "Hobby, if you knew that poor woman's history, you would be more compassionate towards her. She told me she was sacrificed, and I do mean *sacrificed,* as a girl, even before she was a woman, to an older man whose mind and body were contemptible to her. You have met Lord Oxford, so need I say more?"

Hobby tutted sarcastically. "And now, I suppose, you are her white knight come along to bring some joy into her life?"

"No, I am merely her *friend.* Is one not allowed now to be friends with a woman simply because she is married?"

"And not only is she married, she is *forty.*"

Byron glanced over at Lady Oxford sitting beside Lady Jersey. "And so she has reached the autumnal full bloom of her beauty in my opinion."

"She is still a woman of forty, while you are only twenty-four and still a fool."

Byron suddenly clutched Hobby's arm in alarm. "Richard needs to leave – *immediately.*"

Seconds later he had scooted across the floor to the far end of the supper room and out through the door that led to the stairs down to the back of the house.

Without even a glance around him Hobby rushed after him like a schoolboy fleeing from news of the headmaster's imminent arrival – finally catching up with Byron in the back garden. "What? *What?* Was it Caroline Lamb you saw? Has she not gone to Ireland after all?"

"No, did you not see – Lady Melbourne and her *niece,* the one I rashly proposed to!"

"So?" Hobby could not understand the alarm. "She refused you, not interested in you at all, so why the sudden rush?"

Byron's expression was perplexed. "Do you think I

should go back inside and *pretend* to be broken-hearted by her refusal? I suppose it would be the most decent thing to do in the circumstances."

Hobby took a moment to think about it. "Oh, I see your dilemma now. It would be quite outrageous for her to see you happily enjoying yourself within days of her rejecting your marriage proposal. You could of course go into hiding for a few weeks, and then emerge wan and woeful. That is the *customary* thing to do."

After a period of thought, Byron said, "Or I could go to Cheltenham for a few weeks? Lord and Lady Holland have gone there for the benefit of the spa waters and invited me to join them. Yes, that's what I'll do. Tomorrow I'll go to Cheltenham and join the Hollands. Do you want to come along with me?"

"No thank you," Hobby sniffed. "I would rather get drunk on liquor in London with Scrope Davies than spend even a day drinking spa waters in Cheltenham."

"So would I, Hobby, so would I, but remember what we were taught, how we were schooled – 'in deference to the feelings of the gentle sex, a man must do the right thing'."

Byron shrugged and continued walking towards the back gate. "Although I know I shall probably *hate* Cheltenham."

Chapter Twenty-Nine

~ ~ ~

Byron was enjoying his time in Cheltenham, especially as Lord and Lady Holland had insisted he stayed with them at *Georgiana Cottage*. A strange name, he thought, for a large and secluded country house of three floors and numerous bedrooms.

Lady Holland could not believe her ears when she awoke one morning to hear Lord Byron singing.

Amazed and amused, she pulled on her *robe de chambre* and followed the sound of the voice ... which led to Byron's dressing room, the door half open, where she could see him singing as he shaved.

She knocked gently and poked her head round the door to stare at him. "I did not know you *sang*, and so well!"

Byron smiled. "I love to sing, but usually only when I am alone, and feeling happy."

"And *are* you feeling happy?"

Byron rinsed his razor in the bowl as he thought about it. He had been very happy living here with the Hollands, like one of the family ... something he had always wondered about and sometimes yearned for, to be part of a normal family living a normal family life.

"Did I awaken you?" he asked her.

"Yes, but I'm glad you did. It was lovely to wake up and hear a man *singing*. I immediately felt cheerful and ready to enjoy the day, which is quite unusual for me in the mornings, I assure you."

The rest of the holiday was just as cheerful, apart from the quantities of the medicinal and disgusting

Cheltenham Spa waters the three forced themselves to drink, followed by numerous glasses of good wine to get rid of the taste.

When the time for their departure approached, Byron found himself dreading the thought of going back to London with all its glitzy activities and tedious problems. He liked the peace and quietness of Cheltenham so much, he decided to stay on at Georgiana Cottage even after Lord and Lady Holland had left.

The only disturbance to his peace now was the anxious letters that kept coming to him from Lady Melbourne, the first having been forwarded from London. The dear lady was very alarmed that her niece's rejection of his marriage proposal had sent him into a fit of melancholy that had driven him away from London.

She hoped not, because she herself was now so fond of him; and also because Annabella had asked her to suggest (if he would agree) that they enter into some friendly correspondence occasionally, in order to get to know each other a little better. Lady Melbourne's main concern though, was that he should not be staying away from London due to feeling *hurt*, as that would distress her deeply.

Once again he picked up his pen to reply, but this time he decided to be very honest with Lady Melbourne:

My dear Lady Melbourne, — As to your niece Annabella, that must take its own chance — I mean the acquaintance; for it never will be anything more, depend upon it, even if she <u>revoked</u>. I still have the same opinion of her, but I never was enamoured. You were never more groundlessly alarmed, for I am not what you *imagine in that respect.*

Do not fear about Caroline either, even if we were to meet in the future; but allow me to keep out of the way if I can, merely for the sake of peace and quietness.

Yours affectionately, BYRON

In London, the news that Lord Byron had proposed to Annabella Milbanke, who had surprisingly rejected him, caused the stimulation of some new interest in her.

Augustus Foster, a son of the Duchess of Devonshire, bravely sent his own written proposal of marriage to Miss Milbanke.

Annabella was shocked, but Lady Melbourne was delighted – to get Annabella married off would kill two birds with one stone – it would fulfil her duty to her brother in Durham to find Annabella a suitable husband in this her "coming out" season, and would also remove her niece from her care.

"Well, my dear, are you going to accept his proposal?"

"I will need to consider it very carefully," Annabella replied, and retired to her room where she sat down at her desk and considered the proposal with all the calculation of a skilled mathematician.

Augustus Foster had no money of his own, nor would he inherit as he was merely the son of the Duke's *second* wife.

Another fact that must be considered, was that the Devonshires may be rich in assets and property, but they also had gigantic *debts*. It was well known that when Georgiana, the first Duchess of Devonshire, had died young a few years previously, she had left gambling debts of over £100,000, – a truly *enormous* amount of money – and now Elizabeth Foster, her replacement, had brought nothing to the Duke's second marriage to alleviate those debts except three children from her former marriage.

It was beyond Annabella's comprehension why all these London society women were so obsessed with card-playing and gambling. It was *sinful* to gamble money away on nothing more useful than the pleasure of playing cards.

Annabella suspected that the only reason Augustus Foster had proposed to her, was because he had been told that she was an heiress to a fortune. And as he had no title, being no more than the Duke of Devonshire's *step*son, the title would pass on to William Cavendish, the Duke's son by his first wife, Georgiana.

She picked up her pen and began writing a letter in dismissal of the proposal, informing Augustus Foster quite bluntly that — *"I consider it my duty to comply with the wishes of my dear parents to consider only those marriage proposals from men of title and independent wealth, and you possess neither."*

The Duchess of Devonshire was greatly relieved when her son Augustus wrote to inform her that his proposal to the heiress, Miss Annabella Milbanke, had been curtly rejected.

"Do not make yourself unhappy about her," the Duchess wrote back, *"she is truly an icicle."*

Chapter Thirty

~ ~ ~

The only disconsolate thing Byron had against Georgiana Cottage, was that it contained no good books. Well, it contained *a few* good books, but he had read all of them in the past few weeks.

He wrote himself a reminder in his notebook — *Find a good bookshop in Cheltenham town tomorrow.*

Before retiring to his room and bed, he made one last detailed search of the bookshelves, finally giving it up as a lost cause and lifting down the heavy Bible, carrying it over to the library desk, and sitting down.

As a child he had always loved reading the colourful adventures and stories in the Old Testament, so he would read a few now, if only to make him yawn and feel more sleepy.

He opened the book at random, and found himself reading some of the Psalms of David ... understanding them so much better now, than he had ever done in the past when a boy.

Psalm 137 engrossed him, for who could imagine what it must have been like for the Jewish people after the fall of Jerusalem, destroyed by Titus and the Romans, reducing the Holy City to a pile, and forcing the people of Israel – those that were not slaughtered – into a nomadic exile.

His mind was travelling back, far back to that terrible time, imagining what it must have been like to be one of those last few Jews to leave Jerusalem behind them. And seeing all the slaughter, they must have stood on that hill of blood and believed they were the last few

Jews left on earth.

He had always felt great sympathy for the Jewish people. Even now, as they still were, dispersed, trodden down, criticised and condemned, and why? He did not know. All he knew was that it was not right – so it had to be *wrong*.

And now in the silence of the night, his growing emotions were influencing his vivid poetic imagination as he stood beside that last group of Jews on the hill of blood, looking back on the destruction of Jerusalem, the massacre of the Hebrew people, before turning away and beginning their desolate wandering journey into exile.

Where did they go?

According to David's Psalm, they went first to Babylon.

A slow, sad tune was playing in Byron's head, driving him to stand up and find pen and ink and paper and start writing his own poetic version of Psalm 137, which was later to become his first and most famous *Hebrew Melody:*

By The Rivers of Babylon We sat down and Wept

We sat down and wept by the waters

of Babel, and thought of the day

When our foe, in the hue of his slaughters

Made Salem's high places his prey ...

He wrote on until *Rivers of Babylon* was finished, and then, at last, he took himself up to bed.

Yet he still could not sleep; his mind relentlessly wandering back to that hill of blood ... to those last few Jews ... to them the fall of Jerusalem must have been

like the loss of Eden, the only home they had known ...
defiled and desecrated by the blood-lusting savagery of
Titus and his soldiers.

Had the Romans really believed they could butcher
the Jews into worshipping *their* gods – Mars and
Jupiter and Zeus – instead of the God of Abraham?

Minutes later he had candles lighting and was back
down at the library desk in his dressing-gown with pen
and ink and paper, writing a *second* Hebrew poem
about the destruction of Jerusalem, but writing it solely
from the view of one man, one Jew – looking back in
despair at the desolation of his land ...

From the last hill that looks on thy once holy dome,
I beheld thee, oh Zion! when rendered to Rome:
Thy last sun went down, and the flames of thy fall
Flashed back on the last glance I gave to thy wall.

I looked for thy temple, I looked for my home,
And forgot for a moment my bondage to come;
I beheld but the death-fire that fed on thy fane,
And the fast-fettered hands that made vengeance in
vain.

And now on that mountain I stood on that day,
But I marked not the twilight beam melting away;
Oh! would that the lightning had glared in its stead
And the thunderbolt burst on the conqueror's head!

But the Gods of the Pagan shall never profane
The shrine where Jehovah disdained to reign;

And scattered and scorned as thy people may be,

Our worship, oh Father! is only for thee.

This second poem, he realised, did not have a title. He put aside his pen and laid his face down on his folded arms on the desk, closing his eyes to think of one ... a title ... a memorable title ... a *Hebrew* title ...

He was still slumped down on his desk, fast asleep, when Fletcher entered the room in the bright light of morning.

"Wake up, my lord, wake up! It's important to me that you wake up!"

Byron slowly lifted his head, blinking dazedly at Fletcher. "What?"

"I'll have to leave you in the care of the house servants. I don't want to neglect my duties but I must. It's a matter of life and death."

Byron was instantly awake. "What's happened?"

Fletcher held out a letter. "This has just come, asking me to go back to Newstead straight away ... my wife Sally is dangerously ill."

Byron stared. "*Dangerously* ill?"

Fletcher nodded. "So Nanny Smith says, dangerously ill with pneumonia, and you know Nanny is not a woman to exaggerate."

"No, not Nanny," Byron agreed, thinking of the urgent letter Nanny had once sent to him, informing him that his mother was dangerously ill; and so it had proved when his mother died before he had reached Newstead.

"Then I'll go to Newstead with you," he said, pushing back his chair. "Allow me to quickly wash and get dressed and we'll be on our way."

Up in the bedroom, as soon as he was dressed, Byron

saw Fletcher at the wardrobe, hastily trying to fold and pack clothes.

"Leave the packing of the bags and everything else, Fletcher. I'll arrange for them to be sent on in a carriage after us. Come, let's go."

On the ground floor, Byron remembered the two Hebrew poems and rushed into the library to collect them from the desk, pausing to read quickly through the first one entitled – *By The Rivers of Babylon We sat Down and Wept*

While sadly we gazed on the river
Which rolled on in freedom below
They demanded a song; but, oh never,
That triumph the stranger shall know.

Once again his mind flashed back to that last small group of Jews, defeated and bonded, while being mocked by the pagan soldiers of Titus – "Sing us a song! One of your songs of Zion!"

Impulsively, Byron lifted the pen, dipped it in the inkhorn and rapidly added two more lines beneath:

May this right hand be withered forever
Ere we string our high harp for the foe!

Fletcher was calling to him – the horses and carriage were ready.

He quickly glanced down through the second poem, which still had no title –

"My lord ..." Fletcher arrived at the door looking anxious and jumpy ... "the horses and carriage are ready but they can't find the damned driver!"

"*Who* can't find the damned driver?"

"The servants."

"Then *I* will find him!" Byron folded the pages, shoved them inside his coat pocket, and went in search of the driver, whom he eventually found still asleep in his room above the stables.

"They didn't look very far, did they?" he said to Fletcher who was now crying with worry. "Nor in the most *obvious* place."

The driver, still pulling on his greatcoat, followed by his hat, hastily climbed up on to his bench and called down, "Where to, your lordship?"

"Nottinghamshire."

"Whereabouts in Nottinghamshire?"

"Newstead Abbey."

Chapter Thirty-One

~ ~ ~

The autumn-littered earth with its fallen dead leaves covering the lawns, reflected the bleak mood of Joe Murray and Nanny Smith and the rest of the staff at Newstead Abbey. They were a closely-knit household and it saddened their soft hearts to see a grown man cry so much, and Fletcher had been crying every day for almost a week.

The death of Fletcher's wife, so shortly after his arrival back at Newstead, had hit him badly; and now he was blaming himself for not paying enough attention to her; cursing himself for allowing her to have her way and go back to Newstead instead of making her stay with him in London.

"I was a bad husband, a careless husband, and I should have been kinder to her," Fletcher kept saying; which reminded Byron of his own accusations against himself when his mother had died ... "*I should have been kinder to her ...*"

"I need to practice my boxing," he said to Fletcher. "Will you spar with me?"

Fletcher stared at him, the tears still rolling down his face. "Spar? You want me to *spar* with you – even though I'm so grieved?"

Byron shrugged carelessly. "I need to keep up my boxing practice, and I've not had a session with John Jackson for weeks. Come along, Fletcher, you were a bad husband and a careless one, but you can't spend the rest of your life crying about it."

The great hall on the first floor was empty of all furniture, a huge room with oak-panelled walls and long bright windows that Byron had used as a "sporting room" since his teenage years. Unable to participate successfully in any other athletic sports due to his damaged foot, boxing and fencing were the two sports he employed to keep himself fit and strong; and throughout the years his valet, Fletcher, had regularly been his sparring partner at Newstead; a duty which Fletcher had always enjoyed.

Not today though. Fletcher fumed as he followed his lordship up to the Great Hall and put on his boxing gloves, thinking it to be a heartless thing for his master to make him do when he was so grieved in his endless heartache over Sally, his poor neglected dead wife.

Still sulking, still fuming, he walked over to his lordship who appeared to be still tying the cord at the wrist of one of his boxing gloves.

"Do you truly think you were such a bad husband?" Byron asked, his eyes and attention still on the glove.

"I do," Fletcher replied honestly. "The worst husband any unlucky woman could have."

"And a careless one?"

"No, I *did* care about Sally, but I'm sure she found out that I had a mistress when you and me was living in Athens. That's why she left me in London, I'm sure of it."

"How could she have found out?"

"The Greek woman wrote a letter to me, all in Greek, a load of foreign squiggles, but she pressed her painted lips at the end of the paper, by way of a kiss to me."

"How did she know your address? Or how did the postman – if it was written in Greek?"

"She asked me for it, when we was leaving Athens, so I wrote it down – the address of the Hut, not the Abbey – and then when young Robert brought the letter to me in the stables, I thought to keep it, just as a memento of my foreign travels."

"And you think Sally saw the letter?"

"I do. Why else would she suddenly leave me in London and go off back to Newstead ... but she made no fuss, that was not Sally's way, to make a fuss about anything." Fletcher's tears began to roll again, "But now that's she's gone and I didn't get a chance to say sorry to her..."

"Now you hate yourself?"

"Aye."

"And you want to beat yourself up?"

"No. Why would I want to do a daft thing like that? No, but I would've liked it if Sally had tried to give me a belt or two, to show that *she* cared."

"Then let me do it for her —" the sudden and swift hard punch into his jaw sent Fletcher stumbling backwards and onto his back.

He sat on the floor for a moment in shock, and then gave his head a shake in fury, before jumping back up onto his feet and throwing his own hard punch that knocked Byron sideways.

Standing at the half-open door and watching, old Joe Murray was smiling as he left them to it, returning to the Servants' Hall where he sat down with Nanny Smith and reminisced:

"I remember when his lordship's mother died, that was the only thing that helped him out of his guilty misery and brought him back to himself again – sparring with Fletcher. And I remember poor Fletcher complaining to me at the time that his lordship had thrown some brutally hard punches at him, much harder than usual, but Fletcher took it like a man, swollen face and black eye and all ... and now I suppose his lordship is doing the same for Fletcher, either giving or taking some hard punches to give the poor man some relief from all his grief."

Nanny Smith thought it a strange way to console a man. "I think the way women console each other is much better," she said. "A few kind words, and then a nice cup of hot tea to soothe the anguish."

"Aye, happen so," Joe replied, lighting his pipe after Nanny had left the room; sitting back in his chair and watching the great mahogany clock up on the wall. It was an old clock, dating back to the sixteenth century and it had some strange writing on the white face of it – *Tempus Fugit* – which the old Baron had told him was Latin, and in English meant "Time Flies".

Not always, and not today, Joe decided, because the next hour went by very slowly as he sat and wondered how the boxing match in the Great Hall was going on.

Finally, his patience gave out and he made his way to the Great Hall, poking his head inside the half-open door, expecting to see poor Fletcher getting the worst of it ...

But no, to Joe's surprise it was his lordship who looked injured, sitting on the ledge of one of the long windows while Fletcher was busily patting a flannel over his left eye and saying cheerfully, "Never mind, my lord, the bruise will be gone before the season."

Snatching the flannel out of Fletcher's hand, and then seeing Joe at the door, his lordship smiled sardonically. "Do you hear him, Joe? He says that every time I come back from John Jackson with some bruise or cut over my eye – *'Never mind, my lord, the eye will be healed before the season'* – as if one's eye was of no importance in the meantime."

"What season is he talking about? This coming winter?"

"No, the London season of parties and balls."

"And when is *that* season?" Joe asked.

"The London season," Byron said, dabbing the flannel over his eyebrow, "which starts in November, and goes on tediously until mid-June."

"So it's a mighty *long* season then," Joe observed.

"And all of it just to have parties?"

"No, not just that. It's timed to fit in with the opening of Parliament in October. That's when the politicians and the gentlemen of the *monde* settle themselves and their families in London for the winter and all the social life of the metropolis, which goes on until Parliament shuts down in June for the summer recess, and then all retire to their country houses for the less hectic summer season.

"But the *spring* season is the most important one," Fletcher told Joe. "That's the one where all the new young ladies and heiresses do their official *coming out* to find a husband, and I never like to see his lordship scarred or bruised in the spring – not with him being so legible."

"*Eligible,*" Byron corrected. "How many times must I tell you the *'e'* is at the beginning."

Once again Joe Murray left them to it, satisfied to see Fletcher looking more himself again with no tears running down his face. Nanny Smith was wrong: a good spar took the misery and anger out of a man quicker than any dish of tea. Well, that's how they had always done it in Joe's own young days in the Navy.

Chapter Thirty-Two

~ ~ ~

The next time Joe saw his lordship was later that afternoon in front of the house where one of the stable boys was tightening the girth under his horse.

Joe, in his usual way, made a polite enquiry as to where his lordship might be going? And at what hour he might return?

Byron lifted his left foot into the stirrup and then sprang up into the saddle before replying, "I'm just going for an idle canter."

"To where?"

"To wherever my horse decides to take me."

"And you'll remember my long advice and *not* race. We cannot have you falling off again."

Byron looked down at Joe, wondering if he should remind him that he was no longer a boy.

"Not with you being one of the worst horse-riders in the county," Joe added in his old worrying way. "Race and fall off and it will be more than your eye that gets bruised."

"A jog, a trot, a canter, I'll do all those things, but I'll not race," Byron assured him.

Joe watched him as he turned the horse around, thinking of his lordship's right foot which could *sit* in the stirrup, but not *grip* it. And the grip of his knees on the horse was not enough to keep him stable, *not* when he raced.

As soon as the horse was out of Joe's sight, Byron kneed him into a fast gallop, for no other reason than obstinacy, but then he slowed down and allowed his horse to trot along, while gently guiding him *away* from the direction of Annesley – anywhere but *Annesley* and

Mary Ann Chaworth.

True love, he had decided, could only be finally vanquished by keeping well away from it.

The horse trotted on, and the destination was of no consequence; it was the purity of the sweet air around Newstead that Byron loved, and so often longed for when he was in smoky London with all its chimneys puffing up cloudy fumes, especially in autumn and winter when the fires were burning day and night.

He also loved the silence in which he could hear the singing of birds again, not as fulsome as in summer, but still a sweet thin chirruping echoing in the silence.

He looked around him at the landscape and saw the horse was taking him in the direction of Hucknall. Here and there he passed the farm of a tenant where a man in a field would tip his hat to him, or a woman outside a cottage would dip him a quick curtsey. To both he raised his hand and returned a brief and smiling salute.

In the vast surrounds of the Newstead lands, the news that his lordship was back at the Abbey seemed to fly faster than a bird, and so everyone kept their eyes open for a glimpse of him. All loved him, not for his poetry, which few understood, even those who could read it, but for the fight he had put up in the House of Lords on behalf of their downtrodden and unemployed people, replaced by machines.

Parts of his speech protesting against the Death Penalty for the Nottingham machine-breakers had been printed in the Nottingham newspapers, and then read aloud in every tavern or house by those who could read; and those who listened had been proud of him; proud of his sympathy for them and proud of his defiance against his own class.

He had spoken out with all the scorn of scorn, and without picking his words he had shown that House of Lords that he was not afraid of saying things, and *said* them he *did*, and bedamned to the consequences to himself. Some even said he wrote his poetry in the same way, without fear or favour and with no cowardly bowing down to the opinions of others.

Aye and aye, all agreed – Lord Byron may not be a good horse-rider due to his damaged foot, unable to jump fences and hunt the foxes as other gentlemen did, but he had a hard-riding way with words, and a neck-or-nothing political temper. A renegade, a revolutionary, and from the age of ten he had been one of their own – a Nottingham man.

At Hucknall Church, Byron pulled his horse to a halt and sat for a few minutes thinking of his mother, for here she lay, down in the Byron vault, beneath the floor of the altar. He gazed towards the door of the church and saw that it was firmly closed, which was just as well.

He then slowly moved his gaze over the garden in front of the church ... and the rose-bushes she always found fault with, always complaining about their negligent upkeep to the vicar ... All those summer roses were gone now, as dead as she was, and it was not a nice thing to be thinking of.

He wheeled the horse around and rode at a gallop back towards Newstead until he found himself trotting in the silence again, slowing to a walk, glancing down at Leander who was contentedly trotting beside him.

"This is much better than your London walks, isn't it, Lea?"

The dog ignored him, his ears pricking alert, then barking towards the distance as if he did not like what he could hear.

Turning a bend and staring across a wide field, he heard and saw what had alerted Leander – a girl on a horse in a buff-coloured riding habit, galloping as fast as if she was being chased by the Devil, her head bent low towards the horse's neck as she jumped the horse over a low hedge with all the ease of a rider who jumped fences regularly.

Byron had never witnessed a display of such superb horsemanship, staring in admiration until Leander decided to join in the fun of the race and charged towards the horse, barking and yapping excitedly, causing the girl to veer her horse abruptly out of the dog's way, turning around until she had ridden in a circle, slowing to a stop while her horse whinnied and attempted to back-step away from the noisy pest.

"Leander. *Leander!*" Byron called, riding towards the girl. "I beg your pardon, Miss, but he is still a pup and his excitement —"

His words trailed away as he looked into the face of the rider, who was not a girl of about eighteen as he had thought ... but a woman ... a *beautiful* woman, and one who had always been so very precious to him.

"Mary!"

A thick strand of her brown hair had, in the course of her gallop, become loosened, falling in a soft coil onto her shoulder and over the bosom of her riding habit. She wore a shepherdess's straw hat with a ribbon of red velvet, which framed the exquisite delicacy of her features, and she looked, as she had always looked to him ... adorable.

Flustered and shy, Mary gave him a nervous smile. "Lord Byron."

Byron drew in a trembling breath. *One smile from her and all my sense and judgement take flight.*

After an awkward silence, he said quietly, "We meet again rather unexpectedly, my dear Mary."

Somewhat apprehensively, Mary agreed. "We do, my lord."

And yet the path she had taken led to only one place. "Were you on your way to Newstead?"

"Newstead? No-no, I was on my way to Mansfield."

"Mansfield?" Byron showed his surprise. "Then you have come a mile or two out of your way. Surely it would have been quicker to take the path straight up from Annesley?"

Mary was endeavouring hard to compose herself. "Yes, indeed, it would have been ... but I had something to collect in Newstead Village," adding quickly. "I had no thought or intention of bumping into you."

Byron smiled. "How else could the angels fall?"

Mary looked at him with innocent perplexity in her dark eyes.

"Those thousands of angels dancing on the head of a fine needle ... you used to ask me how they could fall off, and now you know ... someone bumped into them."

Mary recalled their old jesting game and smiled. "You remember that?"

"Of course. I remember everything."

"Not exactly though," Mary smiled, relaxing a little. "The question I used to ask you was, 'How *many* thousand angels could dance on the point of a very fine needle without jostling one another?"

"And I still don't know." He glanced up and around him. "But I do know it is about to rain ... can you feel it spitting?"

Mary glanced up. "Yes, rain. I doubt I will go to Mansfield now. I've no wish to get drenched."

"And as we are so near to Newstead," Byron said, "why don't you come and take some shelter and tea until the rain stops? Nanny Smith usually sends up tea around this time of day."

~~~

Nanny Smith was struck dumb when she saw the "friend and neighbour" his lordship escorted into the house.

"You remember Mary, don't you, Nanny? She has come to take tea with us, on her way back to Annesley."

Nanny could do no more than dip a quick curtsey before finding her voice. "Mis-Mrs Chaworth, a pleasure, indeed, to have you visit Newstead again."

Mary smiled. "Thank you, Nanny."

"We will take the tea in the *small* salon," Byron said, guiding Mary towards the stairs.

Nanny quickly dipped a knee again and then bustled back to Joe Murray, whose eyes popped at the news.

"It's been so long since I've seen her, but – for a moment there – it felt like it was only yesterday," Nanny said with some wonderment. "She hasn't changed much."

"Then let's hope *he* has changed, in that matter anyway," Joe replied anxiously, "because there was a time, in their younger days, when either a frown or a smile from that girl could *rule* him – change his mood or his mind in a flash."

Nanny shrugged as she moved to busy herself preparing the tea tray. "Joe, just for a change, why don't you tell me something I *don't* know!"

~ ~ ~

While the rain poured down outside they drank tea by lamplight. Mary sat in a high-winged armchair gazing around her. "I think this is the only room in Newstead that I have not been in before ... or have I?"

"No. This was my mother's private sitting room. No one but Nanny Smith was ever allowed in here."

"And you."

"No, not even me, not unless I was summoned. And even then I rarely appeared, because *this* is the room where she liked to sit and lay down the law, her own law."

Mary's eyes were full of understanding, still remembering Byron's mother so well: a robust Scottish woman with a fierce temper who could not speak without shouting – always shouting – and always about *My George* this, and *My George* that. In time, though, like everyone else, even she began referring to him simply as Byron.

"One day, while you were away on your travels," Mary said, "your mother came over to Annesley demanding to see me, saying she could not find your coronet. She had searched everywhere, in box, cupboard and closet, but no, the precious coronet was nowhere to be found."

Byron frowned. "So why did she go over to see you?"

"Because she wanted to know if you had given me your coronet as a gift. And if you had, she was taking it right back again."

Byron thought it very funny, but all he could say was, "Poor soul, she was very proud of my coronet."

"Have you ever worn it?"

"Yes, twice. The first time was on the night of my twenty-first birthday, just for fun. And the second time, more seriously, on the day I officially took my seat in the House of Lords."

"When was that?"

"Oh, not for some months after my twenty-first birthday, before I went abroad. The delay was due to my official papers not being in order, due to the careless way my great-uncle treated everything."

"But if your great-uncle had been the fifth Lord Byron before you, how could there be any question of your validity?"

"The House of Lords, Mary, is very particular and pedantic about everything. Every detail is carefully scrutinised; and in my case, a particular marriage certificate was missing."

"Oh?"

"My grandfather's marriage certificate, Admiral John Byron. He had married a Miss Sophia Trevanion of Caerhays Castle in Cornwall in 1748, but as the marriage took place in the private chapel of Caerhays Castle, no regular certificate of the ceremony could be produced. So John Hanson, my attorney, was forced to go down to Cornwall to get signed Affidavits and other proofs of the marriage, before I could officially take my seat, which I did, on the 13th March 1809."

"And you wore your coronet."

"A necessary requirement when swearing all the oaths."

"Ah..." Mary could not help feeling a slight sad. "Your mother would have been so proud to have seen you on that day, wearing your coronet in the House of Lords."

"Yet I did not wear it *happily*," Byron insisted. "I am not a champion of kings, nor have I ever wanted to imitate one by walking around with a crown on my head."

"Still, it would have been nice for her to see it. Can *I* see it?

"The coronet?"

"Yes. Do you have it here?"

Byron was not sure. "My attorney may have it in London, or Joe Murray could have it locked away somewhere here in one of the cellars. If you wish, I'll go and ask Joe if he knows where it is."

Mary smiled, not in consent, but at his casual attitude to it all – a gold coronet which may be here, or even there ... but then he had said he was not a champion of kings ... and that was Byron, so different to others, and so different to her husband Jack, who bowed low at the sight of anything royal or above his own station. Had he not married her because she was the sole heiress of Annesley and its lands? Of course he had. That's why he and his socialite mother had rushed her into a marriage in their drawing room – to secure the wealth of the Chaworth estate. Jack had even readily agreed to the stipulation in the marriage contract that he must change his name from Musters to Chaworth, which had greatly upset his father.

And yet ... she had been just as culpable in the calamity, eager to become a woman and rush into marriage with the man everyone called "Handsome Jack" who was ten years her senior. So grown-up, and so different to Byron and his boyish devotion.

She sat back and rested the side of her head against the wing of the armchair, her thoughts sad, her heart sad. If only she had known then, what she knew now. ... If only she was not always so unhappy with her life, so lonely in her heart ... at times her depression was unbearable ...

Byron entered the room, smiling at her, and she loved him for smiling at her in that fun, warm way, reminding her of the past when they had both been so innocent and full of laughter and fun ... the happiest days of her life ...

"Joe knows where it is. He has it locked it away, but has gone to get it for you."

"For me?"

"For you to see it." He sat down. "You do realise it is just a piece of gilded trash."

"You mean ... it's a fake?"

"For what it symbolises, yes. Putting a coronet or crown on a man's head does not make him a more worthy being than other men. No more than a crown of thorns made Jesus a criminal." He smiled mordantly. "Now there's a comparison for you to ponder on."

By the time Nanny Smith brought in a fresh tray of tea and quietly slipped out again, they were talking in the way they had talked in the old days, from gravely serious to silly and funny.

"Now here's something for *you* to ponder on, Byron. It's a well-known fact that no woman would ever eat an apple without peeling it – is that not correct?"

"Indeed, it is a crime against the law of the land, punishable by death if not adhered to. Although a man can gnash straight in."

"So here's the question – if Adam and Eve were the only two people in the Garden of Eden, when Eve peeled the apple and then gave it to Adam, who did she give the peel to?"

Byron rolled his eyes, knowing it was one of her made-up conundrums like the angels on a needle, but she was losing her skill, because this time the answer was so easy.

"It's obvious," he said, "she either threw it away or gave the peel to the serpent."

"Aha, for a Cambridge graduate you are not as clever as you should be, because the part of the question you *should* have pondered was – where did Eve get the knife?"

Byron laughed at the nonsense of it all, turning to look as Joe Murray lumbered in carrying a large wooden box.

"I didn't think I would have to be finding and fetching this up today," Joe grumbled. "I had it hidden away so safely that I couldn't find it myself for a while. Safe as a king's crown it was, and so will it be again, as soon as you give it back to me."

"Thank you, Joe."

Joe's gaze transferred suspiciously to Mary, tilting her a brief bow, "*Mrs* Chaworth," and then turned to Byron. "Do you want me to open it for you?"

No, just leave the key."

Joe reached into his pocket. "There are *three* keys. I like to have three for safety."

Byron smiled at Mary. "Joe believes there is something magical about the number three."

"Aye, the Trinity, my lord. Why else are there three Gods, Father, Son, and Holy Spirit? Never forget the

Trinity is what I say."

"Which is *another* conundrum," Byron replied wryly, "because you say it too often and too piously for a man who never goes near a church."

Joe took a deep breath to stem his annoyance. "I was told, when I was a boy, that when I die I will need to have three keys to get into the Kingdom of Heaven."

"Yes," Mary agreed. "The three keys – faith of soul, goodness of heart, and hands of charity."

"Eh?" Joe stared at her in bewilderment, and Byron laughed. "Is that why you are always collecting keys, Joe?"

And then to Mary, "He even has a few keys to some of the monks' rooms down in the cloisters – the doors are long gone, but Joe still has the keys."

"*Holy* keys," Joe replied. "*Monks'* keys. One of them I found near the monks old burial ground some twenty years ago, and another key Boatswain dug up and brought to me just before the poor dog died. I'm still hoping to find a third holy key and then I'll be well armed when my time comes to go."

"Which is now." Byron gave him a look, which told Joe to scram.

"So you'll send for me when you want it locked up and taken back down again, my lord?"

"I will."

Joe glowered once more at Mary and then turned and walked to the door, his shoulders set stiff and high in umbrage.

"I think," Mary said quietly, "that he has the same thought that your mother once did, and fears you might be intending to give the coronet to me as a gift."

"Well, I *would* have given you a gift of one just like it, if you had waited long enough to honour me by becoming Lady Byron."

Mary stared at him, unsure if he was being serious or flippant; one never knew with Byron. She pretended amusement. "Do you honestly think I would marry any man for the purpose of gaining a title and a coronet?"

"Oh, not *you*, Mary; many other women, yes, but not you. Well here it is," he said flippantly, lifting the coronet from the box, "the gilded trash."

Mary stood up and walked over to inspect it, her fingers moving over the white pearls above the gold base, thinking it was not trash at all, but quite beautiful.

"It's not as heavy as it looks," she said with surprise. "It's quite light."

"It's designed that way, due to the fact that a man may have to wear it for hours at a time during ceremonials. Thankfully I do not waste my time on such events."

Mary gave him one of her impish smiles. "May I try it on?"

He nodded, and then watched her walk to the large mirror on the wall and carefully place the coronet on her brown hair; watching her, adoring her, and feeling all the old heartbreak coming back in a rush again.

"I feel like a little girl again," she said, admiring herself in the mirror, "trying on grown-up hats or wearing little paste tiaras and pretending I was a princess."

"And Maid Marian," he reminded her. "Remember when we went to that masque ball at the Assembly Rooms in Nottingham and you came as Maid Marian."

"Yes ..." Mary thought back, "and John Pigot came as Robin Hood ... and you came as a highwayman."

"At the Masque Balls in London I still occasionally go as a highwayman, and the less people who know it's me behind the mask the better."

Mary was still thinking back to the Masquerade in Nottingham, remembering her Maid Marian costume, which she had loved so much.

"And then *you* spoiled our fun by being sullen and standing and glaring at us all night because we were dancing and you could not join in."

Byron shrugged, philosophically. "When I was a boy I acted like a boy, which is not very strange ... unlike Maid Marian who went on to marry the Sheriff of Nottingham."

Mary stood motionless, her back to him, staring at him through the mirror as their eyes met for a long wordless moment.

She lowered her gaze, removed the coronet from her head, and silently returned it to the box. When she looked up into his face her eyes were shimmering with tears. "That was deliberately cruel."

"Why?" he said archly, as if not understanding. "It's true, so why is it cruel?"

Mary blinked rapidly. "Thank you for the tea and shelter, but now I must leave."

She turned briskly, retrieved her hat, walked over to the mirror and returned it to her head, tying the red velvet ribbon under her chin. Now she looked like *Mrs* Chaworth again, and all the relaxed cheerfulness had gone from her face.

"How have I offended?" Byron asked curiously. "You *did* marry the Sheriff of Nottingham, so why am I at fault for saying it?"

"I did *not* marry the Sheriff of Nottingham," Mary insisted. "I married Jack Musters and he was then only the *son* of the Sheriff of Nottingham."

Byron had to smile at the ridiculousness of her reasoning.

"He was still a bully and a boor, and he is even more so now, or are you unaware of how he is treating the people of your own Nottingham — him and his bullying militia?"

Mary almost choked on her breath, unable to take any more; she had suffered enough from the actions of her husband, *enough, enough, enough!*

Byron saw an ashy paleness come over her face as she appeared to sway slightly. Immediately he was at her side, his hand around her waist, quickly guiding her to the nearest armchair where she slumped in a faint.

"Mary!" He stood for a shocked moment over her collapsed figure, and then grabbed up a book and began to wave air over her face. She looked pallid and ill and he could not comprehend the change in her.

He threw down the book and lifted her hand, slapping it gently and saying her name, while staring anxiously at the soft whiteness of her tilted chin, her colourless face, the dark shadow of the lashes on her cheeks, her lips parted like the lips of a child in sleep.

"Mary?"

Her eyes opened, gazing at him as if drugged, and then moving her eyes slowly to look around her, she came back to herself, and slowly sat up ... saying weakly, "Oh ... I'm sorry."

"Mary, are you ill?"

"No ... but I have fasted since breakfast very early this morning ... so little wonder I took faint."

"Water," he said, "you must drink some water." He lifted the water jug from the tea tray and poured some into a clean cup. Mary took the cup in both hands and took a few sips and then began to tremble like an aspen-leaf.

"Mary, I'm ready to shoot myself for distressing you. What can I do to make amends?"

Mary sat for a number of seconds gazing into the water in her cup before saying quietly, "A hot cup of sweet tea would be more reviving than water?"

"Sweet tea, of course, your usual remedy."

He took the cup from her hands, felt the lukewarm

teapot, and then walked over to the fireplace to pull the rope for Nanny Smith. The rope was gone.

"Oh, I forgot," he said irritably. "After so many bad tempers my mother finally yanked the rope down in one of her rages while I was abroad. I'll go down."

"No, no, please..." but he was at the door and then out of it, and Mary sat back tiredly, resting her clasped hands on her lap.

The lamp on the tea table shone a warm yellow light on her chair, and the flames in the fireplace radiated comfort. The rapid beats of her pulse, the last thing she remembered before fainting, were now slow and calm.

She was glad she had fainted, because she had not wanted to leave, but Byron's offensive words about her husband had made it obligatory to do so, and that had been the most breath-crushing thing of all, especially after she had deliberately rode towards Newstead in the hope of crossing his path.

She knew that whenever he was at the Abbey he always took a ride in the afternoons. There was not much that happened at Newstead which did not get back to Annesley through the servants or tenants, and it was always a subject of great comment whenever his lordship was home and back in residence.

Her mind drifted back, as it had done so many times during the years, to that night in 1808 when Byron had surprisingly accepted an invitation with other members of the Nottingham gentry to attend a dinner party at Annesley Hall.

Would she ever forget that night? In her mind she had still been expecting to see the teenage boy who had been her constant friend until her engagement to Jack Musters, but after his years at Cambridge he had come back to Annesley a man; a divinely handsome young man. For days afterwards the serving maids had been all in a flutter about him. And she, too, had found herself thinking about what might have been.

Her reverie was broken by Byron returning to the room carrying a tea-tray with fresh china, and Nanny Smith coming in behind him carrying a plate and wearing a sympathetic expression on her kind face.

"As luck would have it," Nanny said, "Cook made some gingerbreads this afternoon, and I remembered how much you used to like our gingerbreads, Miss Chaworth." Nanny smiled. "Do you remember how you would always ask me if the cook had made some?"

Mary looked at Nanny who had not only called her *Miss*, but had also remembered such a thing; and then she looked at Byron who was already pouring her a cup of tea – and faced with such care and kindness, Mary felt so affected that her mood immediately lifted and lightened and she was smiling again, her dark eyes brilliant as she spoke to Nanny about the cook at Annesley who was not good at making gingerbreads. "They are always too hard."

"Does she not put a good dollop of molasses in the mix? That's what our cook swears by, plenty of molasses to give the gingerbreads succulence."

Mary didn't know what her cook put in the mix. "But I will ask her, and if she does not use molasses, I will ask her to do so."

"You see," said Nanny Smith, returning to the kitchen and Joe Murray, "any other mistress would have said 'I will *tell* her do so', but she said 'I will *ask* her to do so.' She was always such a sweet and polite girl, and lovely too, so no wonder she had his lordship wrapped around her little finger."

"And *still* has," Joe grunted resentfully. "Only for *her* would he make me go looking for the coronet – all the way down to the cellar! And only for *her* would he come rushing in here looking for the tea – nearly scalded me he did when he grabbed the tea-tray out of my hands, as if he thought I was *too slow and* wouldn't be able to get the tea up to her fast enough."

Nanny sat down and said resignedly, "She's still his idol. Any fool can see it."

Chapter Thirty-Three

~ ~ ~

The following morning Nanny Smith was up bright and early as usual, doing her dusting, pausing in the small salon when she noticed a pair of buff-coloured kid gloves on the Queen Anne sideboard. She knew instantly they were Miss Chaworth's gloves, due to the small and slender size.

"Now then," she murmured. "Isn't this a nice excuse."

A short while later she had donned her cloak and bonnet and walking-boots, and had set off across the fields towards Annesley Hall. It would be good to see Nanny Marsden again and pick up a bit of gossip. Of course, as was the custom in the country, she knew she would have to give some gossip back in exchange.

A sound at her back made her turn to see Leander following her. "Go back, Leander, go back," she ordered, but the dog barked and wagged his tail, eager to accompany her.

"Is his lordship still asleep? Is that it? Oh, very well, you can come along, but you must behave yourself and stay outside in the yard or Nanny Marsden will not be pleased with you."

A long, strong walk brought her to the field-gate which opened from the land of Newstead onto the grounds of Annesley. Walking onwards under the arch into the courtyard, and passing the range of stables where the squire kept his fox-hunting steeds, she finally reached the back door of the kitchen where she found Nanny Marsden having her breakfast with a few of the maids.

"Well, I'll be ..." said Nanny Marsden, looking up and seeing who it was; and then after hurriedly ordering one

of the maids to bring a fresh pot of tea, she escorted
Nanny Smith down the corridor and into her own
private parlour, the usual abode for their chats.

"Who's this?" said Nanny Marsden, frowning at the
dog that leisurely followed them into the room.

"Leander. He's Lord Byron's dog, but his lordship
hasn't risen yet and the poor thing was bored waiting.
I'll take him outside."

"No, don't do that! If he's Lord Byron's dog then let
him alone. Let him stay if he pleases. He's welcome."

Nanny Smith smiled. "So you've still got a soft spot
for his lordship I see."

"Ah, bless him, that I do!" said Nanny Marsden,
fondling the dog. "Well! I never thought I would see a
dog of Lord Byron's in Annesley again."

Nanny Smith sat down. "The last one you saw here
must have been Boatswain."

"Aye, Boatswain. Ah! what a dog! My young mistress
loved it when Lord Byron brought Boatswain here. And
you know, even now, when the master talks in a scornful
and sneering way about Lord Byron, my mistress always
gets very warm in the face in defence of him. She won't
hear a word said against his lordship, not from anyone."

Nanny was surprised – now *this* was something new
to tell Joe Murray.

"So," she said, following the normal routine, "how
have you been since I last saw you?"

"Ah, dear me!" Nanny Marsden flopped her stout
body down in the armchair opposite. "I'm getting on,
getting old, almost sixty now. You know that I have my
own little cottage in Annesley Wood?"

"I do, and lucky you are to have it."

"Aye, and there have been times of late when I've
dreamed of settling there, nice and peaceful like."

"So why don't you?"

"Nay!" Nanny Marsden cocked a sharp eye. "I'd never

leave my mistress, not unless it was her wish to retire me. It was she who secured the cottage for me, although she does often tell me that Annesley will always be my home for as long as I want to remain here."

A maid brought in the tea-tray and once she had poured the tea into the cups, and then quickly left the room, Nanny Marsden sat forward and lifted her cup and saucer.

"With things being as they are," she said sadly, "I often think of Lord Byron and my mistress when they were younger ... In those days, he used to ride over here and sometimes stay three days at a time and sleep in the blue room. Ah! Bless him! He was so taken with my young mistress then; he used to walk about the garden and the terraces with her and seemed to love the very ground she trod on. He used to call her his bright morning star of Annesley."

She sat back, sipped her tea, and sighed. "A soft spot for Lord Byron! And why should I not, eh? He was always main good to me when he came here. Many say it was a pity that he and my young lady did not make a match. Her mother would have liked it. Some think it would have been well for him to have had her, but it was not to be. Mr Musters came along and saw her and that was that."

Nanny Smith had never seen her old friend looking so downcast. "Is there something wrong? Something you can talk to me about? Just between the two of us, *confiding*-like?"

Nanny Marsden shrugged tiredly. "Oh well, if you don't already know then I may as well tell you, seeing as every tenant on the Annesley farms and in the Annesley villages knows all about it. And how could they *not* know, when it's the talk of all Nottingham."

"But not at Newstead," said Nanny Smith. "Mind, we are very cut off there, in our own little world. But whatever it is, I can see it's disturbing you badly."

"No mind about me, it's my young mistress I'm worried about. Ah! So very worried that betimes I cannot sleep at night."

"A worry shared, is a sleepless night spared."

Nanny Marsden nodded. "Aye, happen so."

~ ~ ~

Burdened as she was with a kind and caring heart, Nanny Smith was on the verge of tears when she later left Annesley to return home to Newstead, walking at a slower pace than usual, her heart full of sorrow for poor Miss Chaworth who had been such a sweet and respectable young lady; and still she was, in every part and portion, apart from her insufferable marriage to Jack Musters.

And, according to Nanny Marsden, all the Annesley tenants still adored her ... and now Nanny Smith knew why Mary occupied herself doing so much charity work *away* from her home, becoming Patron of the Nottingham Hospital, as well as all her other charitable duties on behalf of the Nottingham poor.

On reaching the parklands of Newstead, Leander suddenly barked wildly and shot off, deserting Nanny to race on towards the Abbey like an excited hound chasing a fox.

"His lordship must be up and about then," Nanny murmured.

She could hear Leander growling as soon as she approached the yard, turning the corner to see a wild erratic scuffling going on between the dog and his lordship in one of their playful fights.

"Where did you take him?" Byron asked as she approached. "Your long excursion has delayed my return to London."

Nanny looked down at Leander who was now

standing meekly at his master's side.

"Just for a walk."

Byron eyed her shrewdly. Nanny Smith loved her long walks, always returning with rosy cheeks and claiming the breeze had blown all the cobwebs from her mind, but today ... today her face was joyless.

"Nanny?"

"No." Nanny shook her head, "I'm not going to tell you, because it's something I know you will not be happy to hear. It certainly did not please *me.*"

At times like these, Byron considered Nanny Smith to be as bad as Fletcher – getting ink from a stone.

"So where did you go?"

"Oh, just to have a cup of tea with my old friend Nanny Marsden."

Byron stared. "At Annesley?"

"Aye."

It took more than ten minutes of verbal bartering before Byron finally got Nanny Smith into the privacy of the downstairs parlour to tell him what she kept saying he would not be happy to hear.

She sat in the chair with her cloak and bonnet still on, clutching her big old leather purse in her lap with both hands as if it was the only thing keeping her steady.

"It's about Miss Chaworth."

Byron nodded. "Who else at Annesley would I be interested in?"

"Apart from dear Nanny Marsden?"

"Of course."

"And I know you've always disliked the husband."

"Which only leaves Mary – pray get *on* with it, Nanny!"

So Nanny Smith did, and Byron listened as she told him about the awful life Mary was now living, and had been living for years.

"According to Nanny Marsden, the marriage was bad

right from the start, lots of quarrelling and upsets. Mr Musters turned out to be a very different husband than Miss Chaworth had expected."

"In what way?"

"Oh, she soon learned he had other women, lots of women, vulgar mistresses all over the place. Even some of the farm girls from right there in Annesley, as well as one up in Yorkshire. Aye, Mary knew, because there were enough people who came running to tell her, and all of them *gentry,* from her own class, which must have shamed her terribly."

Byron was baffled — thinking back to the girl he had known before her marriage, – a happy girl with a charming and playful temperament —"She was the most beautiful prize in Nottingham."

"Aye, well it seems Jack Musters prized himself more. To him, it was Mary who was getting a prize catch. Full of himself with his own idolatry. One night Nanny Marsden heard him telling Mary that she was a fool if she thought he could be faithful to one woman for all of his life. *'A man,'* she heard him say, *'needs variety in his life, and all sensible wives know that.'*"

Nanny Smith could hardly believe such shameless behaviour from a gentleman. She opened her bag and took out a handkerchief to dab at her brow.

"And then there's the occasional bruises, you see. That's what has Nanny Marsden in such a state of worry."

"Bruises?"

"On Mary's arms, the sort of bruises that come when someone grabs a woman and treats her hard."

Byron's hands were now gripping the arms of his chair. "You mean he is *rough* with her?"

"It would seem so, and a few times Nanny Marsden has seen a bruise on the side of Mary's face. She could not say it was *him* who made them, but who else?"

Byron sprang out of his chair. "I must go to her. And while I'm there I'll demand her abominable husband to come outside for a boxing match with *me!* And if that don't suit him, we can do it with pistols."

"No, my lord, no!" Nanny was up on her feet. "He's not there. He's up in Yorkshire."

Byron halted in his steps and looked at her. "Yorkshire?"

"Aye, that's where he sent Mary when he heard you were back from abroad at the time your mother died. Mary knew she could not go to the funeral, ladies not being allowed to attend funerals ... so she wanted to come over here to Newstead to give you her condolences, but he wouldn't let her come, in case you and she got friendly again ... so he sent her away to Yorkshire until it was all done and over."

The expression on his lordship's face made Nanny very glad that it was not his way to ever use bad language.

"I wish I'd not told you now," she said fretfully. "I wish I'd not gone there to learn it. And at the end of it all, I forgot to hand over the gloves."

"What gloves?"

She was opening her bag. "The ones I found in the small salon this morning. Miss Chaworth's gloves."

~ ~ ~

The gloves were tucked safely inside Byron's jacket as he rode at a gallop over to Annesley. The gate was wide open so he was able to ride on under the arch and into the courtyard without having to dismount, slowing down at the stables where the first person he saw was William Caunt, a lad who had worked at Newstead since his boyhood, before taking up a position at Annesley where the horses were more plentiful.

"*Lord Byron!*"

Caunt was full of surprise and smiles as he reached up to take the reins. "A pleasure to see you again, my lord, aye, a real *pleasure!*"

Byron dismounted. "And my pleasure, William, would be to know if your mistress is at home?"

"She is, my lord. But it wouldn't do for a gentleman of your rank to come in the back way. So if you go round to the front door, I'll tell the housekeeper and she'll be the one to go and greet you. She'd skelp the breeches off my backside if I let it happen any other way."

A few minutes later Nanny Marsden opened the front door like a delighted mother welcoming home a long-lost son.

"Well! I never thought I'd be seeing my Lord Byron here in Annesley again! And you're welcome, my lord, most welcome! Is it my young lady you are calling on?"

"It is. Is she receiving visitors?"

"Ah!" Nanny Marsden laughed as Leander slinked up to her, his tail wagging. "And here he is again!" She bent down to fondle the dog and a daring idea came to her.

"My young lady is in her own sitting-room above the small courtyard. You know it well, her favourite room. So why don't you go up now, and I'll take the dog off to my parlour to give him a rest by the fire."

Byron was not so sure. "Should you not announce me?"

"Ah! It will be a nice surprise for her, if you just pop your head in." And on that Nanny Marsden had Leander by his collar, leading him down the hall to her quarters.

He climbed the stairs silently, the thick panel of red stair-carpet muting his every step. Along the wall going up his eyes moved over all the familiar paintings of the Chaworth ancestors, reminding him of his younger days when he was certain some were scowling at him in accusation because he was a *Byron* – a descendant of the man who had killed their kinsman William

Chaworth.

> *No florid prose, nor honied lies of rhyme,*
> *Can blazon evil deeds, or consecrate a crime.*

So said Childe Harold ... He stepped onto the landing which was very quiet, silent, unlike the old days when she was always playing her piano and singing to herself.

The door to her sitting-room was half open; he looked around it, and there she was ... sitting in a chair by the window, her head bent and her fingers sewing.

"Mary."

Startled, her turn of surprise brought a rush of colour to her cheeks, her dark eyes wide with astonished bewilderment. "*Byron?*"

He quickly apologised. "Nanny Marsden bade me to come straight up." He removed her gloves from inside his jacket and held them up. "You left these at Newstead."

"Oh, did I?" She quickly stood up, then quickly sat down again, looking fleetingly around her as if not sure what to do next. "My goodness ... I'm so taken aback ... because a moment ago I was thinking of you."

"Why so?"

"Because last night I read your book, Childe Harold's Pilgrimage."

"Why only last night? It was published nine months ago."

"Yes, I know, but Jack ... well, that's what I had to collect from Newstead Village yesterday. I ordered it from Hatchards."

"Could you not have had it delivered here? It's only a book."

Mary flushed again, and looked down at the sewing in her lap.

"Mary."

"Yes."

"May I come in?"

Her startled surprise was back, but now there was a smile on her face. "Oh, of course! Oh, my goodness ... I don't know where my head is today! Did I leave that at Newstead also?"

She set her sewing aside and stood to greet him in a formal way, holding her hand out.

He crossed the room and took her hand, but instead of briefly bowing over it, he lifted it to his cheek and closed his eyes while he held it there for a silent and soothing few seconds, just like he used to do in their young friendship days, whenever she told him she was upset about something.

And in those seconds Mary knew that he knew, and her face paled with the humiliation of him knowing. Had William Caunt gone over to Newstead this morning tittle-tattling? Perhaps, and perhaps not. Unfair to blame him. All servants gossiped.

But now she was undone, all her composure gone, although she tried to maintain it. "Oh, Byron, please don't do that ... so much has changed since you used to comfort me in that way."

Byron looked at her pale face with tenderness. "I have not changed, Mary. I will always be your friend and defender, and nothing will ever change *that*."

Mary blinked her eyes rapidly, unable to take it in, that after all this time he still cared for her.

"But ... you are a great man now, Byron, in your politics, and your poetry, and *famous* ..."

"Oh, fame is nothing more than being known to a lot of people you don't know and will never know." His eyes were fixed on her face. "Why on earth did you marry him, Mary? He was then as he is now, so why?"

He could see in her eyes a kind of mute despair as her mind sought for an answer. Her lovely mouth was pale and a little tremulous as she said, "I suppose I was then, as I hope I am *not* now ... soon led, easily pleased, very hasty, and then quickly relenting ... but I know I do still have a *good* heart."

A maid arrived with the obligatory tray of tea, which neither of them wanted.

"Oh, but ..." the maid, a country girl of about sixteen, seemed unsure what to do next, "Cook said to tell you, Ma'am, that after what you told her last night, she has made the gingerbreads for you special like, with more molasses in them."

"Oh, in that case," said Mary, a smile brightening her face, "we cannot disappoint her, can we, Lord Byron?"

Mary returned to her chair and Byron instinctively moved to his old usual place on the window seat facing her. The maid poured the tea and Mary reached for a gingerbread to sample it.

"Delicious," she exclaimed after a bite. "Pray try one, Lord Byron, so that Sarah can give our cook your opinion."

Byron lifted a gingerbread, took a bite, and quickly looked at Mary, before swallowing and smiling at the maid. "Scrumptious! My compliments to the cook."

"Oh, she *will* be pleased when I tell her," smiled the maid, and then turned and ran out to convey the message to the kitchen at all speed.

As soon as she was gone, Byron threw the gingerbread down onto his plate, and then quickly picked it up again and shoved it inside his pocket. "I shall have to tell Nanny Smith the truth though," he said. "Annesley's gingerbreads are still almost as hard as slates."

"I would say even harder!" Mary chuckled and put a hand over her mouth. "Poor Cook, her eyesight is not as good as it used to be, so I hope she didn't put her hands on a tin of tar instead of a tin of molasses – I suppose, dripping from a spoon, they *could* look the same."

"I think not, in fact I'm certain, because the smell of hot tar and hot molasses is vastly different, which would have been clue enough to alert her. Also, tar is a substance made to *stick*, so if her sense of smell is as bad her eyesight, she would still have been unable to get them off the tray – even if she used a sledgehammer."

"Oh, that *is* a relief to know." Mary was still smiling, until it suddenly occurred to her – "But that means her gingerbreads are even worse than ever they were. Oh, poor Cook ..."

She quickly leaned forward and scooped up a handful of the gingerbreads. "Here, put these in your pocket also, so when the tray goes back down and Cook inspects the plate, she will think you have eaten quite a few."

Byron looked at her as he shoved the handful of biscuits into his coat pocket. "You are right, you still *do* have a good heart."

~ ~ ~

Later, when Mary's presence was needed in the nursery, Byron stood to take his leave, but Mary hastily bade him not to go, not just yet.

"Sit down, do! It's probably nothing more than a childish squabble about a toy, and as usual I must be the referee. I shall not be long."

Left alone, Byron found himself free to look around her sitting-room more slowly, recalling all those times in the past they had spent in here together.

He moved to his feet and stood at the window, gazing down on her private little courtyard which had not changed in any way, except the numerous tubs of beautiful flowers which she had always tended so lovingly, were now emptied of all but earth due to autumn's cold bleakness.

A quiet and secluded garden, which had once been a sequestered world of friendship for her, and a world of boyish love and romance for him ... Was it because both were alone with no siblings, and both were the heirs to adjoining estates ... was that what had drawn them so close together in those long summer days of their youth? Once again he found himself journeying back into the past ...

These two, a maiden and a youth, were there

Gazing – the one on all that was beneath

Fair as herself – but the boy gazed on her;

And both were young, and one was beautiful:

And both were young – yet not alike in youth.

As the sweet moon on the horizon's verge

The maid was on the verge of womanhood;

The boy had fewer summers, but his heart

Had far outgrown his years, and to his eye

There was but one beloved face on earth ...

He turned away from the window and the garden below and wandered over to her piano, his hand slowly tinkling out a few notes.

There was one song, he remembered, a Welsh song called "Mary Ann" and because that was her name he regularly persuaded her to play it over and over for him; and sometimes he even sang it with her.

He did not turn when she came back into the room, his fingers still tinkling out notes on the piano ...

"I really must leave now," he said quietly, knowing that if he stayed any longer there was a very real danger of finding himself hopelessly in love again, especially now that she was no longer an innocent girl, but a truly womanly woman.

Mary made no reply, watching him as he removed something from the breast pocket inside his jacket ... a notebook and a pencil ... placing the notebook on the top of the piano, flipping it open and rapidly writing something ...

"This is my London address," he said, ripping out the page and turning to her. "You know that if you ever find yourself wishing for a friend, or need help in any way ... you can always send for me."

She gave him the smallest shadow of a smile, unable to tell him that her life and her wishes could never be that easy.

~ ~ ~

The day after Byron's return to London, his agent, Robert Dallas, visited him in his rooms, only to find his lordship absorbed in the composition of a letter or a poem or whatever it was he was writing.

Dallas could see he had been barely noticed when he entered the room, until his lordship glanced up.

"Pray go on, I am happy to wait," Dallas said, and sat down in a chair near to the side of the desk and read a newspaper for some time.

Finally he put the paper down and looked at Lord Byron, astonished at the complete abstraction of his mind. He had a small smile on his lips, and his eyes were full of the pleasure he felt at what was passing from his imagination to his paper.

He looked up for a moment, and then down at his writing, and Dallas felt convinced that he did not see him sitting there, and that his thoughts prevented him discerning anything about him.

Dallas said: "I see you are deeply engaged."

In the silence that followed, Dallas realised that his lordship's ears were as little open to sound as his eyes were to vision.

He stood up. "I will return another time, my lord," he said, and on his departure from the room Dallas was almost certain that his lordship had not been aware of his arrival or his leaving.

The following morning Dallas called again, and found his lordship in his usual good humour.

"I must say," said Dallas, "it is a relief to find you not so absorbed in your writing as you were yesterday."

"Yesterday?" Byron looked genuinely puzzled. "Did you call yesterday?"

Dallas nodded, and told him of the length of time he had sat looking through a newspaper.

Byron appeared doubtful, a half-smile on his face as if wondering if Dallas was jesting.

"I truly did call on you, my lord, but your mind appeared to be miles away."

"Then I beg to hope," Byron conceded, "that you did not go away thinking I was rude?"

Others may have gone away thinking that, but Dallas had simply put it down to the eccentricities of poetic genius. And as long as Lord Byron kept writing, Robert Dallas would continue to grow rich.

"Rude? Oh no, my lord, not at all."

~ ~ ~

Miles away, in Annesley Hall, Mary was reading Byron's letter, telling her of the pleasure he had felt at seeing her again.

She absorbed every word, like a thirsty child drinking water; relishing every sentence. Yet by the end of the letter, all she could feel was a sad pain.

On the day he had left Annesley, she had felt so empty, so devoid of joy, which was strange after only two meetings in the space of two days, and those meetings coming after two long years since they had last met after his return from abroad.

Nanny Marsden came into the room carrying a cup of hot chocolate, her eyes on the letter in Mary's hand.

"Well, what news of my Lord Byron? Is he well?"

"*I miss him terribly,*" Mary wanted to say, but she knew she could not say that ... not even to Nanny Marsden or to anyone at all ... not even in a whisper.

Mad, Bad, and Delightful to Know

The Third Book in the Byron Series

Gretta Curran Browne

Living amongst the richest people of the highest strata of London Society and being fallen over by its glamorous women, Lord Byron has never quite got over the raw emotions of his unrequited love for his country cousin Mary Chaworth.

Until they meet again, and Mary finds new hope for a happier life with the man she had once rejected as a teenage boy, and now deeply loves.

Byron brings down the wrath of the newspapers for using his poetry to criticise the bloated Prince Regent, and speak up for the starving English poor; but the attacks on his name do not trouble him at all.

Although he remains troubled by Lady Caroline Lamb, who is now stick-thin and gaunt-faced from the pain of her insane love for him; hiding in his publisher's waiting room and sneakily following him through the streets, until he complains in a letter to Lady Melbourne – *"I am being haunted by a skeleton!"*

A story full of humour and drama and colourful events and people from the Regency era, including Beau Brummell; the courtesan Harriette Wilson, and so many others – all mad and bad and delightful to know.

Thank You

Thank you for taking the time to read '*A Strange World*' the second book in the *LORD BYRON* series. I hope you enjoyed it.

Please be nice and leave a review.

*

I occasionally send out newsletters with details of new releases, or discount offers, or any other news I may have, although not so regularly to be intrusive, so if you wish to sign up to for my newsletters – go to my Website and click on the "Subscribe" Tab.

*

If you would like to follow me on **BookBub** go to:-
www.bookbub.com/profile/gretta-curran-browne and click on the "*Follow*" button.

Many thanks,

Gretta

www.grettacurranbrowne.com

Printed in Great Britain
by Amazon

72883365R00190